MINE TO GAIN

MAGGIE RAWDON

CONTENT NOTE

A list of content information you may want before reading can be found on my website: maggierawdon.com/content-information/

To my readers who wish they could have had the brother instead.

1

Beatrix

You know that moment when you've had enough? Where everything in your life has been on a downhill slide, and now, the smallest, most ridiculous thing imaginable is about to send you into burn-everything-down mode? That's me right now. Standing outside the Queen City Chaos football team's auxiliary building in front of a man who I am sure is otherwise a very lovely gentleman but is currently wielding his access power to the team like he is the last bastion between the players and certain doom.

"As I said, I don't have my badge yet. I'm still new, but I'm Beatrix Xavier. I should be on the list. I'm Madison Westfield's assistant and part of the PR team."

"If you don't have a badge, you can't get in." He doesn't bother to look at me now.

"Well, I'm required at this event, and the PR team knows I

don't have a badge. They said I'd be on the list. Could you please call someone and have them double-check? You'll see that I'm on the PR staff list, I promise." I give him my sweetest smile, praying that he'll be reasonable. I glance at the time on my watch. I'm about two minutes away from being officially late and the anxiety turns my stomach.

"Ma'am, I don't have time for personal favors. We have an event here tonight. If you don't have a badge I can scan, you can't come through. Those are my orders." He looks at me dismissively and moves on to the next person behind me in line.

I'm so frustrated I could cry. Nothing has gone right lately. But I fight the tears because I'm not about to let anyone think I'm anything less than professional. Especially not when I'm fighting for any sort of chance I can get at a full-time job here. Some way that I can keep my dreams alive.

"Okay. Well, what if I can get ahold of someone inside with a badge? If they come get me, will you let me in?" I ask as I watch him usher several more people inside the building.

"If they can bring you a badge with your name on it, sure." He gives me the kind of smile that tells me he thinks I'm making shit up, and my nails bite into my palms as I smile back. "But you need to step aside. You're in the way, and we have other people trying to get through here."

"Okay. I'm going to call Madison then. Thank you." I flash another saccharine smile in his direction, willing myself to keep a calm, polite demeanor despite the fact he's toying with my sanity.

"I have no idea who Madison is, ma'am, but you need to get out of the way, *please*." He dismisses me sharply, like I'm a cocklebur stuck in his shoe.

I step to the side and let out a soft growl of frustration as I root for my phone in my purse. I watch as he picks up his walkie-talkie and says something into it, his eyes lifting to look me over one more time while he talks. I have a feeling if I keep pressing the issue, I'm going to be banned from the Chaos's buildings for life.

I don't need this today of all days. I really can't afford to be late or have people wondering where I am when this is a big event for the families. His refusal to even look at the list I'm positive he has somewhere behind his desk or on his phone has me ready to scream. But I can hear my mother's voice in the back of my head, telling me to stay calm and prove him wrong by doing what he asks. Class over crass, she always used to say.

More players and their families easily slide past me, notably without badges. But Mr. Rules over here strikes me as the type that has every single player's name and current stats memorized before the season starts so he can chat them up. Sure enough, he nods, smiling and waving them in quickly.

I press the call button next to Madison's name, and it starts to ring. And ring... And ring. As more people file by, it sends me to her voicemail, and I send a text instead.

I start walking back and forth trying to burn off my nervous energy while I wait, staring at the city skyline, and wishing that I had her brother Easton's phone number. He's the wide receiver for the Queen City Chaos and one of the city's favorite players. I'm sure if he came out here, Mr. Rules would be eating his words. I'm out of luck there too. I try Wren, his wife, instead, but her phone goes to voicemail as well.

I'm guessing Madison is too busy setting things up, and Wren is probably busy greeting other players and their families. I pace the sidewalk again, trying to think of another solution that isn't just bull rushing past Mr. Rules and hoping I can run faster than him. I can't imagine it looks good that I'm missing. I'm supposed to be helping get photos for the day and helping oversee some of the activities the team has arranged for the families.

When the next players go in and Mr. Rules is busy scrolling

his phone for a moment, I approach him again, hoping that politeness can still win him over.

"Hi again. I called my friend, but she's not answering. I'm guessing she's busy helping with stuff inside and can't hear her phone. Is there someone you could call over the walkie-talkie to ask her to come out? Or could you ask for Easton Westfield? He's a friend as well. Either of them would be happy to explain to you that I'm part of the staff and just haven't received my badge yet.

"Ma'am. I'm not going to repeat myself. If you don't have a badge, you don't get in. I'm not bothering any of the players to have them come out here and get you. They're busy enjoying the day with their families and don't have time to be bothered with *friends* right now."

The way he says friends has snapped my last bit of patience. If he wants to pour gasoline everywhere, then I'm ready to toss the match. I open my mouth to speak when an arm suddenly wraps around my shoulder, and I'm pulled close to a hard chest. The scent of a soft, masculine cologne wraps around me and a warm, deep voice I haven't heard in a while speaks on my behalf.

"Hey, Jim. How are you today? Is there a problem here? I see you met Trixie. She's coming in with me today if that's all right."

My heart skips a beat and I close my eyes because I'm being rescued by my ex-boyfriend's older brother. If that's not the cherry on top of everything today, I don't know what is.

I look up, and Cooper flashes me a bright smile and winks at me, squeezing my shoulders before he looks back up at Mr. Rules, apparently, also known as Jim. Jim snaps to attention, his stiffness melting until it's all cordiality and friendliness. Lizzy, Cooper's daughter, is standing next to him, her eyes darting between all three of us as she watches her father charm my nemesis, and she grins with amusement.

"Of course, Mr. Rawlings. I didn't realize she was with you. I apologize."

Raucous internal screaming is happening on my part, but I just flash my own smile at Jim while I bite my tongue and follow Cooper into the building. I take a deep breath after I'm past the gauntlet of entry doors and try to recenter my sanity before I have to go in to work with my game face on. But first, I have to thank my ex-boyfriend's brother for saving me from starting a war I might not have been able to win with Jim.

"Thank you for that. I appreciate it." I give him my first genuine smile of the day.

"Anytime, Trixie. Sorry he gave you shit. He means well, I think, but he's a little overprotective of the team."

"I noticed."

"Trix! I've missed you!" Lizzy beams at me. Lizzy is Cooper's thirteen-year-old daughter. We bonded initially on my first family trip with the Rawlings to their family lake house. She'd been more than thrilled to find out that I knew how to play some of her favorite games and was willing to listen to her stories and flip through her art books with her. The kid is a prodigy, honestly, who is desperately excited to get through school so she can start a career in video game design.

"I've missed you too! How have you been? How was school this past year? You've gotten so much taller." I'm doing the mental math, and if I'm right, she's just finished eighth grade. She's shot up at least another inch in the last year and is coming closer and closer to my five-nine, especially in the platform sneakers she has on.

"It was good. I start high school in the fall. Dad's terrified." She laughs as she looks at her father, and he gives me a sheepish shrug.

"Wow. Time has flown by. How's the designing going?" Last we talked she'd come up with a concept for a game she wanted to develop with her friends.

"Good. I'm going to a designing and coding camp later this summer."

"That's amazing! I'm so excited for you." I want to ask her so many more questions because she's the sweetest kid, but my eyes dodge to the hall I need to hurry down to find Madison before this event gets fully underway.

"You should come sit with us!" Lizzy looks at me hopefully and I smile back, wishing I didn't have to let her down.

"I think she's got some work to do, Lizzy," Cooper says softly to his daughter, picking up on my anxiety. He flashes me a look of understanding, and I answer it with my own.

"Oh. Okay. I get it." She gives me a resigned look of appreciation, and I feel guilty after the two of them rescued me. I glance at Cooper one last time, hoping he doesn't think I'm being ungrateful.

Cooper, the single dad, has always been a bit of an enigma. Mostly because that version of Cooper was the one I knew best, but the one the rest of the world knew was Cooper, the playboy. The guy who dates models and actresses. The life of parties and the forever single guy who never had time for anything else but football and partying, and more secretly, his daughter. He's always worked hard to keep her and their lives out of the limelight.

"If I can get away, I'll definitely come to find you so you can tell me more." I grin at her, and then wave a quick goodbye and nod at Cooper one last time before I start to speed walk down the hall.

Cooper looks nothing like Rob, my ex, despite the fact they share genes. He's taller, with darker-brown hair that's always got that messy, just-woke-up look with short curls, where Rob had always spent hours grooming his. Cooper has deep-brown eyes flecked with gold and warm brown, where Rob's are a crystal blue and hold a sharp gaze that Cooper just isn't capable of. Cooper's jaw is more cut, and he's leaner with a broad chest and the kind of shoulders and traps that would give him an excellent career in fitness modeling if he ever wanted it. Even in his day-off jeans, T-shirt, and backward hat look he has going on today, he's still gorgeous. Whatever woman eventually lands him is going to be lucky as hell. I used to look forward to seeing who he'd end up with, hoping it was someone as fun and laid-back as he is, as I desperately wanted a future sister-in-law to hang out with at the family get-togethers. But now that's all a distant memory. Because while Rob and I had been on-again and off-again for quite a while, the last time we called things off, it was permanent.

"There you are!" Madison, my best friend, beams when she sees me come in the door. She's still putting together swag bags for the families to take home. I hustle to take over the bag prep.

"I'm so sorry I'm late. The guy at the door wouldn't let me in because I didn't have my badge. Acted like I was a dire security risk to the entire team. I called to see if you could get me in, but I guess you didn't hear it."

"Oh no! I'm so sorry, Bea! It's in my purse in the office. I didn't even think." Madison looks at me apologetically. "I've just been rushing around and I didn't even notice the time. I should have known when you weren't your usual punctual self."

"It's okay. Cooper got me in. Apparently, Mr. Rules at the door will let anyone come in as long as they're with a player." I give her a sideways look and shake my head.

"Cooper got you in, huh? Was that awkward? Did he say anything about Rob?" Madison raises an inquisitive brow.

"No, he barely talked at all. Mostly just Lizzy. She was surprised and catching me up on things in her life. She's so sweet. I forgot how much I missed her."

"That's Cooper's daughter, right?"

"Yes."

"I forget that he has one, honestly. With his reputation and everything."

"I was literally just thinking that on the way in. That how I've known him is so the opposite of his reputation."

"Well, he's been working hard on it," Madison quips.

"True. He wants Playboy of the Year as badly as Quentin wants Grump of the Year. How's that going by the way?" Quentin Undergrove is the Chaos's new quarterback, Madison's ex, and the current focus of her PR efforts.

"We're making progress. He's being agreeable. Too agreeable, which I find suspicious." She flattens her lips.

"I told you my theory." I flash a small smirk at her that she doesn't appreciate.

"Yes, well... doesn't change facts."

"You don't still think about him that way?" I raise a brow at her because I don't believe it.

She and Quentin are forces of nature separately. The two of them together? I don't think there's anything they couldn't accomplish. As long as they aren't fighting each other. If they come to blows, they're going to take everyone out with them, possibly this entire organization. Especially considering his uncle is the coach and her brother is expected to be one of his main receiving targets on the field. But Madison can run circles around almost anyone in PR. It's part of the reason I love working with and learning from her. So if anyone can put Quentin in his place—it's her. Assuming they don't kill each other first.

"Do you still think about Rob?" She volleys the question back, and the look on her face tells me she doesn't mean for it to hurt so much as to remind me that we're both in a similar place. She's worse off, really, since she's forced to work with her ex.

"Less every day."

"Then imagine ten years of every days."

I don't entirely believe her, but I'm not going to argue the point now. We need to be on top of our game today. We want to make a good impression on the team and the players going into this year.

"Do the tumblers go in every bag? Or just these ones?" I change the subject.

"All of them. They're cute, aren't they?"

"Yeah, they are. Any extras?" I flash her a conspiratorial grin.

"I think there might be." She hands me one and nods for me to tuck it in my bag. "All right. You ready to load the carts and take them out?"

"Wherever you lead, boss." I grin at her, and we start working to get the bags out into the main hallway.

"So what about Cooper?" she asks as we're loading the last of them.

"What about him?"

"That won't be weird for you—having to be around your ex's brother all the time? I honestly didn't think about it. I was so excited to have you out here when they said I could bring someone on. I forgot about that."

"I don't think I'll have to be around him much. He was always nice to me, and I love Lizzy. So I think we can keep things professional when I have to see him. Hopefully, he doesn't run and tell Rob what a mess I was this morning." I shrug as we start to wheel them down the hall.

"Well, as long as you're okay with it. If it becomes an issue, just let me know, okay?"

"Of course," I answer as though it's an impossibility but now I'm wondering if I should be more concerned about it.

2

C *ooper*

LIZZY'S RUN off with a group of other teens to walk the stadium and check out the setup while I've been rounded up by a bunch of the guys to talk about their latest off season fishing trip. I'm half listening to them regale us with a story about their big catch, but my mind is still spinning from the fact that Trixie's here in Cincinnati. I thought after she and my brother, Rob, broke up, it would be the last I'd ever see her. Never in a million years did I think she'd be here working PR alongside Easton Westfield's sister.

My brother's ex has accomplished things no other woman in my life has managed—like a recurring nightly spot on my mental roster. Because she's starred in nearly every fantasy I've had since I met her. I haven't told a fucking soul about them because I don't even understand it. I'm sure if I saw a shrink, they'd tell me it was some sort of Freudian complex about competing with my brother on and off the field for attention. Or for someone like me, she represents the idea of a relationship—the one thing I can't seem to make happen.

As far as I can tell, it's just her. All the little things about her —from the way she smiles like you're the only person to ever really amuse her, to how she always loved my family like her own, down to silly little things like the way she always divided her candy into colors and ate them one by one while we watched movies. Or the way she couldn't bait a hook to save her life, but was still willing to spend an entire afternoon letting me teach her.

My brother's ex is also one of my teen daughter's idols. She's obsessed with the fact that Trix can keep pace with video game knowledge and knows some of the lore behind her favorite worlds. They've stayed up more than one night together having slumber parties at our family lake house over the years. And despite the fact my daughter is more punk rock and Trixie is quiet luxury, the two of them have spent hours shopping with one another and comparing their favorite playlists and Roman Empire books. The fact that Trixie is the younger sister of Alexander Xavier, the league's best defensive end and my daughter's way-too-old-for-her crush—one that makes me worry about what I'm in for when she hits high school this fall —gave Trix even more bonus points in Lizzy's eyes. I'm half-certain Lizzy would run away to live with Trix if she could. Apparently, it's a family trait that we're all a little fascinated with her.

When Rob and Trixie broke up, I hoped Lizzy and I could both let her go for good. But Lizzy still found ways to mention her, especially whenever we had to spend any time around Rob's new girlfriend. And for my part, she still haunts my dreams despite trying to write her off as a figment of my imagination or some ideal I'd conjured up. A reason to explain why I couldn't date because I hadn't found the perfect woman the way my brother had.

I've been doing better in recent months though. I've even gotten to the point where I'm trying to move on from one-night stands and situationships to a place where I can consider actually finding someone I want to date. Trying to be better for Lizzy's sake, if not my own.

But now Trix is here, blown in like a tornado, and destroyed all my progress within a matter of minutes. Because now all I want to know is how long she's here and if I have a shot in hell.

"Rawlings!" Wyatt Northmore, our kicker, and one of the only guys on the team besides Ramsey willing to call me on my shit, shouts my name.

"What?" I blink, coming back to a reality where Beatrix Xavier isn't sprawled out in front of me in one of the sundresses she used to wear, eating strawberries curled up in an Adirondack chair or playing volleyball in one of her sheer swimsuit coverups.

"You're not even listening, are you?"

"I was listening, I just... ran into someone I used to know. Didn't expect to see them here."

"Don't tell me, one of your hookups is someone's sister." Northmore raises a brow, amusement dancing over his face.

"Or wife?" Ramsey, my closest friend in the world and on this team, adds.

"Oh fuck. If it's the wife, I don't want to know." Garner shakes his head, gritting his teeth as he flashes me a look.

"But if it's the sister, you do?" Northmore looks at him.

"I mean... is she single?" Garner grins. "I don't mind sharing."

"Fucking hell. Let the man speak," Ramsey grouches.

"So?" Northmore asks.

"Neither. My brother's ex." I shrug but I feel like every

thought I've ever had about her is showing on my face given the way they react.

"That's not better. That's..." Ramsey raises his eyebrows with a look of admonishment.

"I didn't fuck her. I just said I ran into her. Damn." I give them all a shut-the-fuck-up look.

"We're just fucking with you." Northmore gives me his own what-the-fuck look and returns to his story about the fish they caught until we're surrounded by the married men on our team, living vicariously through Northmore's very obviously exaggerated tale of the rest of his evening at sea.

"Less of the fucking, maybe? We got kids here." One of the other guys who's just joined says, and I decide to wander off on my own and let the guys do their off-season humble bragging without me.

I check on Lizzy, who's still outside half playing something on her phone and half invested in a conversation happening with some other kids her age. It's really not fair to call her a kid anymore. She's getting so grown up, and by the end of the summer, I wonder if I'll recognize her anymore. Her mom's already told me she's planning some sort of pre-high school makeover with her friends, which is a lot to stomach on its own because my girl has always been a tomboy at heart—all messy hair, stomping through creeks, playing video games in oversized T-shirts and baggy jeans. But recently, she's mentioned boys names she knows and talked about them in hushed tones in the back seat of my car with her friends in a way that says she sees them as more than video game buddies, and I am one hundred percent not ready for that.

When I turn the corner, our tight end, Easton Westfield's standing there looking disgruntled as he sips a drink and glances back out across the room. I raise a brow at him in question.

"The Undergroves continue to annoy me," he gripes, referring to our new coach and his nephew, our new quarterback, Quentin Undergrove.

"Sorry?" I shrug, only partially committed to the apology. "I don't think Quentin's half bad now that I've had more of a chance to know him."

I already struck up a friendship with him, and I honestly like the guy. He seems like a straight shooter and, for all the talk about him being a grumpy asshole with a chip on his shoulder, he's been laid-back and friendly enough when we've gone out for dinner after practice. Plus, he played with my brother back in Pittsburgh. If Quentin could get along with Rob, I imagine he could get along with most of the guys here. Because my brother is a self-assured, self-centered prick when he wants to be, especially when he's in a locker room after a win. Easton's easygoing as fuck in comparison, so the two of them not getting along is a little surprising, even with the bitter family history between the Undergroves and Westfields.

"Not trying to fuck your sister, is he?" Easton grumbles.

"No. But your sister's grown. I think she can make those decisions for herself, can't she?"

"Course she fuckin' can, but doesn't mean I don't worry about her. She takes on a lot, and her trying to make him the city's darling lover boy is asking too much. Even with her PR skills."

I imagine that's why Trix is here. Easton's sister, Madison, has called in reinforcements, and Trix has her own sent of PR skills that saved my brother more than once.

"From what I've heard, they're already making some progress." Quentin couldn't say enough good things about Madison, and for her part, she was working hard to make him a household name here.

East shoots me a look, and I give him another shrug in return.

"The two of you *would* get along," he says sarcastically. I know the Undergrove presence here has him on edge and that the history between those families is long and bitter, but I also know Easton can roll with the punches when he has to.

"Like I said, set your family shit aside… You might like him."

"We'll see. We're stuck with him one way or the other, so he better at least be able to throw a decent ball."

"You know he can."

"He's not a top three," Easton argues.

"No. But that doesn't mean shit if we've got the right guys playing and moving the ball."

East's mouth flatlines, and he chugs the rest of his drink, tossing the container into the recycling bin.

"Like I said. We'll see," he repeats. "Gonna look for Wren. See if she needs anything or if she'll at least get off her feet for a minute. I'll catch up with you later." He gives me a half smile and a nod, and then he's off to find his pregnant wife.

———

A short while later, I find myself in the buffet line with Lizzy while she grabs the food she wants, and I help hold a plate of desserts for her. The girl has a mean sweet tooth just like I do, and I love her for it because it's meant she's always been game for late-night trips to get ice cream or eating donuts for breakfast all weekend. Things her mother overlooks in the name of positive coparenting.

"Oh, and they have s'mores outside!" She whirls around with her plate and grins at me. "Do you think Trix is around here? I want her to sit with us. I can't believe she's seriously here." Lizzy's eyes dart around the room, and they must catch on her because she grins even brighter.

"Trix is working, Lizzy. Let's give her a chance to do her job."

But I follow her line of sight, wanting another glimpse of her to torture myself with.

Lizzy's eyes flash to mine, and she studies my face for a minute.

"You're not gonna take Uncle Rob's side, are you? I know he has a new girlfriend, and we're supposed to just be excited for him, but I miss Trix. Do you think they could get back together when he comes to his senses?"

I hope the fuck not.

"I doubt it. Your uncle's pretty set on the new girlfriend." I didn't like her nearly as much. My parents aren't exactly fans either, and Lizzy has made her opinions well known to everyone but Rob and his girlfriend. But I'm also not rooting for Trix's return to that particular title either.

"Well, he's an idiot. She's not half as smart or as pretty as Trix."

That's true, but she's also half as independent, half as ambitious, and half as well-connected, which means that she doesn't outshine Rob. Or at least that's my guess as to why he's been so enthusiastic about this new relationship. I personally don't give a shit who he dates. As long as she's tolerable and doesn't influence Lizzy, it isn't my business. If it means that Trix is free and clear, well... that doesn't hurt either.

Lizzy leads the way to a table on the other side of the room near where the Paines and Westfields are sitting, and I follow her, setting up her food and then letting her know I'm running to get us drinks. My timing is damn near perfect because just as I pull up to the drink station, Trix is en route to the same place. She doesn't notice me until it's too late, and then her steps stutter. I can see her glance around like she wants an out, and I'm hoping I can reassure her I'm not here to be Rob's spy.

"You're not going to make a run for it, are you?" I ask playfully.

"What?" The guilt is written all over her face. "I just forgot something is all."

"Not just avoiding anyone with the last name Rawlings then?" I raise a brow.

"No, I just—"

"What are you drinking?" I ask when the bartender nods to me.

"Um, just a wheat beer if they have it."

I'm surprised it's not wine since that's what she always drank before, but I ask the bartender for it and order a second for me and a pop for Lizzy before I turn back to study Trix. The closer I look, the more little changes I see. Something about her hair is different and her makeup too, but I don't want to be caught staring.

"We can pretend he doesn't exist if you want. Well, I can't promise Lizzy won't mention him. She has big opinions on what an idiot he is, and honestly, I agree with her. But otherwise, we can just be random people on the team you're getting to know while having a drink and some dessert if you want to come sit with us? Lizzy is dying to talk to you, so I feel like I gotta put in a good word for her."

The uncertainty leaves her face, and she smiles at me, a genuine one that lights up her chocolate-brown eyes.

"We don't have to pretend. You and Lizzy were always kind to me. And I'd love to hear about what she's been up to, if you don't mind."

"Nah. She'd love that, and you can catch us up on what you've been up to."

Things like whether she's over my brother and if she has a new boyfriend.

"Of course. I'd ask the same for you, but I assume most of it wouldn't be safe for Lizzy's virgin ears," she teases me, and the flash of a smirk that crosses her face as I hand over her beer does things for me.

So yeah, whatever recovery I thought I'd done on the whole "not coveting my brother's girl" front? It's forgotten the second I watch her walking in front of me, and lost for good the second I see my kid fall into love with her all over again as they discuss her favorite things, her high school and summer camp ambitions, and swipe through the artwork on her phone that she's been working on while Trixie fawns over them all.

I'm a fucking goner all over again, remembering every single reason I had a crush on this woman in the first place and inventing new ones while I listen to the two of them catch up on life since my brother fucked up. But the beautiful thing about all of this is she's not my brother's girl anymore, and I have all the cheat codes to win her over.

3

Beatrix

IT'S GIRLS' night tonight, and Madison and I are both hanging out in Wren's living room while we catch up on each other's week. We're sipping cocktails and mocktails and eating a million and one delicious snacks that Wren has made for us, including a to-die-for chocolate cake that she's just put on the menu at her sports bar, West Field, that sits next to the stadium.

"What do you put in this, magic?" I blink as I take another bite.

"Something like that." Wren gives me a bemused look.

"Is the recipe a secret? I feel like I need this in my lineup."

"She's obsessed with baking. I don't know how you guys do it. I don't mind cooking a few nights a week but baking with all the measuring and mixing and exacting temperatures—it's not for me." Madison takes another swipe at the dip with her cracker and eats it while she shakes her head in disbelief.

Wren laughs. "It's not that difficult once you get the hang of it. And yes, the recipe is secret-ish, but I can let you in on it as long as you swear to secrecy."

"For this, I'll do whatever you want." I take another bite and close my eyes, savoring how good it is. "Is it just chocolate cake or something fancier? I mean, obviously, there's chocolate in it, but like... Wow."

"It's Better Than Sex Cake." Wren grins as she pulls out her phone and types away. "Just sent the recipe to you."

"I'm sorry, what now? I don't think so. I mean, maybe better than sex with East, but no way is any cake better than *good* sex," Madison argues as I grab the recipe Wren just sent and save it to my recipe folder, along with a note that says, "Learn to make A.S.A.P."

"First of all, I feel the need to defend your brother here, and I don't think you'll want the details." Wren eyes her sister-in-law.

"Ugh. No, definitely not. Please, spare me. Pretend I said nothing."

"And technically, it's not better, but it's damn close. Also... it was sex with East that kind of inspired it."

Madison makes a disgusted face and pushes the plate with her piece away from her on the coffee table while Wren and I both laugh.

"Cake inspired by sex. I like it," I say flippantly, grinning as I take another bite and see Madison cringe again.

"How's the dating app been treating you?" Wren gives me a thoughtful look.

"Meh. I've barely looked at the one I downloaded. Not many prospects. Hard to be interested in anyone, honestly." I shrug.

"Are you still missing him?" Madison asks.

"Missing Rob? No. It's been what... nearly a year? I'm over him. But sometimes, I miss being in a relationship. Not all the work... But the good parts, you know? Having someone to grab dinner with. Watching a movie before bed. Sex you don't have to get all dressed up and go to a bar for." I laugh at the last bit, but Madison and Wren still look worried for me.

"But no dates or hookups have interested you?" Madison gives me a sympathetic look.

"It's been hard since I've been traveling so much. You know that. You've been putting work first too. I haven't really been able to think about it, and when I do, it's an afterthought. Dating is a hard no for me right now anyway."

"Why's that?" Wren takes a sip of her mocktail as she leans back.

"I have no idea what I'm doing with my life. If our business idea to start a PR retreat for athletes will work." I look to Madison. "If it does work, I'm not sure where I'll be living since we've had trouble finding an affordable place. There's no sense getting attached to someone new just to say goodbye in a few months when I need to move."

"Okay, well, we're definitely going to be a success, so erase any other thought from your mind. But I understand what you mean about not knowing where we'll live. It's why I'm still in their cottage." Madison nods to Wren and then grins at her. "Thanks, by the way, for continuing to tolerate me squatting in your guest house."

"It has been a great source of entertainment so far, what with the deliveries and listening to you and East bicker." Wren laughs.

"I wish there was room for another bed, Bea. I'd move you in with me at least." Madison rolls her lower lip into a pout.

"You could always stay in our guest room?" Wren offers.

"No, I couldn't do that to you all." I shake my head.

Wren is already pregnant, opening a new restaurant, and has Madison living in the guest cottage, which she and East built when they first bought the place and were doing massive renovations. I don't want to be another thing on her list of upkeep and to-dos, especially since our friendship mostly exists on the back of Madison's and my friendship right now. I love her and want to keep her forever, and part of that means not wearing on her last nerve now that we get to spend some time together.

"Well, if you change your mind, you know where you can come," Wren adds.

"I appreciate it."

"Okay. Back to the drought. You can't date, but you can fuck, right? I mean, is that against your rules? I know you were raised a little fancier than the rest of us, but then Xander is your brother," Wren muses.

I laugh hard at that. My brother, Xander, was probably the most notorious playboy in the league before my future sister-in-law nailed him down. I have their engagement party to host in Seattle in a few weeks, and there's a whole lot of prep work I need to be doing to get ready for it. It's yet another thing on the list that keeps me from browsing singles apps or hitting bars on what would otherwise be free nights. Not that I'm necessarily complaining because I love being able to help Xander and Harper.

"It's not against the rules per se, but I think I'm bad at it. Like, I don't even know what apps are good options these days or how to find time for it. The last time I dated before Rob was years ago. I don't know that I'm prepared for all of that. And what are people even doing for dates now?"

"You're overthinking this too much. We can find the right apps and things for you to try based on what you want. Are you just looking for the occasional hookup to keep you out of a drought, or are you looking to work your way down your adventure list? How wild are we getting with this? Let's start there." Madison gives me a curious look before she takes another sip of her drink. I've walked right into this because she always has a plan for any problem.

"My adventure list?" I raise my brows.

"Yeah," Madison answers matter-of-factly, like I should just know what she's talking about.

"You don't have a list of things you want to try?" Wren looks up at me.

"Should I?"

"Not necessarily a literal list. But what about a mental one?" Madison presses.

"I have no idea what you two are talking about. Like sex stuff?"

They both laugh, and Wren shakes her head.

"It doesn't have to be sex stuff," Wren explains. "It can be just things you're challenging yourself to try. A bucket list or whatever. But it *can* include sex stuff. Especially if you're single and trying to figure out what you want next time so you're not stuck with someone who doesn't have patience."

"Right. Things that turn you on. Things you want to try. Things you have tried and definitely want to do again?" Madison's looking increasingly concerned about my lack of list.

"I can't say that's a thing I have. No."

"Oh. We need to make you one. Stat. Get your phone out." Madison swallows the rest of her drink and motions toward my purse.

"I think we also need to just get her back to having some fun. It's almost summer. I know there so many things to do with the team, but you should have some fun. Get out and, like, go to the pool or take a hike or visit a museum." Wren looks at me. "You're all work and no play. That's not healthy."

"The fact that you two workaholics are lecturing me about my workaholism has me worried."

"Well, we can all be better about it. Support each other in

taking some time off and just enjoy life instead of always being on to the next. Right, Mads?" Wren looks between us.

"Sure. Just as soon as I unload the biggest pain-in-the-ass client I've ever had." Madison holds out her hand for my phone.

"You secretly love torturing him," I tease her about Quentin.

"I mean, I don't hate it. I've been pushing him to work on his lists too." Madison watches as I search for my phone, which I just put back in my bag and somehow immediately lost.

I extract and unlock it before I hand it over to its fate. She opens the notes list where Wren had given me her secret recipe for the Better Than Sex cake, creates a blank list, and then grins deviously as she starts to type away.

"Her obsession with lists is definitely a kink, right?" I ask as I flash an amused look at Wren.

"It wouldn't surprise me." The corner of Wren's mouth quirks up in a smirk.

"All right. We'll ease into the kinks. Let's just make you a list of things you want to try this summer in general." Madison smirks as she adds a couple of stickers to the note before titling it. "We can call it the Better Than the Ex List."

"Oh. I love that." Wren claps her hands together and grabs another cookie off the veritable tower of snacks she made for us. "What's up first?"

"I don't know. Now you've given me way too many possibilities." I look to Madison for guidance.

"Okay, so let's start with something you've never done but have always wanted to try."

"Stargazing?" I shrug.

"Stargazing." Madison presses her lips together and tilts her head in thought. "I've honestly not tried that either. See, that's a good start. What else?"

"Camping? Maybe? I'm not sold on that, but theoretically, the nature and the s'mores sound like fun."

"You've never been camping?" Wren presses her hand to her chest in surprise.

I shrug sheepishly. It wasn't exactly high on the list of things to do in the Xavier household where things like fundraising dinners and golf outings with business associates took precedence.

"All right. Well, at the very least, we can set you up out here in the woods with a tent. We have half a dozen because East keeps deciding he needs the latest model. Whatever that even means when it comes to tents. Like... as long as it doesn't leak and there's enough room, I'm not sure why it matters. And yet every summer, like clockwork..." Wren shakes her head in disbelief, and Madison and I both laugh.

"Married life sounds like fun," I muse.

"Don't get me started. I love that man, but he also knows how to drive me mad."

"Yeah, I can take you camping if need be. But maybe we can find a cute guy to take you." Madison raises her brows.

"I mean, I have wanted to try sex outside. Always seems so romantic in the movies when they're rolling around in a meadow."

"It's overrated." Wren sighs and gives me a doubtful look. "Bugs, leaves where you don't expect to have them, humidity in the summer... I'm just saying. Go in prepared for the reality rather than the fantasy."

"Speak for yourself. Some of the best sex of my life was outside." Madison types the next item onto the list. Wren and I both raise our heads to look at her even though she's still busy typing.

"Care to enlighten us?" I try to distract her from the list because I think that might be the end of it, and I'm sure she'll tell me it's not long enough.

"No. We're focused on your list. Sex outside because you're into exhibitionism?"

"No. Not really. I mean, I'm not against it, but I think, if anything, I'd prefer to be on the other end of that scenario. What is that called? Voyeurism? Yeah, voyeurism."

"Watching can be fun," Madison muses. "Ooh, what about a sex club then? Have you been to one of those?"

"Can't say that I have."

"All right. Voyeuristic experience and possible sex club added to the list."

"Okay, this is already getting ambitious for me. I need small steps here. First adventures, you know. We're bouncing from camping in a tent in Wren's backyard to sex clubs. That's... a lot."

"Lists should be ambitious. It's a goal list. You want to get as much as possible, but it doesn't have to be *everything* if you don't want it to be. You've got to challenge yourself and put yourself first, Bea. Get out there and see what you like. This is an opportunity. A chance to have a new you—the one you want without your ex influencing your choices." Madison gives a little pep talk on her soapbox.

It's one of the reasons I love her. She's always up for a challenge and pushes me to expand my horizons. I've come leaps and bounds from my quiet, prep-school self since I met her. I might have to amend her list down to size when she's done though.

"There are lots of other fun things you can try at a sex club, too, if you find a guy to go with," Wren offers.

"I'd have to find the guy first, one I feel comfortable with, and again... no dating, remember?"

"No dating doesn't mean you couldn't find a regular hookup. Someone on the same page as you about the no feelings."

"And where am I going to find this guy? My free time is spent around the team, and in addition to the obvious problems with that, I have absolutely sworn off athletes for life. If guys aren't after me for my father's connections, they're after me for an in with Xander. No thank you."

"That's why you've got to get on one of the apps. You can filter those people out. Keep your last name private, and no one has to know who you are. Pick guys who aren't into sports even. I'm adding that to your list. You need to find a new app to try. I'll send you my favorites, but you can mix and match and swipe your way to someone who fits your wants. You're so good at this when it comes to setting up clients. Just use a bit of that magic on yourself."

"Well I'm glad you believe in me. I have my doubts." I shrug, nibbling the edge of a cracker as I stare out the window.

"You're gorgeous, Bea. You're going to be inundated with dicks the second you open a profile and have to try to pick. The weeding through them is a little exhausting. That's how you end up just settling for the guy you hate." Wren jokes about how she met her husband.

"Well... thank you. But it still seems a little overwhelming."

"If you need help setting up your profile or anything... you've got me." Madison gives me a reassuring look.

"You're the best, Mads."

"Okay. So assuming we get you the guy... what's on the kink list?" Wren asks.

"Doesn't sex outside and voyeurism count?"

"Sure, but you've got to have something besides that, right? Something you can try in the sex club when you visit." Madison smirks.

"I've got nothing."

"Nothing?" Wren questions me, raising a brow.

"Not anything I can think of."

"All right. Well, then, I'm adding some suggestions of my own." Her face turns serious as she types away. A couple of moments into her list, though, my phone vibrates, and she looks up at me. "You have an alert that just says 'Cooper.'"

"Chaos's Cooper? Rawlings?" Wren's interest piques.

"Rob's brother?" Madison joins in the sudden inquisition.

"I ran into him at the family event. His daughter, Lizzy, wanted to catch me up on things and talk, so he invited me to sit with them. We were chatting, and he asked about the image makeover we're giving Quentin and wanted to know if it's possible to do something for him too. He wants to start thinking long-term about when football's over and what it's going to take to make that happen."

"Cooper wants an image makeover?" Wren is the queen of suspicious questions right now.

"I think he just thought the idea was interesting and asked me if there was anything I thought I could do. So I set a reminder to look into his public profile. I only really know Cooper, the dad, so..." I shrug and look to see Wren's face turned up in surprise.

"He is... Let's just say, he has a reputation. When he doesn't have his daughter, his house is the party spot for a lot of the single guys. He's dated a few celebrities, too, which caused a lot of drama when they came back to Cincinnati and were spotted out together. I was hoping he'd stay with that one actress he dated. She was sweet and came to a couple of team things, but it fizzled out, I guess. I'm curious what he wants to change."

"Yeah. What's the angle he's wanting?" Madison perks up. "Could he be a client for us, do you think?"

"I think he was just interested in sponsorships and a transition when he quits playing in a few years. Whether he needs to tamp down the whole playboy thing to do it. I'm not sure if he wants to be a client full time or not."

"He could definitely tamp down on the image. Or he could just lean into it. If that's his thing, some brands love that," Madison offers.

"True. I just want to see what the general public's vibe on him is. Is he a favorite on the team?" I look to Wren.

"Oh yeah. He and East are pretty close, except he parties a lot more than East does, so we see him more when he has Lizzy. He has her like every other week, I think. The other weeks, she's with her mom. So he's kind of Dr. Jekyll and Mr. Hyde that way."

"Interesting." I sip my drink and mull over what I might be able to do with that. But I can't help being curious about there being more of a non-dad side to Cooper.

"Well, that's not great. He probably needs to pick a lane." Madison glances at me. "Easier to market him for sponsorships if he's one or the other. I bet you could do some great stuff for him. Maybe it's worth signing him if he's interested."

I nod and watch as Madison looks back down at the list on my phone and grins.

"What?" My brow furrows as I feel a hint of apprehension at the way she's smirking.

"He should be on the list." Madison's grin turns devious.

"Ohhhh." Wren follows with a whistle, but she grins brightly at the idea. "He would be perfect. Probably knows where all the good clubs are. I like that."

"Perfect for what?"

"Sex. Obviously." Madison's typing away again.

"What? Do not put him on the list! Didn't you, literally, just talk about him being a client?" I practically choke on my own words. The idea of Cooper and me is absurd.

"Too late. He's already on it. Better an adventure than a client for you right now." She grins.

"He's Rob's brother, Mads!" I protest.

"That's bonus points for his eligibility, in my view." Madison's eyes light with amusement.

"Because it'll bring all the drama my way?" I give her sideeye.

"Because you already know and like him. Because, like Wren pointed out, he's already got a reputation, so it's not like you're going to sully it. And three, he's the brother. What's not to like about a little revenge sex?"

"And if I take him on as a client?"

"Weren't you just encouraging me the other day to hook up with *my* client?" Madison gives me a pointed look, and I press my lips together and roll my eyes.

"That's different. You've already slept with him."

"A million years ago. It's not the same."

"Neither is this!"

Wren's having a good laugh at the two of us bickering, and I shake my head and down the rest of my drink.

"You're a bad influence."

"Tell me that after you've checked some of these things off your list."

Madison saves the list and hands my phone back to me. Wren's already off to the kitchen to grab some more dessert and a refill for my drink before I look up again. I try to distract myself with another bite of the cake, but now all I can think about is Cooper.

4

Cooper

I FINISH up my last round of reps and head for the showers. Lizzy's with her mom this week, so I'm heading home to get the BBQ fired up for the guys coming over later tonight. Just as I'm walking in the door, my phone dings with a number I don't immediately recognize, and I open it as a second message follows.

UNKNOWN:

Hey. This is Beatrix. I had your number saved from one of the times we were at the lake house. I hope you don't mind me texting.

> I just wanted to let you know Lizzy tried to add me today on my private Instagram account. I'm not sure how she found it. Probably because she's so smart. I've declined, but I don't want her to be upset. She can add me on my public account if she wants or text me anytime. I mean—if you're okay with it! My private account is mostly what I use for close friends, and I just don't want her to accidentally see something she shouldn't.

I'm grinning like an idiot at my phone because now I have her number without having to find an excuse to get it. Although, I'm curious about this private account she has on social media. But first things first. I have to reel it in and act like the good father and professional I am.

> No. Text her anytime. Thanks for the heads-up. I'll chat with her and give her your number to text you, if that's okay?

I type in Trixie and save her to my contacts before I toss my bag as I walk in the door and tuck my phone in my shorts. I make my way to the shower, stripping out of my shirt. I'm exhausted after a long day of offseason practice. My muscles are still trying to remember how the fuck to play football all over again, but I'm not too exhausted to text with her.

TRIXIE:

> Yes. As long as you're sure you don't mind? I understand if you don't want us talking. It made sense when Rob and I were together, but now, it might be weird for you?

> Not weird at all. She adores you. She's been going on about you since she saw you the other day. As long as she doesn't drive you crazy, I'm happy for you guys to talk.

> Okay. I just wanted to be sure! Thanks. Good seeing you both.

Well fuck. I need a reason to keep this going, but first, I have to get showered, dressed, and get things marinating out of the fridge and on the grill before the rest of the guys get here. And fire off a text to Lizzy to find out how her snooping ended with her being on Trixie's private account.

ME:

> Hey Lizzy. Hope you had a good day at school. Trix said you added her on an old private account on socials. She doesn't use it much so she said you can text her at this number if you want to talk more.

I send the number over to her and wait for a reply as the water in the shower heats up.

LIZZY:

> Okay. Thanks. I just wanted to catch up and ask her about something.

> She said to text her anytime. But now I gotta ask, ask her about what?

> Girl stuff.

> Okay, well, don't drive her crazy. Also, what's the account name you found?

> Why do you want to know?

> Just want to see something.

> Not suspish at all.

> Huh. That's interesting.

> What?

Someone just asked me about doing something on Saturday night. Might have to go.

You know we're going to the fair! Everyone is going, and I can't miss.

Are we though? I don't know. Can't seem to remember.

I could just have Emmeline's parents drop me off with her.

Nice try. If you go, I go. Now... give me the info.

It's TrixXTreats.

That's my girl.

Making me sell out Trix so I can see my friends. I'll have to discuss that with her when we chat.

Don't you dare.

Hmm. Just hoping I can get some time with my friends without my dad watching me like a loser.

Smartass.

I learned from the best.

I'm going. Those are the rules. I drive. I stay.

You can stay at the same place, but you can't, like, stalk us around the fair. You're going to embarrass me.

You realize half the guys in your school invite me to their birthday parties every year, right?

Embarrassment. Distraction. Either way. Not cool.

I'll keep a low profile. Like a spy. You won't even know I'm there.

You are such a nerd.

A nerd who loves you. Getting ready to BBQ. Have a good night. Do your homework. Listen to your mom.

Don't eat all the cookies I bought. I want some when I get home. Tell the guys I say hi and remind Rams he still hasn't beaten my score.

Will do.

I'M LAUGHING at how much it's going to irk Ramsey that he can't beat my daughter at his favorite game, and more that she loves to taunt him about it. I copy the name Lizzy gave me and type it into the search bar so I can find the account.

It comes up quickly and is private just like Trix said it would be. A small picture of her in a dress is the only sign it's hers with a bio so vague it could belong to anyone. I have my own private account for friends and family, so I don't blame her for wanting some anonymity in a world where people can turn the smallest thing into a salacious detail. I like having somewhere I can post things that are just between all of us and not having to hear every thought that runs through random people's heads about me and my performance out on the field.

It's one of the few things I hate about being a pro athlete— some people have no boundaries, and others feel like being pro means being flawless all the time. So I can appreciate a space where there's no pressure to be perfect .

I hover my thumb over the follow-request button for a

moment, contemplating whether or not I should. But I'm curious what's behind the privacy wall. Who she is when she's not being the senator's daughter, the good girlfriend in front of my parents, or the public-facing PR person.

I've seen enough to know I like her. More than I should given who she's been to me before now. But I have a feeling there's a lot more to Beatrix Xavier than I've seen so far, and a whole lot fucking more I'm going to like. Which is enough to convince me to push the button.

It's anticlimactic, though, because nothing happens. Just a note that she'll be notified and will have to accept or decline. I tap my phone against my leg and then set it on the counter so I can hop in the shower. I'm more anxious to see how she'll respond than I've been for anything outside of a game in a while. I am playing with fire already, but I like it.

———

An hour later, I've got the grill going, and Northmore is splashing around in the pool with Mira, Kelly, and Daphne, while Ramsey and Garner are busy helping me prep the food. I check my phone again, and there's a notification, but when I open it, it's from a post I made on my main account this morning and nothing from my private account.

"Waiting to hear from someone?" Logan Garner smirks and nods to my phone. "You've been checking it like every five minutes."

"Oh, just Lizzy telling me how you guys can't beat her score in the game and filling me in on her day."

"Damn. I really can't. She's fucking good. I think she really does have a career in it. Aren't there like competitive teams and cash prizes? Maybe she should do that," Ramsey pipes in.

"I've offered, but she doesn't want to compete. She just wants to design. She's always sketching things in her notebook and then running off into her room to work on them. She has an idea for a post-apocalyptic game right now. Honestly, it sounds pretty badass. Her friend's been working with her on it, though, and he's always coming over on his skateboard after school when she's here."

"A guy, huh? You let them hang out?"

"With the door open. They're still young, but her mom said the PTA group chat says a couple of the kids were already caught making out under the bleachers. She wants to go to the fair this weekend with him. He invited her. I guess there's a group of them."

"Kid stuff is a challenge, huh? Fuck, I don't know how you've done it for thirteen years already. Even now, I don't think I'm ready for them."

"Almost fourteen years now. I don't think you're ever ready. I think you just get thrown into the fire and pray you've got enough water every day to put it out."

Garner laughs and shakes his head. "Yeah, I think I can wait a bit for that."

There's a shriek from the pool that draws our attention toward it, and I see Mira splash Northmore with water, laughing and then trying to swim away before he can catch her. Ramsey's making his way to the pool, and Daphne's pulling herself up out of the side in a way that's hard to miss. Water's cascading off of her as she uses a towel to dab at her neck and chest. I'm half-certain it's for his attention, or maybe all ours. She's wild as hell and off-limits for every guy on the team.

"Fuck. She's hot..." Garner curses under his breath.

"Two words: Mayweather's sister."

"I know. But I can look, can't I?"

"At your own risk."

"You wouldn't if she asked?"

"Fuck no." I draw a line at my teammate's sister. My brother's ex, on the other hand... There, my morality's a little on the gray side. At least when it comes to one woman in particular. I glance at my phone again, and there's another notification. It's not from the app, but it's a text. And it's Trix. I nearly drop my phone in my hurry to open it.

TRIXIE:

Did you try to add me, or was that an accident when you were checking up on Lizzy?

> I talked to Lizzy and gave her your number so the two of you can chat. I meant to add you, unless you think I'm not old enough for the content.

She leaves me on read, and I turn around to open the grill again, flipping over the burgers and dogs while I wait to see if I get an answer.

TRIXIE:

Funny. But... is it weird if we're friends?

> Why would it be weird?

The obvious reason?

> Nah. I think it'd be weirder if we weren't still friends. You're not going to hold him against me, are you? I can disown him if need be.

I guess I won't make you disown family just to talk to me.

You and the rest of your family were always kind. I know I said that already, but seriously, thank you. And thank you again for the rescue the other day.

> You act like it's hard. We all just like you. Just between us—you were the only girlfriend of his I liked.

> Well... thanks? I think. I'm not sure what that says about me.

> Probably that he was lucky for once.

Lucky as fuck, frankly. I still have no idea how Rob convinced her to date him. She was out of his league. Out of mine, too, really. Way too refined and smart for either of us. That isn't going to stop me from trying though.

I spend most of the rest of my BBQ distracted and texting with Trix rather than chatting with any of my guests. I can feel Daphne's irritation with me building that I'm ignoring her, but I'd rather let her be Garner's problem than mine. Especially since I'm fairly certain her only interest in me is that she views me as a challenge. The two of them make a lot more sense, assuming he's ready to have his limbs rearranged in the process.

The more I text Trix, the more I'm reminded of how much I like her and how easy she is to talk to. I just wish I could spend more time with her, and somewhere outside of work. Which makes me think about this weekend and gives me a brilliant idea.

> So I'm wondering... do you like county fairs?

TRIXIE:
> That's a loaded question.

> Is it? Bad fair experience?

> I had to go to a lot of them as a kid.

> 4H?

> Worse. A father in politics.

> Oh right... That's fair. Get it?

> Sorry. That was fucking lame. Dad jokes just happen sometimes.

She doesn't answer, and my anxiety builds because I hope I'm not fucking this up. When another ten minutes pass by and I hear nothing, I decide to go for it anyway. Hoping I can salvage it somehow.

> Not even a giggle? Well. I'm still gonna shoot my shot. Confidence of a middle-aged dad, after all.

> I've gotta take Lizzy to one Saturday night. I promised she could go with her friends. But there are boys involved, one in particular I have my eye on. So I told her I'd take her, but I'm staying. It'll be weird if it's just me wandering around checking on them, but if you go... It'll just look like I'm out with a friend. So you could help my image by making me look like less of a creep.

TRIXIE:

> Sorry, I was in the shower.

> The dad jokes are gold. They definitely make me giggle.

> Does she already have a boyfriend?

After my brain short circuits for a moment imagining her in the shower, I answer her.

> I'm not sure. She swears he's just a friend, but he comes around enough that I think he wishes they were more. If I spent that much time on a girl at that age, it was because I wanted to be more than her friend. So I have my suspicions.

TRIXIE:

Had trouble with the friend zone growing up, did we?

I plead the fifth. But seriously... I'll buy you all the funnel cakes and ride tickets you want. Lizzy might even stop complaining about me going if you're there...

What time? I have a date Saturday, but I could go later.

My heart sinks. If she's already dating, that answers my question about whether or not I have a chance in hell.

A date? Already? You move fast.

TRIXIE:

Ouch? Madison's got me on a dating app.

I cringe at my own lack of filter. I don't know what I'm doing when I've got someone like her I'm trying to talk to. Just fumbling around trying to figure things out and making an ass of myself in the process.

Didn't mean it like that. I know you've been broken up for a while. I just meant you haven't been in the city that long.

TRIXIE:

I've been here for a bit.

Where are you living anyway? Got an apartment in the suburbs somewhere?

A hotel.

A hotel? Is it a long-term stay or? Seems like it'd get old after a couple weeks.

Something like that. Still trying to figure out if I'm going to stay here for long enough to justify something other than a hotel.

Well, tell your date he better give you some good reasons to stay. The team needs you.

I'll be sure to let him know you said that. His profile said he's a big Chaos fan, so he might actually listen to you.

Then tell him if he cares about the team, he'll cut the date short so you can go to the fair with me. I have to have her over there at 7:30.

Okay. I'm meeting him for coffee at 6, so I might be able to meet you there. Where's the fair? I'll have to get a ride. Still no car either.

Must be a pain getting to the stadium every day.

I'm staying close. Walking distance. Mads has been picking me up for other stuff, and I've been grabbing the occasional ride. It's been okay so far.

The fair's kind of out in the country. Where are you going for coffee?

The typing bubble pops up and disappears a few times. I'm not sure if she doesn't want to tell me or she can't remember the name of the place.

TRIXIE:

The Perk or Later. Why?

I can come to pick you up. Just text me when you're done, and Lizzy and I will get you on the way. I can take you home too.

Are you sure? I don't want to be a pain.

I'm more than happy to pick her up and even happier to grab her from her date. Not that I want to be a dick, but I also don't want to lose my shot before I even get a real chance.

> You're doing me a favor by going and keeping me company. The least I can do.

I grin at my phone. I'm gonna give her the best fair experience of her life, one so good she's going to forget she even went on a different date earlier in the night.

5

B*eatrix*

I'M SITTING across from my date, sipping on my iced tea, when his eyes suddenly light up as he looks over my shoulder. He looks like a little kid who was just told Santa was arriving any minute, and my eyes track his, looking back to see what he sees. When I do, my stomach somersaults. It's Cooper.

He's dressed in worn-in jeans, an olive-colored vintage tee, and a backward, frayed baseball hat that makes him look like he could just be the guy next door. It's obvious, though, that half the people in the room have clocked their favorite wide receiver at the counter.

Their incredibly sexy wide receiver with biceps that make his T-shirt sleeves stretch and forearms that have me, and half the people in the room, staring. He's at the counter ordering a frozen coffee drink, but when he's done, his eyes start to scan the room, headed straight for where I'm sitting. I turn around abruptly, refocusing on Darren, my date. I've almost forgotten I'm on one, too distracted by thoughts of Cooper, and I don't think I thought through what it would mean to have him pick me up.

"Do you know who that is?" Darren looks at me.

"Yes, I know him."

"You a Chaos fan too?" It's a rhetorical question because he gushes on. "I just fucking love them. I know everyone thinks Undergrove is a liability, but I think he's going to be the X factor for the team. Give Westfield something to fight for, and Rawlings is going to help get them there too. I can't wait to see what they do. I just got some tickets for summer camp open days. Me and some of my friends are planning to go. Hoping they'll sign a few things too."

This was one of the many reasons I kept my last name a secret and hated dating. Too many of these guys, if they knew who I was and the connections I had, would only care about that.

"Oh. That sounds like fun!" I don't know what else to say because there isn't much room to say something that wouldn't be awkward.

Darren hadn't been a terrible date so far, although we'd spent most of the night talking about him and his friends. I'd only learned a few trivial facts that gave me any context on why he was single and what he was looking for..

He's divorced and, apparently, very into his "me and the guys" era right now. I'm very into my "me and the girls" era, so I'm not judging, but I'm also not regaling him with tales of our late-night chats and skincare tips. So I could do with a little less play-by-play of his adventures drinking beer and hitting up casinos on the river. Still, he hasn't completely failed the screening phase yet. I'm trying to give him the benefit of the doubt. Even with those downsides, it was going better than half the dates I'd been on since Rob.

"He's signing autographs. Do you mind if I ask him? I can get one for you, too, if you want?"

"I'm good, but sure, go ahead." I don't know how to tell him I know the guy, and I'm not sure what Cooper is even doing inside right now. I thought he was going to text, and I'd meet him out at his truck.

"Oh shit. He's coming over here," Darren curses under his breath, his eyes dodging around, watching behind me. A moment later, I feel a hand on my shoulder, and I look up to see Cooper smiling down at me.

"There you are. You ready?" Cooper asks.

I can feel Darren's eyes boring into us.

"I thought you were waiting outside." I offer Cooper a small smile.

My cheeks heat because I feel like Darren is probably going to think I'm weird as hell now for not saying something. The confused and slightly irritated look on his face I can see out of the corner of my eye confirms it.

"I texted. But Lizzy wanted something. We were here early, so I thought I'd come in and grab it instead of going through the drive-thru."

I look around for Lizzy and then give him a questioning look that he answers with a smirk.

"She's on the phone in the car. Facetiming her friend about what outfit she's wearing tonight."

"You know each other?" Darren finally manages words.

"We're old friends," Cooper speaks up for us and flashes a bright smile to Darren. "Just picking her up to take her out to the county fair. Have some funnel cakes and ride a Ferris wheel or two. You been yet this year?"

Darren's eyes are wide for a moment, and then they go

heavy. A cloudier look overtakes the bright-eyed optimism of meeting one of his idols, replaced by the idea that another guy is picking his date up to go on a second one after.

"No, I haven't been," he addresses Cooper. "I didn't know you had plans after this." Darren's eyes shift to meet mine.

"It wasn't going to be until later. I promised to go to the fair with—"

"It's my fault," Cooper interjects. "Practically begged her to go with me, and then I'm here early. I can wait in the car for a bit if you want, Trixie."

"Trixie?" Darren repeats the nickname like it leaves a bad taste in his mouth.

"Sorry! Bea. I keep doing that. I forget I'm the only one who calls you that." Cooper grins at me, and I swear if I didn't know better, I'd think Cooper was making this awkward on purpose. I smile back because I don't know what else to do. "Do you want me to wait in the car for you?"

"Nah. I think we're good. I should let you two go. It was nice meeting you, Bea." Darren stands abruptly, glancing between me and Cooper. "Have a good evening."

Darren gathers up his drink and his phone, where he'd been showing me pictures of his latest guys' trip, and heads for the door without another word. My stomach drops because I'm fairly certain I'll never be hearing from Darren again. I can't believe I'm already failing, and it's only the first date I've been on here.

"What was that?" I turn my frustration toward Cooper.

"What was what?" Cooper looks at me like he has no idea what I'm talking about. Like he's just a sweet, innocent boy with a megawatt smile who was trying to be helpful.

"Rawlings!" The barista calls out.

"Hold that thought." He moves to get the drink he ordered for Lizzy while I gather my purse and my tea, moving toward the door where he meets me. As I stand waiting, I can see Darren climbing into his car, and I feel a twinge of disappointment for a moment before I shrug it off. It probably wouldn't have worked anyway, and if his ego's that fragile, I don't need it in my life. But I'm still a teensy bit cranky with Cooper.

"He's kind of an ass, no?" Cooper nods toward him.

"I mean, he was thrown off by your sudden appearance. He *was* a fan."

"He didn't act like much of one." Cooper's brow furrows as he watches the car drive off.

"Well, I think he felt insulted that I had other plans tonight. I was just going to tell him I had to run early and sneak out. I didn't expect to have to introduce you, and I didn't mention that you were picking me up."

"Oops." He gives me a sheepish look and shrugs. "Well, sorry. I didn't realize it would make him upset."

I stop in my tracks before we get to the car because I don't want to have this discussion in front of Lizzy. He stops when I do in the small berm and raises a brow when I stare at him and cross my arms.

"It wouldn't bother you if you were out with a woman on a date and some other guy just showed up and said all right, let's go? You'd just be fine with that?" I knew Cooper to be a pretty easygoing person, but I didn't see him being that laidback.

"Nah." He shrugs. "Wouldn't bother me. If she'd go with him, it'd mean that I didn't have a chance in the first place."

My jaw drops, and I give Cooper a look without saying anything, but he just grins and walks me around to the side of his truck and opens the door. He holds out his hand to help me up, and I take it.

"Here's your drink, Lizzy."

He hands it back to her, his arm brushing my shoulder and his cologne sweeping over my senses as he leans into my space to hand it to her. My eyes track the movement, and I feel a flush at the fact that I'm this close to him in such a small space. She takes the cup from him and smiles at me with a little wave before she resumes her conversation with her friend. Cooper rolls around to his side of the car, cranking up some country music much to Lizzy's chagrin, and we take off down the road.

6

B eatrix

WE MEANDER our way through the fairgrounds until we come to the row of carnival games, and Cooper's face lights up as he turns back to Lizzy.

"Want me to win you something?"

"Dad." She gives him an exasperated look. "I know you know I'm too old for toys."

"It's not a toy. It's a memento. Sits on your shelf to remind you of the time Trixie was here, and we had fun."

Lizzy looks up at me with a question in her eyes before giving her father a skeptical look.

"Well, if she doesn't want one, I do," I pipe in, turning to Cooper. I can tell he's trying to hold on to the waning days of her childhood. The time when he's the cool dad who plays football and not the annoying parent who doesn't let her stay out late with the boy he doesn't approve of.

"I can do that." Cooper's smile lights up, and he hurries over to the counter to lay down money for a chance at the prize. Lizzy and I follow after him, and she takes another bite of her shaved ice as we watch him ready himself for his shot at the stuffed animal. Lizzy lets out a little sigh. I know she's impatient to catch up with her friends who aren't quite here yet, but I wish I could tell her how someday she'll wish she had more of this time with him. That not all kids get the kind of attention and time he gives her.

"You're lucky, you know." I look at Lizzy. "My dad would never play games like this for me."

"I thought you said you went to lots of fairs."

"We did, but he was always working when we went to them. Talking to his potential voters. It was mostly about photos and work. I wish we could have just walked around and rode the rides and played the games. Gotten him to relax and have some fun. But it was all business, and we were just there so he could get some pictures in with his family most of the time. Sometimes, one of his staff members would take me to grab a funnel cake or play a quick game before we had to be off to the next thing."

"Well, that sucks."

"Yeah. But hey. We're here, and now I've got you two to let me do it. So thank you for letting me come with you."

"I'm glad you came. He's less annoying, and you get things he doesn't."

"Like lemon shakeups?" I rattle the ice in my cup and then take another long sip.

"That too." Lizzy laughs.

"All right. Which one do you want?" Cooper looks back at me before pointing up to the wall of stuffed animals.

"Um. That one?" I point to a small teddy bear that's dangling near the bottom.

"That's it? No faith." He shakes his head. "But all right."

Lizzy and I stand patiently by while he plays through several rounds of the game, racking up points and spending tickets to win the prize. He refuses to stop at the small one and instead gets a bear that's going to have to have its own seatbelt on the way home. I'm laughing when he hands it to me.

"Thank you. It's adorable." I grin back at the sweet little stitched smile on its face and straighten the Chaos tee he has on. One that's so fitting despite the fact the fair employee didn't seem to recognize Cooper in his baseball hat and aviators.

"Of course. Anything for you," he answers. I look up, startled by the way he says it, and my heart flutters at the way he smiles in return.

The wink he gives me nearly sets me into a full-blown blush until I remind myself I'm here with him and his daughter. All of my heart palpitations and blushes need to be locked down. I'm praying he can't see them on the surface. Because the last thing I need is to look like, after this short little visit, I'm already falling for another Rawlings brother—one who is objectively a good friend to me and ridiculously off-limits.

But half the time, I forget that he is a Rawlings brother. He's sweet in so many of the ways his brother wasn't. Thoughtful even when you don't expect him to be. Always up for a good time and a laugh when Rob spent so much time brooding and complaining. Sometimes, it's hard to believe they were raised under the same roof.

Then Cooper does little things like this, winning me a teddy bear at a fair. Winking at me before he turns to take us for more sugary sweet things to spoil us for the evening. Things that make me feel like I might still want a relationship with someone after all. If I found a guy like Cooper.

NOT LONG AFTER we win the Chaos teddy bear, we run into Lizzy's friends— three guys and two girls who are definitely having the junior high equivalent of a date night minus their odd man out. As they drift off into the night, chatting and heading for one of the games, Cooper and I sit down at a small beer garden area after we grab some snacks.

"Please tell me that's not what I think it is." Cooper watches as Lizzy talks to guy number three, who I assume is the friend that Cooper is so wary of.

"A group date? Yeah, I think that's what that is." I smile at the way Lizzy's face lights up even from this distance.

"They're in junior high!" He protests the idea of it.

"That's usually when kids start dating. Or at least thinking about it. Hand-holding. Movies. Things like that. Plus, it's the summer before high school. Don't you remember what that was like? Sneaking kisses with the guy you have a crush on. Cuddling at 'the movies. Some of my friends were getting to second base." I look back at him before I dunk my pretzel in the mustard that's threatening to overflow from the small white paper cup.

"I don't want Lizzy doing anything like I did. I'm not ready for her to date. I'm not ready for hand-holding, let alone any base rounding. Do you know what kind of assholes are out there these days? It's not like when we were kids and all innocent." Cooper's brow furrows as he watches them drift off around some booths and down the path.

"Oh, I don't know how innocent we were. I had a pretty tame upbringing, but then I had Xander for a brother, and well... I wouldn't call that influence innocent. His friends and the girls they all brought around were very um... educational." I laugh.

"Really? I'd always pictured young Trixie as a super strait-laced good girl. Was that not the case?" He smirks at me.

"Uh... I don't know. More innocent than most, I think. I was pretty naïve. But Xander definitely wasn't, and he rubbed off on me a lot. At least, being in his orbit meant I was exposed to things I wouldn't have been otherwise. If my parents had a say in it, anyway. They didn't even want me to date until I was nearly in college. Meanwhile, Xander was... well, Xander. I'm guessing you weren't all that different from him."

"Maybe." He shrugs, but his lips quiver in a half smile before he changes the subject. "So tonight... That guy. Are you going on another date with him?" His focus suddenly snaps back to me, and I shift uncomfortably.

Cooper and Rob aren't the closest of brothers. I saw more than one strained moment between them over the years. Enough to know there was tension between them I didn't fully understand. Rob didn't discuss it, and I didn't press for more. It was the story of our relationship. But I still don't know if I want Cooper to know the ins and outs of my dating life—or the lack thereof. I'd rather Rob have as little information as possible about me because, given the current state of my very chaotic life, I'd rather he not know what a mess it is.

"I'm not going to say anything to him, you know," he adds when I hesitate to answer, and I feel some relief. I trust Cooper enough to believe him.

"Yes. Well, sort of? I'm done with dating. Trying this whole hooking up via an app thing instead." I take a sip of my lemonade, and apparently, that's more information than Cooper wants because a look of surprise flashes over his face before he covers it.

"Oh. Is that what I interrupted? No wonder he was pissed then," he says as he breaks off a piece of the pretzel we're sharing, his eyes darting off into the distance as he slips it into his mouth.

"Well, I mean... it was kind of a screening situation. I guess?" I feel awkward explaining this. "It feels weird to be back in the dating/hookup pool, and I'm still figuring out what I want. I just know I don't want a relationship."

"No?" His brow is furrowed as he looks over me.

"Is it that surprising?"

"I mean... not to bring him up again, but yeah. A little. You seemed like the relationship type. You guys were headed for permanent, weren't you?"

"I thought so, but I don't think your brother was."

"So he ruined it for you for good?"

"No. He was just... what he was." I shrug. "I'm not in the right place for a relationship right now. I don't know where I'll be living in a year. Maybe even in a few months. Right now, it's in a hotel, which is good for hookups if my neighbors are any indication, but it doesn't really make me relationship material. Plus, I don't know what I want now, you know?"

"Yeah. I used to feel the same way."

"Used to? Are you dating now?" I raise an eyebrow because, while I don't exactly know his reputation the way Wren and Madison had described it, I know he's been perpetually single. In all the years I met up with his family, Cooper never brought a woman home for a holiday or the yearly summer trip to the lake house.

"Not yet. But I'm finally ready to give the dating thing a try." He grins and grabs a fried Oreo, popping it in his mouth like it's a tiny, little morsel.

"You think?" It's my turn to ask vague, probing questions. Because I'm curious about the Cooper who dates, and even more curious about what it could mean for his image reform.

He nods and smiles as he finishes chewing, takes a sip of the Coke he ordered, and wipes his hands on a napkin.

"Yeah. Lizzy's getting older, and it just feels right. I don't want it to always feel like a frat house when she's not there either."

"I mean, I don't think you have to date someone to change that."

"No, but I think... I'm getting older too. If I was going to have more kids or if I want my wife to know Lizzy, better sooner than later, right? Time's probably running out on that front."

I freeze up at the mention of kids. I have no idea if Rob ever told Cooper or anyone else in his family the real catalyst in our breakup: the fact that we couldn't have them, and I wanted to adopt, and he didn't. It had been the final straw on a mounting list of problems. But I can't imagine Cooper bringing it up so casually in front of me if he had.

"I suppose so. But I still think you should do it because you want the relationship. That it's something you want for yourself, not because it's something other people want for you or something you should do for Lizzy."

I didn't mean for it to come out quite so soapbox-y, and I can feel him studying me intently. Hear his cogs turn as he takes in what I've said.

"That what you and my brother were? Something society told you you should do by a certain age?"

"No." I shake my head, laughing. "We were the opposite of that. My parents hate that I'm involved with football and sports at all. My dad nearly died when he found out I was dating a football player."

"Your parents not much for sports?"

"No. Well, my mom is mostly just content for us to do whatever we want to do as long as we're happy, but my dad hates the fact Xander plays. Although I think he's secretly proud of him, he can't stand that I'm involved in it at all. Thinks my talent's being wasted on 'children's games' when I could be making a difference in the world." I hold up the air quotes.

"What does he want you to be doing?" Cooper frowns but doesn't say anything bad about my father.

"Politics. Like him. He wants Xander to follow in his footsteps and me to do PR in his world. Ever since Rob and I called it quits, it's all he talks about. He's... well, it's an open secret he wants to run for president, and he's hoping my brother will be done with football and take up where he left off in the Senate. He wants me to run the campaign for my brother and wants me to get my feet wet by working on his team now."

"But you don't want to?" Cooper probes further. I'm surprised he's this interested in my family's political machinations.

"No. Not really. I mean, if Xander asked me to, I would do it for him. But being back in my dad's world means being back around all the people I grew up with. All the money and politics and backroom dealing. I don't think I have the stomach for it."

"But you have the stomach for guys with massive egos and brand deals and all the team politics?" He gives me a look, and I can tell he's teasing.

"I mean, fair point, but it's not the same. I make my own way here. With Madison's help. I'm sure our last names give us an advantage, but it's not the same way it would be in politics with my dad. There, Xavier means something else entirely."

"Much better in this world where it means don't piss Xander off if you don't want to end up face down in the turf."

We both laugh, and I shake my head.

"Be nice. He's been better since Harper. He's like a different guy, honestly. Mellowed out and happier. It's been good to see the change in him."

"Yeah, I still get why your dad thinks he'd make a good politician though." Cooper grins. "Very cutthroat."

"True..." I take another small sip of my lemonade, hitting the end where the sugar's settled and it's extra sweet. "I'm sorry for dumping all that on you. I doubt you wanted to know it all. I'm just at a bit of a crossroads. I didn't really want to admit that. But I guess it's not easy to hide either."

"I'm happy to listen, Trixie. I asked." He gives me a small smile. "So what are you doing here then? Hoping you can stay and work with Madison, or do you have other plans?"

"We had a whole plan out in Colorado, and it fell through. We're working on Plan B, but we both need to work while we wait. She found this gig. She didn't exactly plan on it being Quentin, but it's work for both of us while we figure out what to do next."

"What was the plan that fell through?"

"We were going to start a PR resort for athletes. A place to help them work on their image and get away from everything while they do it. We had investors and a place up in the mountains on a gorgeous piece of land. That fell apart thanks to wildfires, droughts, and some interpersonal politics, so now we're looking for a new spot and new investors."

"You mean I can go to a resort while you work on me?" He laughs. "Sign me up. I could use more time in the pool. I don't get enough in my own."

"Yes, well... someday, hopefully, if this works out. I'm just not sure if it will..." I trail off because, seeing how Madison and Quentin interact, I have my doubts about whether she'll be ready to leave this place. I'm fairly certain Quentin's plan is to do anything he can to get her to stay.

"Well, if you need an investor, tell me where to sign."

"I barely told you anything about the place," I scoff.

"You're smart and driven. So is Madison. That's all I really need to know." He shrugs. "Plus, like I said, if it means I get to make resort visits while you all reform my image, I'm in."

I study his face for a moment and smile as I watch him break his second fried Oreo in half and eat part of it.

"So you're deciding to seriously date then? Is that why you want the image makeover?"

"Part of it. That and the fact that I know my days playing

football are waning. That I have to think about what's next, and my reputation may not help me in the next chapter."

"Your reputation here doesn't match the Cooper I know. Why is that?"

He stops mid-bite, and his brow furrows.

"I do my best to be on for Lizzy. Be the good dad. Give her the kind of home environment my parents gave me growing up. Then I guess when she's not around, I revert to my old habits. Didn't really have the motivation to do things differently."

"Well, that's fair. It makes a big difference. What happened that makes you want to change?" I'm curious from the perspective of wanting to help him in a professional capacity, but I'm also curious as his friend.

7

C *ooper*

"I GAVE up on the things I wanted. Thought I couldn't have them. It still seems like I might not be able to, but now I want to at least give it a chance. Know I tried. Then, if it doesn't work out, at least I can say I gave it my best shot."

Her eyes shift over my face as she studies me.

"Well, we're alike there." She grins.

"Then we'll make a good team, right?"

"I think you're going to be an easy case. I just have to let people see the real you. The one I always see with your family, and they'll fall in love."

"Fuck, I hope so." I smile at her before I put the last of the Oreo in my mouth, trying to keep myself from saying something more obvious than I already have.

I think she's honestly oblivious—that I'm so deep in the friend zone for her that doesn't even register that I'm flirting with her most of the time. Knowing now that she has no interest in a relationship has put a damper on those hopes. But I'm not ready to snuff them out just yet. What's that thing they always say? Hope springs eternal? That's me when it comes to Trixie.

"Think that teddy bear needs a friend?" I nod toward the bear she has propped on the seat next to her.

"I think I already don't know where I'll put him in my hotel room. You sure Lizzy doesn't want him?"

"Nah. He's yours. You're stuck with him. If you don't want him to have a friend, then I guess you better win something for me."

She laughs, and the sound of it hits me hard. The way she smiles and pats him on the head. I realize it's been a long time, more than a few visits back, since I've seen her look this carefree. I never asked Rob why they broke up, figured it wasn't my business. But knowing how incredibly sweet she is and how patient she was with all of Rob's ups and downs, I know it must have been rough for her. It makes me wonder how he fucked up for good in the end. But I'm enjoying her laughter too much right now to ask.

"Win something for you? I'm not very good at those games." She gives me a skeptical look.

"I can teach you. No problem, Trix." I wink at her and hold out my hand. She takes it, and I haul her up to her feet, only reluctantly letting go when she needs both hands to carry her prize. She grabs the bear, and we make our way back out through the fair.

"So are we spying on Lizzy or just hoping we run into her?"

"Just hoping we conveniently run into her and walk past a few times. I trust her. She's smart and can handle herself, but I just want to be sure that kid doesn't give her trouble. She doesn't tell me about things like her crushes. Saves that stuff for her mom, so I have no idea how she feels about the whole thing."

"You could ask her."

"I've tried, indirectly, and I could tell it wasn't her thing."

"You and Evelyn get along really well, don't you?"

"Yeah. Evelyn's a good person, and she makes the whole co-parenting stuff pretty easy, honestly. Have to give her credit for that."

"Evelyn never made you want to get married?"

"Nah. We had a lot of fun, but we never made sense together. She's a good friend. I'm so grateful for Lizzy, that we have her and get to raise her together, but neither of us wanted anything beyond that." He shrugs as we continue to walk.

"Well, I'm glad that the two of you get along so well. And Lizzy is such a great kid."

"Speaking of Lizzy." I shift my eyes to where she and her friends are standing, doing a quick once-over to make sure everyone's behaving themselves. Trix follows my line of sight and makes a little nod of understanding in my direction.

"We better hurry then so she doesn't think we're following her."

"All right. Let's go to the end. I want my own bear to take home."

"I think you're putting a little too much pressure on my nonexistent abilities."

"Not pressure, *faith*." I wink at her, and she looks up at me with something I can't read in her eyes, almost bumping into a group of people walking in the opposite direction. She stumbles toward me in trying to avoid them, and I catch her by the arm, steadying her back on her feet.

"Sorry." Color lights her cheeks.

"You're good." I run my thumb over the inside of her elbow. I'll take any excuse I can get to touch her. Her skin is so damn soft, and she looks beautiful in the purple sundress she has on. I've been trying not to stare and only sneak glances when I can, but every moment the night goes on, it's harder to do. Just like letting her go is, but I force myself to do it.

When we get to the booth, I pay the guy and hand her the three darts. She smiles at them and then up at me.

"Which one do you want?"

I glance at the wall of prizes and nod to the lion with the mane that looks like he's stuck his paw in an outlet.

"The lion who took fashion advice from Einstein."

"He has quite the look about him." She laughs.

"Which is why I need him. All up to you."

"I really am bad at this, and I haven't tried since I was a kid. I hope you're up for winning yourself one after these end up on the floor in front of the balloons." She starts to line up at the marker and draw her dart up.

"I'm sure you've improved with age. Come here." I step closer to her, putting one hand on her hip and gently pushing to swivel her body into place. "Stand like this and set your shoulders like this. It'll give you better aim."

"Oh." I can feel her tense a little under my touch and then relax. "Okay."

"Set your eyes on the target. Yep. Just like that and then here..." I slide my hand up her arm and around her wrist. "Use the dart, line it up where you want it before you pull it back. Set your aim and then pull back and throw."

We're standing so close I can practically feel her heart beating, and I can feel every breath as her chest expands. Her eyes shift to mine and then back to the balloon wall with a small intake of breath; she sets her aim. I step back to give her space, and she wields the dart like the weapon it is, aiming and then releasing it. It pops a balloon on the wall, and she lets out a little shriek of joy.

"I did it!"

"High five!" I hold my palm up for her, and she uses her free hand to reciprocate. "Now do it again."

She goes again and hits another balloon. But her excitement is too much, and she draws back too quickly on the third and misses, groaning when she does.

"Two out of three's not bad. But you need all three to win a prize." The booth owner looks back at us to see if we want to play again.

"I told you. You're gonna have to win your own." She gives me a defeated look.

"Nah, you got this." I lay down another five-dollar bill, and the owner takes it and lays down another three darts in front of her. "That was just a warm-up. You're gonna get it."

She looks at them doubtfully, but when her eyes rise to meet mine, I nod at her. "Go get 'em."

She grins and takes them again, stepping back and releasing each of them; one by one, she nails a balloon every single time until she's jumping up for joy and high fiving me again. The booth owner hands her the small, frazzled lion, and she presents him to me, grinning proudly.

"Your small but mighty Einsteinian lion, sir."

I press him to my chest. "My new cherished buddy."

She laughs and looks up at me. My eyes fall to her lips. They're so plush, the perfect shade of pink, glossy from some balm she put on after we ate, and I just want to lean forward and kiss them. Taste the happiness I can see on her. Know what it feels like to have her kiss me back. I'm lost in the daydream for a moment before I snap out of it when her phone dings. I blink, and something must be on her mind too because she looks similarly dazed before we start to slowly walk back through the booths together.

8

B eatrix

"SOMETHING WRONG?" Cooper asks while I'm stuck just staring at the screen on my phone.

Everything is spinning. That's what's wrong. I'd been half daydreaming about what it would be like if I was really on a date with Cooper when my phone buzzed with an alert.

I've been tagged in a picture on my main public profile. Not the secret one Lizzy discovered first, but the one everyone knows about. I opened it, wondering if the article the PR Professionals group wrote about Madison and me was finally posted online. What I found instead is stealing my ability to think straight.

It's a photo of Cooper and me at the fair, eating together at the picnic table and laughing. I'm tagged in it, but he isn't. There's no caption, and the account has very little information as I scroll through, trying to make sense of why someone's documenting our trip to the fair. There's no photo, just a little black circle where the person's profile picture should be.

My hand shakes as I turn to show it to Cooper. His face clouds with worry as he looks down at it, but I'm not prepared for the way his eyes darken and his brows grows heavy. There's another ding on my phone as he looks at it, and I lean over his shoulder to see. It's another tag. Another picture. One of us from just a few minutes ago when I was attempting to win him the lion. This time, there's a caption and he's tagged too.

'*What are you up to, Beatrix Xavier?*'

My stomach churns, and I see Cooper's eyes follow the line of text.

"What the fuck?" he snaps as his eyes search the crowd around us, and I do the same, as if somehow, we'll be able to figure out who took these.

"I don't know. It's weird. Right?"

"Has this happened to you before?"

"No. Never."

"This is fucked."

"I don't know who or why someone would take pictures of me like this. I mean... you're in it. It could be you they're photographing." I stare at the screen. "Local media that likes to comment on you? A blogger or an overly enthusiastic fan?" I study Cooper's face as I ask the questions.

Cooper is gorgeous, a phenomenal player, and has a reputation. He's been linked to several celebrities before. It's entirely possible he has a very big fan, maybe even someone toeing the line of being a stalker. Someone might have figured out who I am and decided they want to be the first to report us. It isn't unheard of, and being a player's sister doesn't mean I'm a celebrity, but it definitely still makes the gossip rounds in the sports social media world.

"No. Not that I know of."

"Maybe one you don't know of?"

"That would know *your* name?"

"They could have seen me on the staff roster. With the Undergrove and Westfield drama. It could have come up. Maybe?"

"I doubt it. If they know your name, it's likely you they're after." His eyes search the crowd again, and he looks down at me.

"What would they want from me?" I'm truly puzzled. Cooper's a celebrity, and I'm no one in comparison. I might have famous family members, but I've always been a behind-the-scenes, fade-into-the-wallpaper sort of girl. The only exception being when my father ran for office and people became overly interested in his family. I can't imagine this is any sort of paparazzi situation if it isn't about Cooper.

"I think we should get Lizzy and get going. I don't like that someone's watching you like this. Or photographing us while they're doing it." Cooper's hand is on my lower back as he interrupts my thoughts and hands my phone back to me. It sends tingles zipping up my spine, and I chastise myself for having them in what's otherwise a serious moment.

"Okay," I agree. "What if they're following me, though, and going to find her gets her photographed? I'd hate to have her on the radar of whoever this is." I stop dead in my tracks. I couldn't live with myself if I somehow got her involved in whatever this is.

"I'll keep an eye out for anyone pointing a camera our way."

"Maybe I should stay back or find a ride to the hotel so you can get her home." I worry about being a burden. Cooper has been so kind to me already, and I hate that this is happening when our renewed friendship is so fresh.

"No." His answer is sharp, drawing my eyes to his in question. "I mean..." He takes a breath. "I don't want you off on your own right now. Until we know what's going on with whoever is doing this. It's too strange, and they could still be here. Just stay with me, please?"

I can't disagree with him. I don't exactly want to be alone either. My need to be polite sometimes outweighs my need to be safe, and I feel relief that he's insisting on keeping an eye on me too.

I nod my agreement to his plan, and we start crossing the fairgrounds. He stays at my side, never drifting far and constantly keeping watch around us until we come up on Lizzy and her group of friends. Cooper stops short when he sees her because the boy who had been the spare in their grouping before is now holding Lizzy's hand, just like the rest of the couples.

"Fuck..." I hear him mutter and shake his head before he starts again.

"Be nice. They're just holding hands."

"That's how it starts." There's another grumble I can't hear, and then a moment later, we're next to the group.

"Mr. Rawlings." The boy yanks his hand back from Lizzy's and stares up at Cooper's impressive form towering over him. Cooper doesn't say a word; his eyes just shift back and forth for a moment before he smiles at his daughter.

"We need to get home a little early. Something came up for Trix."

"Trix?" Lizzy looks worriedly around the side of her father.

"I'm okay. Just need to get home." I smile brightly at her, not wanting to scare her or ruin what was otherwise probably a good night. I know at her age, I would have killed for a boy to hold my hand, but having a brother like Xander meant that even if there was one who liked me enough, he was way too scared.

My eyes shift to the boy who'd been holding Lizzy's hand,

and he's still looking nervously up at Cooper, but Cooper's already moved on to the next thing as Lizzy says her goodnights and shuffles off in my direction to head to the car. When we cross the fairgrounds and the gravel parking lot and get back to the car, Lizzy hops in right away, too busy texting to notice how slow we are. Cooper gives me a meaningful look, and I pause before I open my door. I look at him with a question, and his lips flatline for a second before he returns with a more serious expression than I've seen before.

"Listen... I've been thinking, and I think you should stay the night with us. We can make up an excuse for Lizzy so we don't scare her, but I really don't want to take you back to the hotel alone. You can stay in our guest room."

I stand there for a moment considering the possibilities, mulling over the idea of Cooper Rawlings having a guest room in the first place. Then my mind drifts back to a reality where someone might be following us. I wasn't going to admit it because I can handle myself just fine. I've spent plenty of nights on the road in less-than-stellar situations, but I am a little scared to go back to the hotel alone. If they are watching me, however far-fetched that might seem, I don't want them to find out where I'm staying. But I'm also not exactly prepared to stay the night somewhere. My purse has a few of the essentials, but it's a poor excuse for an overnight bag.

"I don't have anything with me."

"I've got plenty at the house to get you through the night. An extra toothbrush and everything." Cooper grins at me, the worried look on his face lifting a little as he tries to put me at ease.

"Okay. I think you're right about the hotel tonight. I don't exactly feel safe going back there, but what are we going to tell Lizzy?"

He shrugs. "We can just tell her there was an issue at the

hotel. No power or water or something, so you're staying with us."

"I'll let you do all the talking then. Are you sure though? I hate being a burden." My voice hitches a little in my throat as rub my thumb over the side of my phone anxiously.

"Trix, you're not a burden and that..." He glances down at my phone in my hand. "Whatever that is, I'm worried about you. I'd rather know you're somewhere safe until we get to the bottom of it."

"Well, I appreciate it. Thank you."

He grabs the door handle and pulls my side open, nodding for me to get in. "Thank me less, and let's get you somewhere safe."

LIZZY TAKES the explanation of why her would-have-been aunt is staying in her home for the night in stride. After giving me a quick hug and a goodnight, she disappears into her room for the evening. Cooper shows me to a guest room that looks like an old girlfriend might have decorated it, if he ever had one, and promises to return with supplies.

I spin around once, taking in the big picture window behind the bed and the cute wallpaper decorating the wall that frames it. Even the quilt on the bed matches the color scheme, and a mess of decorative pillows piled on top bring the whole thing together. I can't help but smile at it before I remember why I'm here. My stomach tumbles at the thought, and I turn to pick up my phone out of morbid curiosity to see if my photographer has stayed silent or not.

I open the app and sink onto the edge of the bed while I stare at the two photos of us. Nothing about the angle or anything in the image is particularly helpful in revealing the culprit. It could have been any one of the hundreds of people at the fair tonight. Someone blithely snapping photos and not even knowing we were in them could have taken them if they weren't tagging me and using my name in the captions.

"You okay?" Cooper asks, breaking through my thoughts as he leans against the doorway. He's out of his shoes and hat now, his hair disheveled from being under the ball cap all day, and the look on his face is full of worry. My eyes flick to his upper arms, where his bicep flexes as he leans, then back to his face, and I tell myself to get a grip.

I don't remember ever noticing Cooper this much before. I've always been logically aware of the fact that he's attractive. I can understand why he always had plenty of women and an attitude about never settling down. But I never looked at anything beyond that surface when I dated Rob. But now, knowing he's worried about me and kind enough to bring me back here, it's hard not to feel something for him even if it's just overwrought gratefulness.

"Trix?" he asks, and I realize I've been staring at him.

"Sorry." I shake my head, trying to clear my confusion. "I'm just trying to think who would even be doing this. And feeling awkward that you're having to have me here tonight."

"Don't feel awkward. You were practically family, and I still think of us as friends. You need somewhere safe to go, and we've got a place for you. Did you tell Madison or not?"

"I didn't tell her. I don't want to. She has so much on her plate with Quentin right now and resolving all the issues between their families. Everything is on the line for her. I'm supposed to be here helping, and I don't want to cause her any stress. After all, it could be nothing, right? Just a fan of yours or a silly prank, maybe?"

The look on his face tells me he's not buying my simple solutions.

"Pretty fucked up prank if that's what it is. Do you know anyone who might do that? Do you know anyone in the area?"

"No. Not that I know of. I mean, it's possible someone I went to school with or something lives here now. It wouldn't be out of the realm of possibility, but I have no idea who would care enough to play a prank like this. I don't mean to keep putting the focus on you. But you're the celebrity. Are you sure you can't think of anyone?"

He shakes his head and looks into the distance again like he's racking his brain for an answer, but nothing's coming up from the well for him.

"No. Like you said, it's possible there's a fan or something I don't know about. But I've never had anything happen like this."

"Not even when you were involved with Sahara or Nikki?"

His mouth flatlines at the mention of some of his more famous dates. He never brought them home to meet his parents or the rest of us, but he definitely attended his fair share of red carpet events with them.

"There were some paparazzi involved with them. More photographers than usual. A gossip reporter digging into my life a little, but I shut it all down quickly."

"None that would have stayed interested in you after?"

"It was so long ago. I can't imagine they would."

"All right. I just wish there was a simple explanation. I'd almost feel better if you had a huge fan or something. Someone who was mad that you were dating. I mean... Not that we're dating. Obviously, we would not be dating. We're *not* dating. But I can see how it could have looked that way from the outside. Maybe." I trip over my words and hedge a glance in his direction, seeing the way his mouth crumples for a moment. It's hard for me to tell if it's a cringe or amusement that triggers it, but he clears it almost immediately.

"Right." He nods.

"Hopefully, it was just a random thing."

"Hopefully," he agrees. "I'm just down the hall if you need

me though. Or you've got my number in your phone. I keep it next to me. If anything else happens, you let me know, okay?"

"Okay. Thank you." I force a smile despite the awkwardness of this. "And thank you again, for letting me stay."

"Anytime, Trix. Anytime."

9

C *ooper*

THE NEXT MORNING, I barely get a chance to talk to Trix before she leaves to go to the stadium for some early PR appointment that Madison and Quentin have. She's playing a support role. But I talked to her long enough to find out that she was tagged in another picture from the fair. That whoever is doing this hadn't just taken a few rogue pictures to prank her but is tagging her again this morning.

It made me nervous to even watch her leave on her own, but she was in such a hurry to get out the door and run by the hotel to change her clothes, I could barely argue with her. I want her out of the hotel, period. Her going back there, even in the bright light of daytime, seems like a risk if they're following her. They might already know where she's staying. They might already have watched her walk from the hotel to the stadium every day.

It makes my skin crawl and my fingers twitch around my cup.

"Dad?" Lizzy asks, and I realize that while I've been imagining scenarios in my head, she came into the room to gather cereal and a bowl for breakfast.

"Yeah?"

"What's got you distracted? Is Trix still here?"

"No. She left early to go to work."

"Is something wrong?"

I turn the words I want to say over in my head, looking for something that isn't a lie but a believable half-truth. I'm not ready to have a conversation about how Trix makes me feel with anyone, let alone with my daughter who already adores her, or tell her what's actually going on in terms of Trix's safety.

"Not wrong exactly. Just thinking about Trix in that hotel."

"I was going to say... Maybe you should ask her to stay here? You guys could commute together. No one ever stays in the guest room. She's just here for the summer, right?"

The summer is short. Too short. I want her longer than that, but I'll take a summer if I can get one. It's better than her being gone permanently. A strange part of me was upset when she and Rob broke up, not that I wanted them together but that I thought I'd never see her again. No more holidays with her there. No more summer trips to the family lake house. No more seeing her in one of her sundresses, laughing as my parent's dog chased after the ball she'd thrown for him, or her curled up next to Lizzy on the couch playing video games together.

"Yeah. I think so. She's got plans going forward." I think about her work with Madison and the looming potential she disappears from our lives again.

"Uncle Rob's an idiot for leaving her and for that woman he's dating now. She's so rude and standoffish and not nearly as pretty or smart as Trix."

"Be nice. She might be your new aunt the way he's been

talking." I couldn't debate the merits of her argument. Rob's new girlfriend is standoffish and a little rude. She's nowhere near as pretty as Trix, at least not in my opinion, but my brother has shared enough details for me to know that he has other reasons why he likes her. None I can share with Lizzy.

"Gross. I hope Trix finds someone better. Maybe we could set her up with one of your friends. Or someone on the team? Maybe it could get her to stay here longer?" Lizzy looks up at me hopefully.

Over my dead body am I setting Trix up with someone. I've had enough torture for a lifetime watching her with Rob. Seeing her on the date last night is enough to know I won't survive another round. I can handle the idea that she'll never want me, given that she dated Rob. I want her to be happy. I just don't need to watch it unfold. Especially not after last night. The way she smiled at me, teased me, looked at me when we were at the fair. Fuck... if the alerts about the photographs hadn't come, I might have been stupid enough to try to kiss her.

But now we have bigger problems on our hands. Namely getting to the bottom of whoever is fucking with her on social media. Whoever is getting close enough to photograph her. I have to figure out how to deal with that first before I can let my feelings about her get in the way.

"Let's not try to play matchmaker right now. She's got a lot going on, and the goal is to help her."

"Finding her a guy could help her." Lizzy grins as she eats a bite of her cereal. I can only imagine what devious plan she's already working over in her mind for Trix. She's been so boy crazy lately, plastering her room with images of the band she's into now, and on her phone constantly, planning for the school dance that is coming up at the end of next week.

"Yeah? And don't think I missed you and your friend holding hands last night. We're going to talk about that. Does your mom know?"

"Mom knows about Billy. He's just a friend."

"You hold hands with all your friends?"

She rolls her eyes at me and shakes her head.

"It's not like that. It's just that everyone else is all hooked up, and we're the single ones, so it kinda pushes us together."

"Hooked up?" I nearly choke on my protein shake. "No one better be hooking up. You guys are way too young for that."

"Not like that. And Dad, I hate to tell you, but there are people in my class who already have boyfriends. Some of them have done more than just kiss. You're going to have to accept that I'm older now. Mom knows I've been thinking about dating." She says it with the voice of someone who's a decade older, and it's unsettling. I'm not ready for adult Lizzy just yet.

"Dating is one thing. Holding hands, fine. Kissing, if your mom knows, okay. Anything more than that, you'd better be having a conversation with one of us first. I don't care what other kids are doing. I care about you. Are you and Billy kissing already?"

Lizzy blushes, and I feel bad for being so direct, but lately, it feels like she's growing up fast, and I'm barely hanging on anymore. I'm trying hard to skirt that line between staying her parent, being an authority figure for her, and still trying to stay coolheaded enough that she can tell me things she might not otherwise. I want her honesty. So does her mom. That was something we agreed on a long time ago about raising her. But I'm worried her high school years are going to test all of those boundaries.

"No, Dad. Billy and I haven't kissed."

"Have you kissed someone else?"

"Dad..." There's an exasperated sigh.

"I just want you to be careful. I was your age once."

"I know. A million years ago. You weren't that much older than me when you and Mom had me." She levels me with a look. One that cuts me to the core and reminds me that she's mine—the same attitude and independence that drove my parents crazy.

"Which is why we want you to be careful. You know we love you. I'm glad it all worked out. But we were lucky we still got through college, had you, and had help to raise you."

"I'm not having sex, Dad. There are no babies to worry about. I had sex ed, and Mom and I talked. I told her I'd talk to her first. You know this."

"Okay."

"Meanwhile..." She rolls her eyes.

"Meanwhile, what?"

"Meanwhile, you don't practice what you preach. When was the last time you even had a girlfriend? Not counting Nikki because I hated her."

My daughter recalls the actress I dated. One she had loved when she was five and saw a movie with her as a princess but grew to despise when she met her just after her eleventh birthday. I roll my shoulders and stand up from the position where I've been leaning over the counter.

"I'm working on it. Finding someone takes time."

"Maybe instead of us helping Trix, you should ask her for help. She said she was helping Madison work on Quentin's image. Finding him some dates with smart women. I bet she could find you a date."

Like I said. This kid is mine. Great minds think alike. I just have a much more specific idea of who Trix could find for me.

"I've thought about trying to work on my image a bit too. But Trix is busy with Madison at the moment."

"She'd have more time if she wasn't running back and forth to a hotel. If she was here... you could talk to her more. She might be able to fix you."

"Fix me," I echo my daughter and raise my brow at her. "I think what you mean is if she was here, *you* could talk to her more." I know how Lizzy's mind works.

"We'd both have perks. Yeah." She grins. "Just please think about it. Don't say no yet."

I'm at least glad Lizzy is clueless about how much I want Trix here. Maybe I'm a better actor than I thought. Because I'm not about to say no to the idea. I'm too busy thinking of ways I can convince Trix.

"I won't say no," I reassure her.

"How's the power in her hotel room anyway? Do they have a new room for her?"

"I don't know. She was in a hurry to get to her appointment. I have to check in with her after work." At which point I fully intend to convince her to come stay with us now that I've been given the Lizzy stamp of approval without even trying.

WHEN I ENTER the locker room after practice, Quentin is the only one left, taking his time packing everything up. He and Easton are still moving around each other like they're trying to decide who the alpha of this pack will be, and I can see the tension still riding in his shoulders as he tosses gear into his bag.

"So you know how I talked to you about Trix before? Wishing I had more time with her? I'm thinking of asking her to move in," I say when I figure it's better to distract him than ask about what Westfield problem he has today.

"Oh yeah?" He smirks. One of our post-practice dinners had involved him confessing his past with Madison and me admitting I've got my own issues when it comes to Trix.

"I figure it could help everyone involved. Gonna go talk to her when I'm done here."

"You got the speech figured out, or are you just gonna wing it?" Quentin raises a brow in question.

"Wing it. Why? You writing speeches at night for Madison?"

"Fuck no. She'd see through that shit so fast. I'm just doing what she tells me to do when she tells me to do it." He grins, and I can tell—despite the vice grip she has on his balls right now—he's happy.

"Oh yeah?" It's my turn to smirk.

"Yeah. I like seeing the way she lights up when she gets what she wants."

I let out a choked laugh. "I bet."

"I know Bea. She's not quite Madison, but you'll still be on a short leash if you go down that road. You sure that's what you want?"

"I've never had a leash before, so I don't know what I want yet."

He lets out a low whistle. "I feel sorry for her then. She had enough trouble with your brother. She's a good one, you know. Deserves someone good for her. You better decide what you want before you go too far down that road."

"She's been pretty clear that she doesn't want a relationship. That she's just looking for fun and a hookup here or there." I have zero intention of doing anything to hurt her.

"She told you that?" Quentin seems as surprised as I was when she told me at the fair.

"She told me enough." I lean against the locker. If anyone gets hurt, it'll probably be me for making the mistake of wanting more from a woman who might only ever see me as a friend.

"So what, you're just planning to be in the right place at the right time when she needs a little help on that front?"

"Figured it couldn't hurt." I grin.

"Well... Good luck. You'll need all you can get with her." Quentin grins at me before he nods and takes off out of the locker room, and I ponder if I really know what I'm getting myself into with this girl.

Not that it's going to stop me from trying.

10

B eatrix

I'M WALKING out of the office when I hear someone call my name. I look up, and Cooper's just down the hall, so I pause and wait for him to catch up.

"You headed out for the day?" he asks.

"Yeah. Need to grab some dinner and then get back to the hotel." I hadn't talked to him much before I left this morning. I was in a hurry and I'm still not sure what protocol is when you're a house guest at your ex's brother's house.

"Where do you want to go? My treat."

"You don't have to do that. You did enough letting me stay at your place."

"Nah. I'm keeping an eye on you. Kind of like a personal bodyguard." He flashes one of his charming grins, and my heart kicks at the sight of it.

"Oh, I see. Going to take bullets and throw your coat down on puddles for me?"

"Little short of coats this time of year, but if it's needed, it can be arranged. Maybe a jersey toss. Got a couple of extras in the bag. That work for you?" He pats the bag at his side and glances at me, a smirk forming.

"I'll have to think about it." I grin. Something about Cooper just makes me feel light. The second he's at my side, I forget everything I should be worrying about.

"So dinner...?"

"I feel like it's gotta be West Field if we're down this way. Don't want to betray Wren by visiting the local competition."

"We could do that, but I've got my truck. I can drive you to one of my favorites if you want. You like BBQ?"

"It's been a bit, but yeah, I like BBQ."

"All right. There's a place off Montgomery. It's a little bit of a drive, but worth it. You up for it?"

I tap my fingers against my laptop bag. I should be going home and doing some of the brand research I need to get to. Not to mention vetting the list of local businesses Madison and I are working on for collaboration opportunities with Quentin. But I do need to eat dinner.

"All right. I can't stay too long though. I've got some work I have to finish tonight."

BEFORE I KNOW IT, we're halfway through dinner, where he's managed to make me sample half the things they have on the menu in a bid to convince me it's some of the best BBQ there is.

"It's good. Definitely better than anything in Seattle when it comes to the pulled pork and the ribs. But the salmon... You need to come to Seattle sometime so I can show you what good salmon tastes like."

"Deal. Just let me know when we're making the trip. Maybe before the season?" He grins as he leans back against his chair and sips his beer.

I laugh at his eagerness and shake my head.

"The only time I'm heading there, I've got my brother's engagement party to host. Which will be an *event*."

"I imagine, given his reputation, it's going to draw quite the crowd." A small smirk plays across Cooper's lips.

"That, and my parents' need to let everyone in their orbit know one of their children is finally getting married."

"Excited for a sister-in-law? Is she a good one?"

"She is. She's lovely, and she adores Xander. I think I'll like having her around."

"That's good. Don't want to be stuck with an annoying one at the holidays." He grimaces.

"Hey now..." I raise my brow at him.

"Not you. You would have made a good one. The current prospect though... not loving her."

"Ah." I nod, not knowing what else is appropriate to say because I'd rather not chat about Rob any more than necessary, so I change the subject. "So did Lizzy buy our story? I hope she wasn't totally weirded out that I stayed at yours."

"No, actually she loved having you. She and I were talking, and that guest room is open most of the time. My parents don't come visit very often, and if they do, there's a whole suite downstairs they usually stay in because there's a small kitchen and a big couch for my dad to spread out and watch sports on."

"I can see that given how protective he was over the den at the lake house." I smile thinking about his parents. I miss them. That's the shitty part about breakups: you lose the family you like too.

"But the guest room. It's open. It'd be cheaper than a hotel. Safer too. Plus, you'd make Lizzy's whole life this summer if you were around to chat and play games with her..."

I spin the bite of key lime pie on my fork around for a moment while I think about the offer. I want to say yes. Cooper and Lizzy were some of the family I hated giving up in the breakup, and I had lots of fun with them at the county fair, but I worry about being an imposition. Especially on Cooper's personal life.

"What about me being there with your... friends around? Won't that be weird? Them wondering who I am?"

"I could just say you're the nanny." A wry grin spreads across his face, and I shake my head.

"A nanny to your almost *fourteen-year-old*?"

"I'm kidding. I generally only have people over when it's just me, and honestly... like I said. I'm trying to turn the page on that. Lizzy was giving me shit this morning actually, saying that I need to start dating. So... it's perfect really. You can help me stay on the road to reform."

"So I get safe, rent-free living, and you get Lizzy entertainment and a live-in cockblock then?"

He laughs, and his eyes go soft as he looks me over. "Yeah. I think it's a pretty good deal. Very little work on your end for lots of benefits."

I feel the slightest flutter in my chest, and that right there should be enough to tell me that this is a bad idea. That letting myself get any closer into Cooper's orbit means I'll get sucked in completely. But I ignore it and agree to the deal with the devil.

"All right. I suppose that's too good of an offer to refuse. When do I move in?"

"Tonight, if you're up for it. We can stop by the hotel on the way back and get all of your things. Easy."

So easy. Just like that I'm moving in with my ex's brother to solve all my problems.

11

B eatrix

I'M SETTLED in my bed when Cooper comes into the room to check on me. He's got a glass of wine and cookies for some reason, like we're about to have a midnight snack. He's wearing nothing but his sweats, and they're hanging lower than usual on his hips. My eyes are drawn down, and while I desperately try to tell myself to stop ogling my new landlord, my dream turns into a nightmare.

Cooper disappears, and the room goes dark. The wine and cookies vanish as quickly as he did. There's a flash of light at the window, and I see a figure standing in it, silhouetted by a flash of heat lightning in the background. Then there's a flash of something else—car lights, maybe? But it doesn't make sense since Cooper's house is off the main road.

The dread inside my chest grows when the person outside steps closer to the glass. I can feel them watching me, staring at me in the bed. I try to move. Try to get up and run for the door, but nothing in my body cooperates. Not a single muscle or limb does what I ask it to. I'm stuck in the bed, and the panic wells in my throat.

I try to scream. I try to yell for Cooper or anyone who might hear me. I hope that Lizzy can't. I don't want her to come running. Don't want the man outside the room to see her. But I remember that she's with her mom tonight. I'm alone with Cooper, and if I can just yell loud enough, he might be able to come help me.

Except when I scream, it comes out like a whisper. A barely audible "help," and it turns my stomach. I can't move. I can't scream. I'm trapped, and the man outside could get in and kill me before anyone would even know it was happening. I try again in vain to scream. Attempt one more shot at getting out of bed. But none of it works.

Then I realize what's happening—I'm still asleep. The stress of everything lately has given me another round of sleep paralysis. I just need to wait it out, give my body time to wake up, and realize that the projection around me is just that. There's no man at the window. I've not been hurt or drugged. I'm safe in bed, and I just have to wake up.

It only takes a moment or two more before I can move freely again, but it feels like an eternity. I blink and shake my head, sitting up the moment I can and looking around the room. Just like I suspected, there's no man at the window and no storm outside. There's just the gentle hum of the air conditioning and the sound of my heavy breathing from being startled awake.

It doesn't change the fact that my cortisol levels are sky-high, and my body still feels like it needs to flee the intruder I thought was outside the window. My mind is still wholly convinced I was just about to die, and my heart is pounding in my chest to the rhythm of panic.

The only thing that works in these instances is getting up. It might mean losing some sleep tonight, but there's no way I'll drift off now. Even if I did, I'd likely just start the same dream over again. The risk of another round of sleep paralysis has me getting out of bed to grab my laptop.

I glance back at the window. I know there was no man standing at the window watching me. But the hairs on the back of my neck still stand up, and I have this strong feeling in my gut, an instinct, telling me to get away.

I'm too embarrassed to go out into the living room and watch TV. Explaining to Cooper that I'm a grown woman who still gets whole-ass, full-body nightmares like this is more than I have in me right now, even though I know he wouldn't judge me for it.

UNFORTUNATELY, my hiding out doesn't last long because there's a soft knock at the door, and I call to tell him he can come in. He opens it gently, and his eyes drift to the floor, where I'm sitting with a pillow at my back, playing on my phone, and absently watching some documentary I found on a streaming channel.

"Everything okay?"

"Yeah. Just couldn't sleep."

"Any particular reason you're down there instead of on the bed?" His brow quirks up at my position on the floor, and he leans against the door frame. He looks much like he did in my dream, only he's unfortunately wearing a shirt this time.

"I..." I let out a sigh. Trying to come up with an excuse on the spot is more difficult than I thought, so honesty it is. "I get sleep paralysis. Have you had it before?"

He frowns and shakes his head no.

"It's like a waking nightmare. My eyes are open, and I can

see the room around me, but my mind is still dreaming and projecting things into my environment. It feels real. Sometimes I wake myself screaming for help, and it takes a while to come down from it."

"Fuck. That sounds horrible. I hate it when I have a regular nightmare. I couldn't handle that."

"They're not fun. I have to sit up for a bit after. Watch TV and distract myself. Bring the adrenaline down and try to get into a place where I can fall back asleep. You know?"

"I can understand that." He nods. "But why the floor?"

"I swore I saw someone out the window. A male figure staring at me and trying to get in the house. Obviously it was my dream. Just feels better to be away from it right now."

"Jesus. Okay. Well, you know you can come out into the living room?"

"I didn't want to bother you."

"Trix. You're not a bother. I was already out there watching some TV. I was about to head to bed to finish watching the show when I saw your light on. Why don't you come watch with me?"

"Oh, I..." I'm short of excuses again, and he grins, stepping forward and holding out his hand for me.

"Come on. We'll grab some snacks and set up in my room. Watch a movie and then if you fall asleep and have another nightmare, I'll be right there to wake you up."

A SHORT WHILE LATER, I'm sitting in Cooper's bed, propped up against a pile of pillows while he flips through streaming services, looking for a movie we can watch. We have snacks set up between us.

"What are you in the mood for? Action? Fantasy? Rom-com?" Cooper's brow furrows as he moves through the suggested list.

"Documentary?"

"Documentary?" He gives me a curious look.

"I mean, if the goal is to fall asleep..." I trail off.

"Okay, documentary it is." He starts scrolling through the list of documentaries, but most of them are unsolved crimes, airplane crashes, or shows about cults. "You sure these are going to help you sleep? Because..." He gives me a worried look.

"Okay. Maybe not a documentary." I laugh.

"Don't they make any like... cute nature ones anymore?" His teeth run over his lower lip in a distracting way as he scrolls through a list of about twenty more crime documentaries. "Lizzy used to love watching them all the time when she was younger. It was all we could put on TV. You know how most kids like cartoons or those educational kids' shows?"

I nod and take a bite of the puppy chow mix we put together in the kitchen while Cooper had me explain more about my sleep paralysis.

"Well, not her. It was nature documentaries. All the time. All day. All night. And like... some of those shows are pretty graphic."

"Oh yeah... I've had to turn them off sometimes. Too gory," I agree, remembering one where a raptor was tearing a poor animal to pieces.

"Yeah, well, that and all the..." Cooper waves his hand around. "Mating stuff."

"The mating stuff?" I giggle when I imagine Cooper having to watch horrified as animals got it on on the screen in front of his poor, innocent daughter.

"Listen, kids ask questions, okay? And then I have to give answers to tests I didn't study for. I don't know how to explain all that." His brow furrows, and he looks stressed just remembering it.

"Well, at least you didn't tell her *Jaws* was a documentary. Xander did that to me. Made me watch it and then told me it all really happened. I was scared to get in my bathtub for a week and refused to take a ferry or get anywhere near the Sound or Lake Washington for months. My parents wanted to kill him."

"Oh, fuck..." Cooper laughs. "I can see Xander doing that too."

"Yeah. He was always giving me a hard time. I was happy when football gave him someone else to terrorize."

"Sibling rivalries are tough." Cooper shakes his head, his laughter fading slightly.

"Yes. Lucky for Lizzy, she doesn't have to deal with that."

"Just her dad trying to explain to her what mating is without actually explaining it." He laughs again.

"Dangers of being a single dad, I guess."

"Unfortunately, there's the occasional downside."

"You're really good with her, you know. I know you like to keep things private. I respect that so much. But sometimes I'm a little sad that people don't get to see you the way some of us do."

"Yeah, well, most of the world doesn't deserve her. I dread it every time that Billy kid comes over. Constantly telling her to keep the door open. I'm going to have to keep an eye on him, make sure he's not turning *Jaws* on or anything just to get her closer."

"It is a very romantic movie," I muse sarcastically.

"Okay. We've talked about it enough, now I feel like we have to watch it." He returns to clicking through the menu and eventually finds it.

The opening music starts to play, and the couple takes off running across the beach a few minutes later. Cooper cringes when the naked woman stops laughing and starts screaming.

"You need me to hold your hand?" I tease, running my fingers over the back of his as he grips the remote.

"I might." He tosses it to the side, grabbing the bowl in between us and putting it in his lap before he takes my hand and pulls me closer. "You gotta keep me safe from the sharks." I hesitate at first, my heart rate kicking up in my chest at the thought of cuddling up to him, but when his arm wraps around my waist and he squeezes me, I realize it's his way of comforting me after everything that's happened the last few nights. So I lean in, resting my head against his shoulder.

"If anything, I might need to let her watch this to show her the dangers of dating fuckboys who fall asleep when you need them most," Cooper mutters as we watch the woman scream for help while her companion falls asleep with the tide lapping at his feet.

"I kinda feel for him." I yawn, realizing I'm finally starting to feel sleepy myself.

"Sleep if you need to, Trix. Lizzy always tells me I'm a good pillow." He grins at me, and his fingers run up and down my side in reassurance.

I smile back at him before my eyes feel too heavy to keep open anymore. Because, to his credit, he is a good pillow, but he also makes me feel safe enough that I'm not even worried about more sleep paralysis tonight.

12

C *ooper*

THE NEXT MORNING, when I wake up, she's curled up next to me. Her ass is snuggled up against my hips like this is how we always sleep. I can't take it this early in the morning. I slowly ease my way out from next to her, doing my best not to tug on the covers or move the mattress as I leave, and praying she doesn't wake up and see how hard I am from the way she felt against me. I'm like a fucking teenage boy around her, and it's embarrassing.

She stirs a little as I move away, turning over to her back and making a soft sound that's sending even more blood pooling south. Even worse, her shirt rides up with the movement, and the lace bra she has on is incredibly sheer. Her pale pink nipples bead up from the cool morning air, and I feel like I'm being tortured—by a sleeping woman who has zero idea how much of a hold she has on me.

I don't even need to glance down to know I'm hard enough to be showing through the shorts I have on. I need to get the fuck out of here if I don't want her to have a rude awakening. As I round the bed, she wakes up, and I'm just thankful I've made it to the door of my bathroom and can use it like a shield.

"Sorry, Trix. Did I wake you up?"

"No." She blinks, her eyes searching for me as she starts to open them fully, and her brow furrows when she finds me behind the door of the bathroom that I've left partially open.

"I'm just gonna get ready. You can stay in bed if you want." I try not to let my eyes wander. Mercifully, like she's suddenly aware of her state, she looks and tugs her shirt down hard. Her cheeks pink, and she sits up.

"I should get ready too. I'm sorry. I didn't mean to sleep this late. I'll get out of your hair." She rushes out of the bed like it's just turned to lava, and I'm glad I woke up first so she didn't find out how close we actually were for half the night.

"You're fine. You need the rest. " I shake my head.

"Well... Thank you for letting me sleep in here after everything last night. I'm sorry again about all of that. I'll meet you in the kitchen. I can cook something. Maybe eggs? Or toast?" She's rambling in an effort to distract me from her wardrobe malfunction. I just want to let her go so her misery isn't prolonged and I can end mine.

"That sounds good. Whatever you want. Have at it." Because there's only one thing I want right now, and judging by her current reaction, I have a snowball's chance in hell of getting it.

"Thank you. See you out there." She gives me a quick nod and then hurries out the bedroom door, shutting it behind her.

I turn on the shower to let the water heat and strip out of my clothes. I can't remember the last time I was that turned on just by a hint of nudity. These days, I'm so bored and jaded, it usually takes a hell of a lot more than that to get me anywhere close to interested. But she has that kind of hold on me. The temptation of being so close I could actually touch her. The luck of having her in my bed, but for all the wrong reasons, even if I loved being the one who could make her feel safe. The touch of huskiness to her voice when she spoke is just enough to send me over the edge.

I can't go out to have breakfast with her like this. Getting hard at every little thing she does or says. I *need* to take the fucking edge off. But the guilt is there when I wrap my hand around my cock and start to stroke, imagining I'm peeling the rest of her clothes off and laving my tongue over her nipples before I move lower and sink my face between her pretty thighs.

13

B *eatrix*

I SNUCK BACK into Cooper's room, hoping to grab my phone without him noticing. I need to put myself back to rights after a rough night with a shower and some makeup before making breakfast. But when I go to grab my phone, I notice the door to his bathroom is still cracked open. The sound of rushing water from the shower and steam rolls out into the bedroom. I see a flash of skin behind the door and the curve of his hip. His thighs look like they were carved out of marble, and getting to see a glimpse of the whole work of art is too tempting right now. Especially after falling asleep in his bed and having more than one not-so-innocent dream about him. It's wrong, but curiosity gets the best of me, and I find myself shifting subtly on my feet to get a better look. I lean to the side, and my jaw drops a little when he finally comes into full view.

He's naked and so ridiculously beautiful. Where Rob was

heavily tattooed—with some very regrettable day-I-turned-eighteen type tattoos that had aged poorly—Cooper has none. He's a blank canvas, and I'm... not hating it. I always thought I was a tattoo girl, but staring at him, I'm questioning everything. Every single curve of his back, shoulder blades, ass, and thighs is on full display with nothing to distract from them, the shadows and the light playing over them to spectacular effect. His arms are roped with muscle, the scar up the back of his elbow moving as his fist pumps back and forth.

I blink. And then blink again as I realize what he's doing when a throaty sound follows a string of curse words. He leans forward and braces himself against the quartz countertop as he starts to work himself over at a faster pace. His eyes are shuttered, and I can see most of his profile in the reflection of the mirror.

"Oh fuck. So fucking close..." he mutters.

I roll my lower lip between my teeth. I should leave. I have to leave. I really need to uproot myself from this spot and get into the shower. Probably a cold one because I'm half-ready to join him in his morning activities.

I should get cleaned up and try to erase this sight from my head. Because the last thing I need is to be thinking about Cooper like this. Obviously last night has thoroughly messed with my head, and waking up disheveled in his bed like we'd just spent the night together made it even worse. Not to mention I'm violating the man's privacy after he just spent last night protecting mine and making sure I felt safe.

But I can't stop watching. It's the hottest thing I've ever seen in my life, and the only thing I want right now is to watch him finish. Well. The only thing I want in this particular moment, if I'm truly honest, is to be the one helping him finish. Since that's impossible, I'll take the consolation prize of watching him come all over his hand.

"Fuck, Trixie. Just a little more."

I gasp silently, the sharp intake of breath freezing in my lungs as I try to make sure I heard him right. I can't have, but I swear... I swear he said *my* name. The flush of that realization spreads down my neck and over my chest.

My mind is whirring with all the consequences of what that could mean as he starts to come; it spills over his hand and some onto the counter before he grabs a towel to catch the rest. His fist moving over his cock in rough strokes while his chest shudders in tandem.

A soft, guttural moan comes out of him as he finishes. He's bent over, leaning hard on his free hand, his head down as his chest rises and falls, and he starts to move the towel over his abdomen and dick. His eyes are only half-open, and he looks drunk on his release as he wipes his hands and tosses the towel in the hamper. He takes a deep breath and runs a hand through his hair and over his face.

"Fuckkkk," he groans again, but this time, it's the sound of regret rather than pleasure. "Get a grip, Rawlings. Get a fucking grip."

He turns toward the shower, and I jump back out of his line of sight, turning quickly to the door and practically running through it down the hall. My phone nearly falls to the floor, but I catch it just before it does. I move faster down the hall than I have anywhere outside of the gym. When I finally get back to my room, I shut the door and lean against it, trying to catch my breath from my sudden sprint and the realization that Cooper just said my name.

14

B*eatrix*

LATER THAT WEEK, I'm home alone with Lizzy while Cooper has an offseason practice and training session that's running long. She's finally out of school for the year and enjoying it by playing video games and lounging by the pool outside. I'm busy following up on some inquiries Madison sent out and emailing a photographer in Seattle we'd both love to see do some work with Quentin if she's willing to while we're all out there later this summer.

But midway through, I hit a wall of fatigue, and I don't think I can bear to open one more email. Writing line after line of polite professional jargon is almost as exhausting as doing time on the elliptical, and I need to give myself a break. A snack wouldn't hurt either, so I wander into the kitchen and start working on some small cucumber sandwiches and a fruit bowl. I end up making more than I need since I don't think Lizzy's had much other than the big pancake breakfast we all had this morning, so I put it on a tray to take outside, figuring I can use some vitamin D too.

"Hungry?" I ask.

She pulls down the headphones that she has on while she floats in the pool and grins.

"Yes! Starving. Hang on." She kicks her way around and makes for the edge of the pool.

I set our snacks out on a table between two loungers and take up my spot, slipping out of my shoes and putting my sunglasses on. I could get used to this life. One where the pool is just outside the back door, and work breaks involve getting to lounge outside. Lizzy pulls up next to me a moment later and sprawls out on the neon-colored beach towel she has spread out.

"So I was just thinking..." She nibbles away at one of the sandwiches, finishing it with some of the lemonade I brought out to go with them. "Dad's birthday is coming up next week when I'm already at camp."

"Oh, is it?"

"Yes. It's that Friday, and normally, I do a whole thing where I bake him a cake and send invites to Ramsey, Garner, and the rest of the guys. But I won't be here to do it. I know he'll say he doesn't care and that we can celebrate it later, but I know he loves having everyone over for the pool and BBQ. He won't do it for himself though."

"Yeah, I know that about your dad." Cooper is always very focused on his friends and family, always making sure everyone else has a good time.

"So I was wondering... Since you'll be here, and I know you bake the most amazing things, would you be willing to host it for him?"

I stop mid-bite of my fruit salad.

"Me?"

"Yeah. You guys are friends. You work with the Chaos, so you could get the invites out to them. We could get the groceries for the BBQ delivered if you don't have time, or we could even have a BBQ place cater. That might be easier. I have a credit card for emergencies."

She's already thought this whole thing through and has the entire plan ready to be put into action. I really don't have a good excuse not to do it, at least not from her perspective. Honestly, I love the idea and figure Cooper could use the break from all the practices and end-of-year parent responsibilities he's had with Lizzy's school.

But then I worry about what it'll look like when the woman who's moved in with him is baking him cakes and throwing a birthday party for him like she's a girlfriend. Especially after the other morning when we clearly flirted with a line we shouldn't cross if I'm going to be living here for the summer.

Lizzy eats the last of her sandwich and then frowns while she waits for me to say something.

"If you're too busy, I understand."

My heart sinks. I don't want to let her down. Especially not when she wants to do something so thoughtful for her dad. I really don't want to let Cooper down either, given how generous he's been with his home and his time for me as I navigate the mess that is my life right now. We're both adults and I can do something to help his daughter celebrate him.

"No. No. It's not that. I can do it. If you plan it and put the invitations together this week, I'll deliver them to the guys before the end of the week for you. I'll just tell them I'm stepping in for you since you can't be there. Just want to make sure you get credit for all the hard work." I smile at her.

"Will you bake him a cake though? I know we can order one, but we both always loved the stuff you made at the lake house when you were with Uncle Rob."

"Yes. I can do that. I have a recipe I've been wanting to try anyway. Your dad likes chocolate, right?"

"He loves it. It's his favorite." She grins, and then it fades. "Sorry for mentioning Uncle Rob. I know that probably made it weird. I didn't mean to."

"No, it's fine. We were together for a while. It's how you and I met. He's still your uncle. You're allowed to mention him to me. There are no hard feelings there."

"Well, I have hard feelings. His new girlfriend is nowhere near as fun as you are. I don't know what he was thinking. But I'm glad you're here with me and Dad for the summer."

"Yeah, I heard you played a significant role in that. Thank you. You're really thoughtful, you know?" I smile at her.

"Don't get too excited. It was a little bit selfish on my part. It meant I got to spend more time with you. And you make Dad laugh a lot, like the way he was at the fair; I'm glad you guys can have fun together."

"Me too." I grin.

"I'm just sad I have to go to camp now because it means I don't get as much time with you." She rolls her lower lip into a pout.

"I'll still be here when you get back."

"But then we're going to the lake house. You know it's my birthday then... and I might need you to make my cake too." A wry grin forms on her face, and she wiggles her eyebrows.

"Okay... let's take this one thing at a time." I give her a look.

Going to the lake house is a nonstarter, not that I want to tell her that. It's one thing to hang out with her and Cooper here. But Rob and his new girlfriend would most definitely be at the big family summer get-together, and I don't need to be the odd woman out for that. Or worse yet, looking like I'm still pining after him and trying to find ways to see him.

"Fine. But I'm still going to be plotting for it."

"You do that. In the meantime, tell me more about camp. Is

it a programming camp or design? What all are you doing there?"

"Yes! It's like a boot camp for game designers. A bunch of other people my age will all work on a project together." She starts telling me all the opportunities she's going to have and I listen. My heart is so happy for her, to know she's getting to do something she loves so much, and that her parents are so supportive of her pursuing her dreams.

15

B *eatrix*

I'M NECK-DEEP IN FLOUR, butter, and cocoa powder with them half-splattered around the kitchen. I'm lucky that Cooper is one of the most patient men in existence because while I might be a halfway decent baker, I am also one hundred percent a messy one too. So I'm hoping he doesn't get home a half hour from now and die at the state of it. Not exactly the surprise birthday party Lizzy imagined for him. As I start to run the mixer, I feel like I'm missing something, and I scan the ingredients on the counter again.

"Trixie?" I hear him call from the front hallway. So much for getting this done before he got home. I guess they let him loose early the day before his birthday.

"In the kitchen!"

Cooper comes in a moment later, blinking as his eyes shift back and forth at the mess I've created.

"I'm going to clean it up. I'm sorry. Wren says it's worth it," I apologize, cringing a little as I look around and see how bad it truly is.

Cooper laughs and shakes his head.

"Okay, well, maybe we need to order in or go out for dinner then?"

"I ordered some food already." I grin at him, trying to cover for the fact that his surprise party's going to be here shortly.

"Oh, okay. Perfect then. So what's so special about this cake?" He sidles up to the counter and peeks into the mixing bowl.

"Wren says it's Better Than Sex cake. It's some inside joke between her and Easton that I'd rather not ask about, but she's planning on serving it at the new restaurant, and she let me try it. It was so good, and Lizzy said you loved chocolate. So I decided it'd be good for your birthday. It was supposed to be a surprise." I'm hoping admitting to part of the secret will keep him distracted from the bigger surprise to come.

"You made me a birthday cake?" The smile on Cooper's face spreads.

"Yeah. I couldn't let you down. With Lizzy at camp, someone's gotta hold down the fort." I grin.

"Better than sex, huh?" He eyes the batter skeptically.

"So Wren says."

"I'll have to give East shit for that one."

I shake my head at him and give him an admonishing look.

"Something's missing though, like I missed an ingredient." I wipe some of the splattered batter off the edge of the bowl.

Cooper turns his baseball hat backward and leans over the counter to grab a spoon out of the holder. He dips it in the edge of the bowl and then licks it. He makes an approving face and a little grunting noise.

"Wren might be right."

"You don't think something's missing?" I ask.

"Tastes like chocolate cake batter to me." He shrugs and hands me the spoon where there's still a little batter left, and I lick it. It's good. Really good. But I still feels like something's just a touch off.

I frown at the bowl and then turn to grab my phone before I realize my hands are still covered in batter and flour. I brush them on the apron without much luck. So I huff and decide to have my phone read it out loud to me.

"Hey Siri, can you read me the Better Than Sex cake ingredient list?"

"Better than the Ex Adventure List. Go stargazing. Go camping. Have sex outside. Voyeurism?"

My cheeks turn bright red, and I'm furiously wiping my hands on a towel before I realize how silly it is to worry about my phone getting food on it when it's literally reading off a list of kinky, post-breakup things I want to try. I can't even risk a look at Cooper right now for fear of spontaneously combusting.

Cooper.

Cooper is on the list.

"Stop. Siri. Stop!" I practically scream the words, but she doesn't. She keeps going.

"Rough sex. Impact play. Degradation."

If I've ever had any luck in my life, I'd like to use it all right now to get this phone to stop telling my ex's brother every fantasy I've ever considered in the middle of his kitchen.

My fingers fumble over the buttons, and it refuses my first entry. I try again, but she's dangerously close to the end of the list.

"Temperature play. Cream pie. Get a tattoo."

Oh my god. I feel the sand running out. I've gotten it unlocked and my finger's half a millisecond away from exiting the app when she does me dirty.

"Sex with the ex's brother."

I hate Madison and Wren right now. I hate myself for not

deleting that the second they wrote it there. I hate the fact that I'm seemingly never able to remember an ingredient list to save my life and for being messy enough that I couldn't just look at the list.

"What was that?" Cooper's voice is rough, and I can feel his eyes on me.

No good deed goes unpunished.

I click out of the app, pretending to be focused on my phone, even though she's already betrayed me. Cursing the fact that there's no time machine app to take me back and stop all this from happening in the first place.

"Uh... that was nothing. Just a joke list the girls put together for me. Madison and Wren were just being funny the other night. We were drinking and talking. Just being silly. You know. I'm sure you do the same with the guys." I swallow hard and then risk raising my eyes to get a look at him, a flush burning across the skin on my cheeks and chest.

I don't think I can live here anymore. I'll need to pack my bags and head back to the hotel. Listening to my neighbors fuck and worrying about a potential overzealous fan is a hell of a lot better than Cooper knowing how I want to get fucked. That I've thought about *him* that way.

And what if he tells Rob that I have a list like this? That he's on it. I'm sure they'll have a long laugh at it. Or at least Rob would. Cooper isn't like that. Really, Cooper wouldn't share something like that with Rob at all, or at least, I don't think he would. That's my only solace here. Focus on the positives, right?

"Do you have a sex list?" He's recovered now. Amused even. I can hear it in his voice even though I've returned to staring at my phone.

"It's not like that. It's a... a challenge list, and there's just some sex stuff on there," I say dismissively and scroll the ingredient list, pretending to have lost all interest in what just happened. We can just move on. Especially when I figure out what ingredient I forgot. "Vanilla. I forgot the vanilla!"

"I'm not sure that list includes anything vanilla. Can you play it again?"

"Cooper."

"I just want to hear the last one again." He hovers as I go to get the vanilla out of his pantry, looking at me expectantly.

"No, I just need to get the spoon for this." I dodge around him and go for the measuring spoons.

"So I didn't hear it right?"

"I don't know what you thought you heard." I shake my head and measure out the vanilla, pouring it into the cake batter and restarting the mixer like my phone didn't just tell my ex's brother I've thought about fucking him.

I stare into the cake batter like if I look hard enough, it might just take me down into its little vortex of chocolatey goodness and let me disappear from this kitchen. I'm contemplating other exit strategies when I feel his hands brush over my shoulders and down my upper arms. Just that soft touch has goosebumps lighting up my skin.

He leans down, and I hear his breathing change before he speaks, and when he does, it's a tone I've never heard him use before. One that has every little part of me paying attention because it's so soft, I have to focus to make sure I hear him right.

"I've thought about you so many times, Trixie. If it was really a joke, I'll never bring it up again. But if it wasn't... tell me."

My heart is in my throat. It must be because I can feel every single little flutter of it, and I can't find words. This can't be real. Now it's me who didn't hear him correctly.

"Not entirely," I say softly. I can admit that much. The whole list wasn't a joke, but I still have some plausible deniability since Madison wrote it for me.

One of his hands slides the rest of the way down my upper arm, over my elbow, and his fingers brush my waist. He bends closer until I can feel the slightest whisper of his breath over the shell of my ear. His fingers inch slowly over me, and I don't move away.

"Are the other things on the list a joke?" He asks quietly, so much so I barely hear him over the pounding of my own heart.

"No. Well... It's like I said. Like an adventure-challenge sort of list for the summer. Things I want to challenge myself to try."

"Because if I'm already on your list, you might as well use me to make your way through it. I could help you with some of them. All of them, really." His voice is so soft and deep that I might be lost in it.

"All of them?" I nearly choke on my own words. I'm already imagining him doing those things to me. The naked version I saw in his bathroom the other morning using me how he sees fit, and I'm ready to confess everything.

"Any of the ones you want." There's a soft, half-nervous laugh from him that puts me enough at ease that I feel like I can admit some of the truth.

"I want to..."

"But?"

16

C *ooper*

SHE DOESN'T ANSWER, but she doesn't move away from me either. I can feel the way the tension is rolling off her, hear it in the way she's breathing. If I've ever had a chance with her, this is it. So I take it and hope like hell it doesn't sink our friendship if I fail. I've gotten too attached to more Trix in my life, too needy to have her any way I can, to be ready to lose her. But I need to know if there's anything more for her there.

"You've been on *my* list for a long time, Trix."

"I didn't think you had room on your list." She teases me, a small smile tugging at the corner of her mouth.

"You're at the top, and if anyone else was ever on it, I don't remember."

"How did I end up on this list exactly?" I can hear the hesitation in her voice, the confusion at us even having this discussion. But I've waited for this opening with her for so long, I can't let it go without trying.

"A sundress."

"A sundress?" There's a small, stuttered laugh that falls from her lips.

"Remember a couple of summers ago when we were all supposed to go fishing? But then Lizzy wanted to sleep in, and you and Rob had that fight?"

"Yeah. I remember. I had no business being on a boat, let alone fishing."

"But you came anyway. With a sundress and no sunscreen. I had to put some on your shoulders, and your skin was so damn soft, Trix. You were so sweet, and I could see where your eyes were still red from him making you cry. It killed me."

"I was embarrassed. Your parents heard us fighting, and I just wanted to be anywhere that wasn't the house." Her brow furrows at the memory.

"I know. Which is why I took you out on the boat even though it took all my self-control not to say anything. Especially with the way you looked. How quiet you were. So I just promised myself I'd make you laugh and forget things for a few hours. Teach you something to get your mind off it. Try to get my mind off you in the process."

"You did. I had a lot of fun that day. It felt like I could forget for a bit, and I honestly didn't want to go back to shore."

"Me either. I wanted to kiss you that day. So fucking bad it hurt."

"I'm glad you didn't," she whispers, and I still my hands in response.

I can hear my heart pounding in my ears, and I'm nervous I fucked up by confessing it to her. I don't know what I'm doing with her, even when I think I do. I start to pull away, but she stops me, her palm over the top of my knuckles, and a soft sound from her has me holding still. "I wouldn't have appreciated it then the way I would now. If you'd kissed me at the fair..." She trails off, and the pounding in my ears is nearly deafening.

"I'll kiss you anytime you want. Anywhere you want."

She must like my confession because she tilts her head and looks up at me, the ghost of a smile crosses her face before her eyes drop to my mouth. It's all the encouragement I need from her before I lean over to kiss her. I'm careful, so careful, gently brushing my lips over hers and giving her the chance to push me away if she wants. It's almost too good to be true. Like for once in my life, birthday wishes are real because I'm finally getting something I've wanted for ages.

Except she doesn't push back, she returns it—kissing me like she wants me. With a kind of greediness that makes me think I'm not the only one who's imagined this before now. She tastes sweet like the cake batter she's fixing, and I brush my tongue over her lower lip for another taste before hers darts out and tangles with mine. I thread my fingers through her hair, and her hands wander down my chest.

For a moment, I have everything I've ever wanted. But then her hand presses down gently, and she takes a step back. Her lashes fluttering, and her gaze falling to the floor.

"We shouldn't be doing this," she whispers, and the words crash through my daze. Battering my thoughts as she retreats, and putting the ocean of what-ifs back in between us.

"Why not?" My brain honestly can't come up with a single good reason, but if she has them, I'll listen.

Her brow furrows, and she looks at me for a moment and then away.

"You're my landlord now, for starters."

"That's temporary."

"You're his brother."

"You said you wouldn't hold that against me."

She levels me with a look. "I don't, but... this can't go

anywhere. Not really. I mean, not that it could anyway. You don't do serious, and right now, neither do I."

"So it doesn't have to be serious. It just has to be fun. And you already know I'm fun." I'm bargaining with her. Bargaining with myself, really, because I'll take whatever she gives me.

She smiles, one that's sincere and travels all the way to her eyes as she looks me over. "You are a lot of *fun*."

"So I don't see the problem."

Her eyes dart back to some distant spot behind me, and she fidgets with the spoon in her hand like she's still trying to reason herself out of this.

"I'm on your list. You're on mine. We're both adults. You've already kissed me. Slept in my bed. Might as well take full advantage of the hospitality around here." I give her a laundry list of reasons we should jump into the deep end. Ones I've told myself a million times.

She shakes her head and laughs again before it fades to a smile, and then her brow furrows.

"Speaking of taking advantage and your bed..." She twirls the spoon between her fingers, and her cheeks flush slightly, her lip worrying between her teeth. "I watched you the other day. I didn't mean to. I went back to get my phone after you went to shower, and the door was open..."

"Watched me?" I'm confused at first, and then the pieces start to fall into place when I remember the state I was in after she slept in my bed. My little self session to get her out of my head. Doing it all while I imagined her spread out in front of me. Fuck... "Oh." I swallow down the awkward feeling. If I was capable of blushing I might be doing it right now.

"I'm sorry. I shouldn't have. It was just... and then you said... Or I thought you said..." She stumbles over her words as she looks up at me.

"Your name." *Fucckkkkk.* "Yeah, about that..." I grab my hat, taking it off and putting it back on again. Straightening the bill out on the back like it'll make a difference in my ability to explain away what she saw. It's a nervous habit of mine I can't help. One I'm doing while I try to explain the fact I get off while I think about her.

"It was hot. Honestly." She saves what's left of my ego. "You were... I thought about walking in there, and then I ran off and wondered if I needed to confess my sins somewhere or something. I was torn between that and taking my own shower." The smile she gives me then makes my heart stop.

"Your own shower?"

"Shower..." She uses air quotes and presses her lips together as her eyes dart off to the side.

"Did you? Fuck... Tell me you did."

"No. I felt guilty, and I was in your house."

"Right. You were in *my* house. You should have come to me. I would have taken care of you."

Her tongue darts out over her lower lip, and she glances at me before she starts to turn away again. I catch her chin and sweep my thumb over it, bringing her eyes back to mine.

"I can take care of you right now if that's what you need."

"I..." She looks at me, and I can tell she's considering it, that she's curious, but thinks it's the wrong thing to want. I'm too desperate to hear her come to care what's wrong right now. "I have to finish the cake."

"You can finish it while I finish you. Not a problem, Trix."

"What?" Her fingers turn the spoon over again and then slip down over the handle. It's a simple act that has me imagining more.

"Finish making the cake. You were doing such a good job before I interrupted. I want to watch you finish it." I stand and gently press my hands to her hips, turning her around so she's back facing the counter.

She sets the spoon down and reaches slowly for the spatula, and my hands coast over her hips, playing over the soft bit of skin between her shirt and her waistband. I can hear her breathing shift again with anticipation, feel it in the way she moves like she's waiting for what I'll do next.

My lips are at her throat of their own volition. I can't get enough of the feel of her soft skin, the smell of her perfume, and the soft sound she makes when I kiss my way down her neck. My fingers follow a similar descent, making their way under the skirt she has on and teasing my way slowly over her skin before I go to slide my fingers under the band of her panties.

Until there's a shrill sound that knocks us both out of the moment.

The doorbell rings, and I pause, racking my brain for who the hell could be here. Lizzy's with her mom. I didn't make any orders yet. I don't live in the kind of neighborhood where people just stop by.

There's a small exhale on her part, and her lashes flutter open.

"You should get that," she says with a touch of reluctance in her voice.

"You know who it is?" I guess she did say she ordered something.

"Yes. Your birthday party." She smiles up at me and then breaks out into a laugh. "Surprise!"

I bite my lower lip and shake my head until I can't help but laugh too.

"Fuck... I'm gonna tell them to go around to the back, and then I'm finishing what we started. They can wait on us for a few minutes."

"I should get the cake in, or it'll never be ready in time. I'm late as it is. Can't have a birthday without cake, you know."

I run my hand under her chin and tilt it up so her eyes meet mine, raising a brow.

"Respectfully, fuck the cake."

Another spate of laughter rolls through her, but she nods her agreement. I hurry to the door, and sure enough, my guys are out there. I greet them quickly, thanking them for showing up as they yell surprise and give me shit about being another year older.

"Trix is finishing the cake and doesn't want anyone seeing the mess. Can you go around back and give me five to help her clean up, then I'll be out?" I ask, nodding my head toward my back fence.

"The wife making you a cake instead of buying it? So domestic." Ramsey gives me a shit-eating grin.

"Wife?" I hear Daphne ask as she walks up the path with her friends. Apparently, they were invited too.

"Our boy's got a girl living with him now," Garner answers her, nodding toward the fence as he heads that way and explains to the girls what's going on.

I'm not sure if Trix is ready for the party she planned for me or how wild these guys can get, but the least I can do for all her trouble is give her an orgasm. So I haul ass back to the kitchen where she's already got the cake in the oven and is cleaning up the mess she made with the batter. It amuses me that someone who's otherwise so prim and proper can't seem to bake without it exploding through half the place. It's another thing about her on a long list of things I love.

I come up behind her as she wipes down the island. She glances outside when we both see the movement of people filling the backyard.

"I told them we needed a few minutes to finish cleaning up in here, so they're out back." I wrap my arms around her waist and kiss the side of her throat.

"It's fine, really. I've got to make the fruit salad and get the drinks out of the fridge and into the cooler."

"I'll take care of the drinks, and the fruit salad can wait."

"Cooper, it's fine. Really. I can wait." She gives me an

amused look and resumes wiping the counter. I kiss my way down her neck and over her shoulder while she works until she pauses again and tilts her head to the side so I have better access, sighing as I hit the spot I'm learning she likes just under her jaw.

"Maybe you can wait, but I can't. I've waited too fucking long already to hear you come for me." I slip my fingers back under the waistband a moment later. "It's my birthday wish. You wouldn't deny me that, would you?"

"I wouldn't," she murmurs, her eyes closing as she speaks.

My fingers glide lower, brushing over her clit and then inside her. She's soaking wet, and I'm desperate to know she's coming thinking of me.

"You're so fucking sexy, Trix. I wish I could have seen you watching me." I circle my thumb over her clit, teasing her with the slightest touch, and she rocks forward.

"Oh god..." she whispers, and her lashes flutter again as she lets go of the cloth she was using. She grips the edge of the quartz slab as I start to work my fingers inside her, my thumb gently beginning to stroke over her clit in tandem. Her eyes open again a second later when she hears voices, and she watches as they start to unstack the chairs and set them up on the deck just outside the door.

"The door's unlocked. They could come in," she says softly.

"They could, so you should focus on coming first," I answer, pumping my fingers in and out of her a touch faster as she rolls her hips forward to counter the sensation.

A chair clamors against the concrete as it comes off a stack and another burst of laughter distracts her.

"Coop," she says, concern lacing her tone.

"Forget them, Trix. Imagine you're watching me again. My hand wrapped around my cock while I think about you. You watching me through the crack in the doorway while you get so wet you can hardly stand it. Desperate for relief. Just like you are right now. So close for me..."

"Oh fuck," she curses as I make my circles around her clit tighter and tighter. Her hips rock forward of their own volition, and I do my best to keep my rhythm for her as she starts to breathe heavier. She's so wet, the sound of my fingers slipping over her skin is practically echoing in the kitchen, and even if someone couldn't see the state I've put her in—they could hear it. A sound that's going to play on a loop for me every night. I need it from here to eternity.

She cries out a moment later as she hits her release, and I swallow the sound with a rough kiss that mutes it before anyone outside can hear. They're too distracted by their own laughter to notice, but I know it'll be moments before one of them decides to burst in and destroy this little bubble I have with her right now. She kisses me back roughly and then sweet as I finish her off, slowing the pace of my fingers and then eventually slipping them free. Her lips are against mine as her breathing slows.

"Fuck that was hot, Trix." My heart is pounding in my chest.

"Thank you," she answers softly, a somewhat sheepish look of satisfaction on her face. I can't help but grin that this beautiful fucking woman is thanking me when I should be thanking her for that experience. She takes a breath, and her eyes dart to the commotion outside again.

"We should get out there," I say before she can.

"Let me just get changed, and I'll be right there."

"Okay." I nod, putting a little space between us so she can get around me and the counter to her room.

"And Cooper?" She stops halfway down the hall and turns back before I can open the sliding glass to the deck.

"Yeah?"

"Happy birthday!" She laughs and then takes off the rest of the way to her room.

I open the door, and Ramsey's standing there, his brow quirked at me when he sees the massive grin on my face.

"The cake that fucking good then?" He smirks before he takes a sip of the beer he brought with him.

"Only had a taste, but I can already tell it's the best I've ever had."

He rolls his eyes and hands me a beer out of his cooler.

"Happy fucking birthday then!"

17

B *eatrix*

THE SUN'S GONE DOWN, and I've cleaned up most of what's left of the party food and drinks. Ramsey is sprawled out on a lounge chair half-asleep, and Garner and Daphne are wrapped up with each other in the hot tub. Cooper swims up to the edge of the pool where I'm sitting, dipping my feet in and swishing small circles in the water, watching it form little sparkling waves in the illumination from the lights he has strung around the pool.

He runs a hand through his hair, sweeping it back, and several droplets highlight the rise of his cheekbones and the sharp cut of his jaw. The man is too pretty for his own good. Making him seem like one of the good guys for this PR project will probably be more difficult than I anticipated since I can't even look at him without having dirty thoughts. Something that he must be able to read on my face when he grins and reaches out for me, wrapping his palms around the backs of my calves and gently massaging them.

"Water's warm if you want to come in?"

"I'm not a very good swimmer." I'm not keen to embarrass myself in front of him or the company.

"I don't think you give yourself enough credit."

"Treading water is about all I can manage."

"We'll have to add it to your list. We can work on it this summer. If you want." The playful grin he gives me melts any protest I might have. This man can teach me anything he wants.

"Do you mind if we stay in the guest room?" Garner's voice breaks through my daze, and I turn to look up at him. His fingers are intertwined with Daphne's. She smiles at me, and I return it. I look back to Cooper to see what he'll say since I'm currently occupying the space with suitcases and a dresser full of toiletries I have no permanent home for at the moment.

"That's Trix's room right now. You can have the room down-stairs if you want."

"She's not sleeping with you?" Garner blurts out, the alcohol he's had leaving him with no filter, and I tense. I see Cooper flash a look of concern in my direction.

"We're just friends. I can move my stuff if you need it though," I say before Cooper can speak.

Garner looks at me with a flicker of remorse on his face, like he knows he fucked up but also knows there's not much he can do to walk it back at this point.

"No. No. You're good. Downstairs is fine. I didn't realize. I'm sorry." He nods before he squeezes Daphne's hand, and the two of them take off into the house.

"Fucking Christ, that boy's a mess." Ramsey's behind us now too, shaking his head and then looking at me with sympathy. "Don't fucking listen to him. He's too dense for his own good sometimes."

"It's okay," I answer softly, giving Ramsey a grateful smile anyway because I'm glad someone understands that this is awkward enough as it is.

"You care if I crash on the couch downstairs too? I don't think I can drive right now. Didn't drink that much, just exhausted."

"Nah. Go ahead. But you better have some earplugs." Cooper smirks.

"Garner's a screamer? Why am I not surprised." Ramsey laughs. "I'll be all right. You two have a good one." He nods a goodnight to both of us and then heads inside, sliding the glass behind him and leaving us with a tidal wave of awkward silence.

"Ramsey seems nice," I say when the quiet stretches on too long for my liking.

Cooper laughs and shakes his head. "Ramsey's anything but nice, but he's a good guy."

"You can be both?"

"He makes it work somehow. He's a damn good friend. I'll say that much."

"Well, I can appreciate that. You're a good friend too, you know. For letting all of us stay here. Looking out for us. Being so kind to me when you don't have to."

Cooper shrugs and looks off into the distance for a moment. I can tell compliments like that make him uncomfortable, so I splash him gently and grin when he gives me a shocked face before his hands are on me again.

"Come in. I'll give you your first lesson."

I pull off the swimsuit cover-up dress I still have on and toss it to the side. His eyes rake over my body, and the look on his face makes me feel about fifty times sexier than I've ever felt in my life. Cooper just has that sort of magic about him. That no matter what, he makes you feel like you're the center of his attention. It's the kind of thing I could get used to if I wasn't careful.

He holds out his hand, and I take it as I slip into the water. It's a little deeper than I am tall at this point in the pool, and I have to kick a little to stay afloat. But he wraps his arms around me and pulls me close, helping to keep me steady in the water where he more than touches the bottom. My hands are resting on his shoulders, and I can feel the way his muscles flex subtly as he holds me in the water.

"I think I need too much practice for this to go on my summer list."

"I'm a good teacher. You might be surprised."

"Oh yeah?"

"I taught Lizzy to swim. You can ask her for a reference."

"I might do that. Make sure you're not overstating your skills and won't lose your patience with flounderers."

He laughs. "You know Lizzy. If there's anything she's taught me, it's to have a fuckton of patience."

"She's a pretty good kid though."

"She is. But we had some rough years there for a while. She's mellowed and found things that make her really happy, and that makes me happy. I just hope high school isn't too hard on her."

"I think she'll be okay. She's got a good group of friends, and once you've got that, high school's not so bad. Even when it does get hard."

"Speaking from experience?"

"It wasn't the easiest time in my life. But then I didn't realize how much harder being an adult would be at the time. It must be nice to live that kind of bliss. Do you think they're getting around to inventing a time machine so we can go back and appreciate it while it's happening?"

"Hmm. I doubt that. But we can work on right now. What else is on that list of yours? Remind me. I got a little preoccupied with one part of it." He grins at me.

"I don't think we need to do that."

"Oh, I think we do. It sounded like a good list." His brow furrows like he's thinking, and he looks up at the sky. "Stargazing was on there, I think. Camping, too, right?

"Yes."

"And there was definitely something about sex outside. Was that during the stargazing or the camping?

"Cooper..."

"Either is probably a good goal to have. It was the next round. The rough sex and the getting spanked is where I got a little distracted, so you're going to have to refresh my memory."

"Oh my god. You know talking about this with you makes me want to die a little, right?"

"Is that what those sounds were that you were making while you finished the cake? Dying?" he pokes.

"Stop!" I laugh and put my hand over his mouth, attempting my most threatening look on him. He laughs, and then he reaches up to gently pull my hand away.

"Why does talking about this with me make you want to die?"

"Because I thought you were going to be my brother-in-law, and you were in that brotherly friend box."

He makes a face that tells me he's concerned about my well-being if that's how I interact with my brotherly type friends.

"Obviously not after earlier but..."

"But..." His hand slips under my chin and runs down my jaw.

"I don't know," I mumble the words because I don't really have objections right now. I know the ones I should have. The things I should say. But none of them manage to make it past my lips.

"You've never been in any sort of box for me. If anything, you run wild in my imagination."

"Oh." I'm winning awards for how eloquent I am right now. My high school English teacher would be impressed.

"So like I said, I'm more than happy to help you with any kind of list you have."

"So helpful." I can't help the smile that erupts, and he echoes it.

"Think of me like a Boy Scout, Trix. Trying to learn to pitch a tent? I got you. Want to know how to start a fire? No problem. Need me to grab you by your throat until you can beg for me in another language? I'm all yours." The smile he gives me ruins the last of my resistance.

Obviously, he didn't forget everything on the list. I shift in his arms, and my fingers slip back over his shoulders to bring us closer. Because tonight, I think I'm his.

"It's your birthday. Shouldn't we be focused on your list?" It's my turn for a devious grin.

"I told you. My list only has one thing on it." I can see the restraint in his eyes, the way he's making sure I know what he's saying.

"So cross it off."

His mouth is on mine a second later, and right now, I'm a little bit sorry I ever kissed any man who wasn't him. I know I shouldn't compare. But Cooper makes his brother look like a fumbling schoolboy. Especially when it comes to the way he kisses and the way he uses his hands. So I'm dying to find out if the rest will follow suit.

His kiss is all-consuming, and we move through the water until he has me pinned against the wall. His hands drift down my sides under the water, and I wrap my legs around his waist as he grips my thighs. I grind against him as my nails dig into the back of his neck, and he answers me by slipping one hand up my thigh to cup my ass, his fingers digging into my flesh. It sends sparks through me, leaving me wondering what it would be like to have him handle me how he wants.

"Fucking hell, Trix." His eyes search my face when he comes up for air like he's seeing me for the first time.

"I'm sorry, I—" I start to say, but he cuts me off.

"You're not sorry, and neither am I. Not for this."

I run my hand down his chest and over his abs until I hit the top of his board shorts, and he runs his teeth over my lower lip as he kisses me again. He groans into my mouth when I make my way under the band of his board shorts and wrap my hand around him.

"Sorry for this?" I tease as I stroke him.

"Nah. But I have to tell you the truth too."

"The truth about what?" I ask, nerves bubbling up but not enough to stop me from my goal.

"Earlier, you admitted you watched me. But I didn't finish admitting how much I think about you. Imagining it's you there with me." Every word is a labored whisper as he starts to breathe heavier against my lips, kissing me intermittently as he confesses what I already secretly hoped was true.

"What was I doing when you were imagining me?"

He lets out an almost inaudible groan and takes a breath before he answers.

"You were spread out on a bed for me, letting me eat your sweet little pussy while you grabbed my hair and pushed my face down, begging me for more."

I let out a muted laugh, surprised by the answer as much as I am by the man. I slow the pattern of my hand and study his face.

"Not on my knees for you?" I raise a brow. I was almost sure that was what he was imagining when I watched him.

"No. I mean, I wouldn't say no if you were offering, but I

can't stop thinking about what you taste like. How you'd sound coming while you curse my name. Feeling your fingers dig into the back of my scalp, and one of your pretty little skirts hiked up around your hips." He kisses his way up my throat and then nips my earlobe. "I'd fuck you so good like that if you'd let me, Trix."

"I think I need you to fuck me."

His eyes light with the admission, falling over my face with a hint of surprise in them before a wicked grin forms in their wake.

"I can do that."

He kisses me again, rough, like he wants to make a point, and then he's pulling me out of the water in one swift motion, setting me on the edge of the pool. He follows me a moment later, and I watch as his muscles flex and the water rolls off him like we're in some slow-motion thirst trap.

He grins at the way I have to pick my jaw up off the floor and then stands, holding a hand out for me. I put mine in his, and he hauls me to my feet, placing another tender kiss on my lips.

My heart is pounding out of my chest when he walks me to the oversized cabana he has out here by the pool. He pulls the drapes on three of the sides, and as each one falls shut, my heart beats harder. What we did earlier was... well, it was one thing. It was wrong, but it wasn't this wrong. It wasn't crossing the Rawlings Rubicon.

My fingers tease along the finished edge of the last curtain before I look up at him again. I'm scared he's going to have the same sudden brush with the truth that I am right now and change his mind. But when I look in his eyes, there's nothing there but pure, unadulterated want.

His mouth is on mine, kissing me roughly, and his hands roam over my body. I'm lost in him all over again. The way he tastes and the way he feels is so different from anyone I've had before. His fingers pause as they reach the edge of my swimsuit. He doesn't ask permission, but every touch on my body is a request all the same.

18

C *ooper*

MY FINGERS PULL at the wet swimsuit bottoms she has on, peeling them slowly down her legs as I kiss a trail behind their retreat, making my way down her legs until she steps out of them. I toss them on the cabana bed behind her and move to the bikini top she has on, tugging it slowly and carefully off her. She helps me as I pull it over her head and toss it next to its other half. I stare for a moment when I have her completely naked. All the curves of her body are so fucking lush and perfect. I've never cared about a woman's size before—skinny, thick, somewhere in between. It didn't matter as long as we liked each other. But seeing her standing in front of me now, I think I've finally found my type. The sweet curve of her hips, the slight indent in them, the arc of her stomach, and the teardrop shape of her full breasts are exactly the way I want them. Like she was made for every single fantasy I've ever had. I turn her so I'm standing next to the cabana bed, and she's got her back to the pool, loving the way the light halos the curves of her body. I drop down to sit in front of her so I can take her all in.

"Straddle me," I say without thinking about it, and she obeys immediately. Her pupils flare, and she climbs onto the mattress. One of her knees is on either side of my thighs as she lowers herself onto my lap. The way her lashes flutter and her mouth opens slightly when she feels my cock nestled between them hits me, just like the realization she wants to please me. She likes it when I take control. "You like being told what to do?"

"I like you telling me what to do."

I can barely take how fucking hard it makes me to have her like this. I've built her up to be a lot of things in my head, and I've had very little experience with the reality. Some part of me is worried that the sweet girl I've always known won't be able to take the kinds of things I want in bed. Even if she has an ambitious list tucked away on her phone.

But if she keeps this up, I'm going to be well on my way from obsession to a full-blown addiction. I don't know how I'll ever let her leave this house. But that's a problem for another night. My only focus tonight is getting us both off as many times as possible. I deserve it for being patient enough to wait until she was single, and she deserves it for having had the wrong brother first.

She resumes kissing me, gentle at first and nibbling my lower lip before she deepens the kiss and grinds against my cock. She moans softly into my mouth, and my fingers dig into her ass, encouraging her.

"You sure you don't want me on my knees? It *is* your birthday."

"I'm sure. It's my birthday, and I'm going to have all the

fucking cake I want. But first, I want you so desperate and wet that you're begging for my tongue."

"I don't think it'll take much," she mumbles as she rolls her lower lip between her teeth. She circles her hips again and closes her eyes, a muted moan coming from her throat.

"So good for me. Keep grinding on my cock like that. Imagine how good it's gonna feel when you ride it." Her breasts sway with the movement of her body, and I take the weight of one in my palm, using my thumb to brush over her nipple as it starts to peak from the attention. I lean down, running my tongue over the tip, and she rewards me with another moan. When I suck it into my mouth, her fingers dig into my shoulders, and she grinds down hard on my dick.

"That feel good?" I whisper the question, raising my eyes to watch her face. She looks like she's in heaven, and I grin. I could sign up to be her plaything every night of the week if she needed.

"So good. Everything about you is *so* good."

I run my thumb over her plush lower lip before I kiss her again, and her tongue tangles with mine. She kisses like she's been starved for this sort of attention, and that's a fucking travesty.

"I can be even better if you ask for it."

"Please?" she asks softly.

"Please, what?" I taunt her, and when she gives me a shy grin, I return it. "I want to hear you ask for what you want, Trix. Tell me how to fuck you, and you can have it. But I want to hear you say it."

"Please fuck me with your tongue. I want to feel it on my clit. Need it," she whispers against my lips before she kisses me again.

So I do as I promised, grabbing her up and flipping her over onto her back. She slides up against the pillows at the back of the cabana bed, watching me while I strip out of my board shorts. Her eyes wander over my body and then land hard on my cock, licking her lower lip as she drags her focus back to my face.

I kiss my way up the inside of her leg and over her thigh as she spreads for me. The light from the pool glistens off her skin, and I press a delicate kiss between her legs. She lets out a soft sound of approval and spreads further for me, so I wrap my arms around her thighs. I drag my tongue through her wetness, and the taste of her has me going harder, grinding my dick into the mattress for a little relief.

"Fuck, Trix. Why is everything about you so much better than I imagined?" I wonder out loud, and when I look up, there's a bemused look on her face. I grin in return, flashing her a smirk before I flick my tongue over her clit, using just the tip to torture her.

"Oh my god," she mutters, cursing under her breath, and she spreads wider, canting her hips and begging for more of me. I keep up the pressure of my tongue on her clit, giving her just enough to make her whimper for more and sliding two fingers inside as she counters each pump of them with a roll of her hips. The two of us create a perfect rhythm, and she starts to come apart for me a few moments later. Her fingers thread through my hair, and her nails bite into my scalp as she fucks my face, riding my tongue like she's never had it like this before.

"Coop. Oh... my... fuck... god. Coop, please. Please." My name is like a prayer on her lips. One she keeps repeating over and over, and it's like a drug in my veins, spurring me on and taking me under at the same time.

She comes hard, tightening around my fingers and so wet that my face, her upper thighs, and the mattress are soaked with her. I grin at the mess, half wishing my brother was here so I could show him how well his ex comes for me. How good she sounds when it's *my* name echoing against the walls instead of his.

"That was really... Just really fucking good," she whispers when the silence stretches on as I kiss my way over her abdomen and up between her rib cage. My cock drags over her inner thigh, and I lift my hips to keep from torturing myself. But she spreads her legs as I do it and wraps one of them around the back of my calf, locking me in place.

"Trix..." I warn because I'm tempted to slide inside her just like this. But she needs time to come back down, and I want to work her up to begging again. "I don't have a condom out here."

"Then let's get inside," she offers, smirking at her double entendre.

She doesn't have to ask twice. I wrap her in the towel she's lying on top of after I pull my shorts back on. I carry her into the bedroom and set her down on the carpet. She shivers a little as the AC whips over her skin, and I kiss my way up her throat as I undress myself and then peel the towel off her. I want the view while I work on the condom.

I grab one out of my dresser drawer, tearing it open and rolling it on as she crawls backward over the bed. I'm waiting for someone to show up and tell me this is all a dream. That I don't actually get to touch her, let alone fuck her like this. But when her legs fall open for me, and her fingers dance over her nipples as she gives me a playful smile, I know I've won the fucking lottery.

Normally, I like to fuck a woman from the back. With her on her knees, while she's pinned up against the wall, or in the back of a hired car while she fucks me reverse cowgirl. And while I want every single one of those positions with Trix, I want to watch her face when I fuck her for the first time. I want to hear every moan and feel every breath she takes when I claim her for myself.

So I climb between her legs and lean down to kiss her,

brushing over her lips with mine and then down her jaw and neck as I slowly press my cock inside.

"Oh fuck..." she whispers. "It's been a minute since I've... I don't know if you'll fit."

"You can take me. Just breathe." I stroke the backs of my knuckles down her cheek, and she lets out a soft breath. "Oh fuck. Oh fuck..." She moans as I slide the rest of the way in, slowly and steadily until I've filled her tight little cunt, and she tightens around me. I hold still, letting the warmth and wetness of her perfect body soak my cock. The way she looks at me makes me feel like a god, and her fingertips play over my shoulders as she studies me.

"You good?" I ask, wanting to be sure she's with me.

"Yes," she answers softly, her warm-brown eyes drifting over my face and down my chest.

I start to move, slowly at first to let her get used to the feel of me and to give myself a chance to regroup. I need to focus, distract myself with a few unsexy thoughts every now and then to keep from falling apart immediately. Just this little taste of her tells me I'll need her again and again.

"Fuck me..." she moans. "Is it your birthday or mine? Your cock is perfect, Coop." A playful grin crosses her face.

This woman is going to be the death of me, one way or another, and I'm pretty sure I'll beg for it any way it comes.

"It's definitely mine." I lean forward, pressing my lips to hers, and she kisses me back softly. She utters another delicate curse against my lips when I rock my hips and take her deeper.

I kiss my way down her neck, and she turns her head, giving me more access. Offering up every part of her body I want as my hand skates down over her breastbone and under the curve of her breast. My thumb teases over her nipple as it beads up for me, and she rolls her bottom lip between her teeth.

Her hips lift as I pick up my pace and, I run my fingers over the curve of one of her hips, drifting over her abdomen and then back up her body again. Every single part of her is gorgeous. I'm finally getting a reward for being so patient when I hear her breathing shift; she mutters how good I am and then begs for more of me.

"Harder, please," she whispers, her lashes fluttering when I pick up my pace. One of her hands grabs the pillow over her head and the other grips the sheets underneath her as she starts to come. She's softer when she comes this time but more effusive in her praise, and I can't believe I get her twice in one night like this.

Listening to her is more than I can take, all my unsexy thoughts drift out the window, and her sounds and her voice invade all my senses as she takes me over the edge a second later. It's been forever since I've come like this, watching a woman like she's mine, and we mean something more than just a quick fuck for fun.

When I've taken care of the condom and come back to the bed, she sits up and smiles at me. A pure unadulterated smile of satisfaction and amusement, and I lean forward to kiss her; once, twice, and then her eyes open, and she looks thoroughly sated.

"Can I use your shower?"

I pretend to consider the idea, relenting finally when she raises a brow and smirks.

"Yes. Towels are in there. I'll grab you a T-shirt too."

"Thank you."

I want to join her in the shower, but I need a moment after that, and I think she might too. After I watch her disappear behind the door, I collapse on the bed trying to process how I managed to get in this deep with her so fast.

19

B eatrix

THAT MORNING when I wake up, I forget that I'm in Cooper's bed and wonder for all of ten seconds where I am and how I made it here. The night before comes flashing back to me, and my heart skips in my chest.

Right. The Rawlings Rubicon. I crossed it. More like leapt across it.

I lift my head just enough that I can see Cooper still fast asleep beside me, and I slip out of bed. I look to the floor for my clothes when I remember I don't have any in here. My swimsuit was abandoned outside along with my coverup. I cringe. I'm not ready for the morning after with Cooper. I need time.

I can streak across the house. Lizzy isn't home for a few more days, so I don't have to worry about her seeing me running across the house naked from her dad's room. But I have no idea if Ramsey or Garner are still in the house, and that would be more than a little awkward.

I spot one of Cooper's T-shirts lying on top of a chair in the corner and reach for it. It's better than nothing, and it'll at least cover the essentials until I can get real clothes on again. I slip it on and sneak out into the hall, across the living room, and by the kitchen. Almost.

"Good morning." It's Ramsey's baritone, and I stop in my tracks and give him something that I'm sure looks like half a wince and half a smile.

"Morning." I try for a peppy tone and fail.

"They had an amazing season this year. Didn't realize you were a fan." He nods to my shirt, and I look down to realize it's a Cincinnati Queens Guard hockey shirt.

"Oh. Uh... yeah. Anything Cincy related; you know."

Ramsey's green-gold eyes light with amusement that I'm playing along with this ruse. He takes a sip of his coffee, and I start to walk away before he speaks again.

"Decided to bunk up together after all, huh? Wish I'd known. Could have come up here when Garner started cater-wauling. I don't know what she was doing to him, but he seemed to be enjoying it in between sounding like he was on the brink of death."

I burst out into laughter and shake my head. "Oh my god. It's too early for those mental images."

"Yeah. Especially before coffee. You coming out here to get some for you and Coop? There's a fresh pot."

"Oh, um... I'm just..." My brain stalls out, and I can't think of a single good reason or excuse.

"Gonna be hard to do the fuck and run when you live with him, darlin'."

The bluntness of his statement hits hard this early in the morning.

"It's not that, it's just—"

"That you're sneaking out of his room before he wakes up on his birthday?"

"I didn't think he was the type to want women to still be there in the morning."

"You think you're 'women' when you're living in his house, and he lets you spend time with his daughter?"

"That's only because I used to date his—" I stop short.

"I know you were his brother's girl. Which is why if you care about him, you'll get two mugs and go back in there." Ramsey's voice is just above a whisper, but it still feels like a threat on behalf of his friend. I raise a brow at his bossiness, and he matches it. It's enough to make me reconsider, though, and my eyes drift back to the hall I just escaped from.

Ramsey's probably right. It's better to have the awkward morning after conversation than have a more awkward afternoon one. We could get this out of the way over coffee and move on with things. I slip past Ramsey, who's still perched at the breakfast bar, and into the kitchen to grab two mugs.

"Good girl," he whispers under his breath, and I look back to raise my brow higher at him, and he laughs and looks back down at his phone. When I slip back past him to Cooper's room, he's still wearing the bemused expression, and I shake my head at him, which elicits a low chuckle.

WHEN I GET BACK into Cooper's room, he's just waking up, and he grins when he sees I have coffee.

"Happy birthday. Officially." I smile as I hand him his favorite mug.

"You're a lifesaver, Trixie." He studies my shirt and his grin brightens. "And you look damn good in that shirt."

"Ramsey asked me if I was a fan."

Cooper winces. "Was he out there? Fuck. I'm sorry."

"It's okay." I take a sip of my coffee and stare out the window.

His house backs up to a patch of woods, but he also has a huge garden that runs the length of the back of the property, and I can see the landscapers already working out back this morning.

"So..." I can hear him thinking, and he sits up against the pillows, and I sit down in the chair near the bed.

"Last night was fun."

"Oof." His brow furrows.

"What?"

"I haven't heard that one since college."

I laugh and shake my head. "I'm out of practice. It's been a while since I did the one-night stand thing, so give me a pass, please?"

"Is that what it was? One night? I thought we had a list."

I grit my teeth and shake my head. "I don't know if that's a good idea. I mean, it feels complicated with everything. You trying to reform your image probably isn't going to be improved by sleeping with the help?"

"You're not the help."

"I sort of am. Your PR help anyway. Kind of extra help around here. It won't look good for you if people find out, regardless of what we call it. Let alone if Lizzy would." I look up from my cup and his eyes search mine. "It didn't take Ramsey much to connect the dots. It makes me nervous. With everything else going on right now, I just don't know that it's a good idea to keep it up. Even if I had a lot of fun."

"So I have Ramsey to thank for it then. Noted. I'll make him pay for that later." Cooper's playful smile returns.

"No. It's not his fault. Just that in the morning, things feel different, you know?"

"I can respect that." He nods, looking at me thoughtfully.

We fall into silence for a moment, and then we both start to talk at the same time before I laugh and shake my head.

"You go," I say softly.

"I was just going to say, if you change your mind and still want some help, I'm happy to earn more badges." He flashes another smile, and it melts my resistance a little. It makes me wish I met him first. Because if I'm honest, one night with Cooper was better than the entirety of my relationship with Rob. But that feels like a heavy thing to say when we haven't even had breakfast yet.

"I'll keep that in mind." I look down at my coffee. "For the record... that wasn't a line or something. That really was the most fun I've had in a long time..."

"Is that your way of telling me I'm better in bed than my brother?"

"I wasn't going to put it exactly that way, but..."

"You should. It's my birthday." He grins before he takes another sip of his coffee, and my heart riots in my chest. I'm trying to decide exactly how much to tell him—how much to confess—when there's a knock at the door.

"You two decent? Your gardener wants to talk to you." It's Ramsey.

"Be right there," he calls back.

Cooper's brow furrows, but he stands and grabs a pair of sweats and puts them on, apologizing to me as he makes his way out. I follow behind at a distance, curious about what's going on but still not keen on being half-naked with his teammates still in the house.

When he gets to the door, the gardener's already in the entryway, and he nods his hello.

"I'm sorry to get you up. We were just out there working, and I noticed there are footprints in the beds around the front and side. A few of the plants are crushed. We can fix it, but did you have someone working out there? You might want to tell them to be more careful."

"Out where?" I ask, forgetting that I'm in what is essentially an oversized nightgown with messy hair. The gardener notes my appearance but doesn't blink.

"I can show you guys if you want."

"Yeah. I think we'd like to see." Cooper flashes a concerned look in my direction and back at the gardener.

"Just give me a second." I sprint to my room to grab shorts and tie up my hair before I join them on the porch.

We follow the gardener around the house with Ramsey in tow, and he points to tracks in the mud—a place where the flowers had clearly been tamped down under heavy boots. I look up slowly, hoping it's not the window I think it is, and feeling my stomach tumble when I see it is. My window. The one I'd sworn I'd seen someone outside of the other night.

Dread climbs up my spine and wraps around my throat, making it feel tight and scratchy. Cooper's eyes meet mine with sympathy before he turns back to the gardener.

"Thanks for showing us. If you can fix it up, I'd appreciate it. Just charge me whatever you need to do that. I'll see what I can do about keeping people out of the beds in the future." Cooper wraps an arm around my shoulder and walks me back to the house. Ramsey studies us as we pass him and then follows us in.

"You know who did it?" Ramsey's brow is hard-set, and he and Cooper exchange a look.

"No."

"Do you know?" He turns to me.

"I wish I knew." I shake my head.

"Gonna fill me in?" Ramsey looks between us.

"Do you mind?" Cooper asks my permission, and I give it. He drains the last of his coffee and puts the mug in the sink before he leans on the counter. "It's the reason Trix is staying here with me. She's had weird pictures sent to her on social media. It's been quiet the last week, or so we thought, except...

she woke up the other night and thought she saw someone out the window. We both thought it was a dream."

"But obviously it's more than that." Ramsey finishes the thought as Cooper's brow furrows with worry.

"I can't believe they'd come here. You'd think they'd be more worried about security with you being who you are." I fold my arms over my chest, feeling vulnerable even talking about this.

"Do you have security?" Ramsey asks.

"I've got an alarm system. I don't know how it didn't trip." Cooper shrugs. "I've never needed more."

Right. Because I brought this into his life. Into his home. A home where he has a daughter who could be in danger too because of me.

"Maybe it's time for me to move again. See about another hotel or an apartment."

"No." Cooper doesn't miss a beat in his answer. "I'm not letting you out of my sight. If he's bold enough to be following you like that. Coming outside the window? No way in fuck am I letting you be out there alone."

"But you and Lizzy live here too."

"Don't worry about me. I can take care of you and Lizzy."

"You got a gun?" Ramsey asks. "Because a security system won't do shit if he comes through the window."

"I've got one in the safe."

"You need to get one that you can keep by your bed. I'll send you some suggestions. Show you what I got. Hell, I can come stay for a while if you need. Or you can come to stay with me. I was planning on going camping for a few days, but I can change that if I need to," Ramsey offers.

"I just wonder if I'm a liability. I couldn't live with myself if something happened to you guys because of me." I look worriedly at Cooper as my anxiety starts to bubble. My stomach is turning, and the anxious feeling is starting to spread. Cooper turns to me and takes my arms, rubbing them and giving me a reassuring smile.

"Trixie, listen to me. I want you with me. I want to keep an eye on you, and I appreciate you being worried about Lizzy. But Lizzy's got that camp for the next few weeks, so she's safe there. When she comes back before we go to the lake house, we can make sure things are locked down. But in the meantime, I'd feel better if you stayed with me."

"I'm just worried."

"I know. But I promise, I've got you." Cooper wraps his arms around me, and I hug him tight.

"What if you come camping with me?" Ramsey pipes in.

I hear Cooper make a grunting sound, but then his head bobs back and forth like he's considering it.

"Get you away from the house and out of the city for a bit," Ramsey adds, looking between us.

"Hey. Maybe that's not a terrible idea. It's on your list anyway, right? We could get away for a few days. I can drive us separately so we've got the extra car," Cooper adds.

I mull over the prospect of being stuck with these two in the middle of the woods. On the one hand, it's not a terrible place to be. On the other...

"My friend was planning to come too. So you all don't have to worry about me if you want to go off and do your own thing." Ramsey smirks.

I watch Cooper flash him a look and the subtle shake of his head, and Ramsey frowns in return. His eyes fall to me with a question in them.

"Okay," I agree.

The alternatives of telling Madison or running home or being alone at a hotel are all there, but none of them are great. They all have a laundry list of downsides, and if camping means getting away from here for a couple of days, it seems worth a shot. I'll definitely feel safer with these two in the middle of nowhere than in a hotel in the middle of the city.

"All right. I've gotta stock up on supplies and pick her up. Then we can head out bright and early tomorrow if that works for you two."

"Works for me. We can get packed and pick up some things too." Cooper smiles at me. "This one's never been camping before, so it's going to be an adventure."

"Never?" Ramsey looks at me surprised.

"Never." I shake my head. Camping was not a thing in the Xavier household. The closest we ever got was glamping in Montana once, and there was a private chef and cozy mattresses with high thread count sheets. I don't think it counts.

"Well, then we can give you the whole experience. Keep your mind off things here. Coop can teach you all kinds of things." Ramsey grins and winks at me.

20

C*ooper*

"So is he always your wingman?" Trix asks as we set up for dinner together at a picnic table at the campsite.

Ramsey and his friend have taken off to grab dinner at a local diner and left us to have our first campsite dinner. Thankfully, I've got a fridge and an outdoor kitchen on the side of Ramsey's RV to make it a little easier.

"Did he say something?"

"I mean, he's said a lot of things. If you ever decide to date, I think he might be a good asset." She glances up to smile at me before she resumes making the salad.

"Should I be worried?" I feel more than a little nervous about what he might have said to her. Besides Quentin, he knows the most about how I feel. I didn't even tell him. He guessed because, apparently, I'm that transparent when it comes to her.

"No. They were all good things. He looks out for you too."

"What do you mean?"

"I think he's worried about what my intentions are with you. Moving into your house. Stumbling out of your bedroom in the morning for coffee. That sort of thing."

"Ah. Yeah. Well, he's never seen me let a woman besides Lizzy stay at my house, so I think he's just a little thrown."

"He knew I dated Rob. Did you tell him?"

I run my fingers over the bill of my hat. When she questions me like this, I feel like I'm transparent.

"Yeah. Originally, when you moved in. He knew I was trying to date or at least take it more seriously and wanted to know quote 'how the fuck that was going to happen when I had a smokeshow running around the place.'" I laugh and shake my head.

Her laughter peels through the air, and it warms my heart. Since we've gotten to the campsite today, she's relaxed more than I've seen her since she found out about the footprints. She refused to sleep in my room last night and said she had to face her fears, but I spent most of the night in the living room dozing off and watching for lights under her door in case she needed me. I was happy to be somewhere where I could keep an eye on her more easily and fucking thrilled that she seemed to be able to breathe a little easier.

"He is... very blunt. Is he always that way?"

"Most of the time. He doesn't sugarcoat anything, but I kind of love him for that. The guys on the team love him for it. It's nice to know you get whatever he's thinking, good or bad."

"I don't know if I could handle quite that much honesty every day."

"You sure he didn't say something?"

"He just... warned me, I guess you could say. About you and Lizzy. Just the kind of thing a good friend does. I'm sure

Madison would be all up in your business too if she suspected this was anything more than us being friends."

"She's a scary one. Quentin's terrified of her. Should I be worried if she finds out?"

"Quentin's in love with her, and I'm fairly certain she's in love with him and just in denial. And no reason to worry. Unless there's something concerning in your background you haven't told me about."

"Well..." I tease.

"There better not be. If I have to sell you as Cincinnati's hottest eligible bachelor, I need to know." She flashes me an amused look.

"No, we're all good." I'd completely forgotten I asked her for help with that. Now it's the last thing I want.

"When we get back, I can start working on it more by the way. I didn't forget, just got a little distracted by everything that's been going on lately. Do you want me to set you up on some dates?"

"About that. I think we should hold off on that."

"Why?"

"You've got a lot going on. We need to figure out this stalker situation. Who to get involved to help us figure it out. If we should call the cops or—"

"I don't want to call the cops. Once they find out who I am, they'll contact my father's security team to see if they have information that could help, and he'll drag me back to Seattle. I need to find a private investigator or someone who can look into it discreetly. I'm still fairly certain it has to be a fan of yours. Especially if they came to your house..."

"Maybe. But it didn't start until you showed up."

"If it's a woman, the fact that you've been out with me and then had me move into your place could have set her off. She could think I'm your girlfriend."

"I guess that's possible. I've never had anything like that happen before."

"But you've never been serious with anyone before, have you? I mean, I know there were a couple of celebrity relationships. But I assumed those were more for show than anything."

I wince. They had been. Neither I was particularly fond of remembering since both women had pretty much hated being set up with me.

"Something like that."

"Ah. That bad, huh? Now I see why you don't want to be set up. I promise I'm much better at it. You can ask Quentin. I mean... he obviously wasn't going to change his mind, but if he wasn't obsessed with Madison, I'm pretty sure he would have liked my picks for him."

"I don't doubt your talent, Trix. I just don't think it's for me."

Especially not now. When I'm practically in the same boat as Quentin. I don't know about being in love. I've never experienced it, and I don't know what the early stages feel like. But if they start by being singularly focused on one woman who haunts you day and night, I'm in trouble. Because she's it for me right now.

"All right. Well, if you were giving me a shot at it, what would your type be?" she asks as I set the food out for us, a mix of BBQ meat and veggies, including baked potatoes roasted on the fire. She's got a salad and fruit all prepped for us along with some wine as I take a seat across from her.

"My type would be... Tall. Curvy. Long, dark-brown hair with some waves to it. Deep-brown eyes. A gorgeous smile. Long legs. Smart as fuck. She has to keep me on my toes and keep up with Lizzy. A little bossy when it's about the important things. Up for new adventures. Doesn't mind the outdoors or hanging out around my guys. You want the dirty list too? She'd have to be up for that." I risk a glance up at her, and her face tells me she's knows what I'm up to.

"The dirty list?"

"I have my own adventure list, Trix. Don't look so surprised."

"I have a hard time believing there are things you haven't tried."

"There are. Plus there are things I haven't done in a long time. Got to knock one of them off the list the other night."

She gives me a curious look and a tentative smile. "Like?"

"I haven't done missionary since... I don't know. High school?"

"Oh." She looks down at her plate. "I'm sorry. I didn't think about... I didn't mean to make that awkward. We could have—I would have been fine with—"

"No." I grab her hand instinctively, and she stares at the spot we're touching like it might burn her. There's panic in my chest that I fucking said this all wrong. "No. I mean I liked it. I wanted it that way. Wanted you that way. You're beautiful, and I wanted to watch you. Wanted to hear every sound you made for me. It was good. So fucking good." I'm tripping over my words like I'm in high school and hating myself for not being able to charm her the way I could charm almost any other woman if I had the chance.

Her fingers move again, the tips of them circling over the inside of my palm before she tilts her head.

"It was good," she agrees, looking off in the distance before a smile returns to her face. "So what else is on your list?"

"You still haven't told me the rest of yours."

"You heard the whole thing. Loudly. In your kitchen." She lets a pretend shiver go down her spine as she takes a sip of her wine.

"I told you. I was in shock, and then once I heard I was on it, things short-circuited. You'll have to tell me again. But hey, that means we knocked at least one thing off."

"Two things now." She smiles.

"Which things?"

"Sex with you. And camping."

"Damn. We're doing so well. You sure you don't want to keep going?"

She gives me a teasing sideeye and a flutter of her lashes that has me thinking about what it would be like to try the one about sex outside. See how she likes sex on top of a picnic table.

"What's on your list besides revisiting missionary?" She presses on.

"Going on a real date."

"What does a real date look like?"

"Asking her out. Planning it. She says yes and gets dressed up. Bringing her flowers or something nice."

"Another thing you haven't done since high school?"

"More or less. Right up there with meeting the parents."

"You want to meet the parents? I thought most guys hated that. At least if they're not power hungry and wanting to meet your senator father. Rob hated meeting my parents." She grimaces a little like she's remembering it.

"If she wants you to meet the parents, it means she thinks there's a future. Right?"

"Right."

"So... I want to meet the parents. Take her out on a couple of real dates."

"You're making my job way too easy with all of your charm, Coop."

"What else is on your list?"

She rolls her eyes, but she pulls her phone out and brings up the document that I've already had read out loud to me. I'm fibbing a little. Some of the other things on the list definitely stuck with me, but I want to see if they're still there, and I want to know how serious she is about them.

"Am I reading this or just showing it to you? Because

here..." She slides her phone across to me, and sure enough, it's all still there.

"Am I allowed to check off completed items?" I look up at her while my finger hovers over the checkbox seated next to camping.

"Sure."

I click it, and the one that mentions having sex with me.

"Unless it meant another ex's brother. I guess I never thought about that," I tease her.

"It was you," she admits.

"This sex outside... did last night count, or do you think you need to try again?"

"We probably need to try again. The cabana had drapes and a lot of privacy."

"We? Do we get to try again?" My heart skips.

"That was a slip of the tongue."

I have to bite mine to keep from making a joke, and she sees how hard I'm trying not to say anything and shakes her head.

"I guess if you keep making me slip up... Maybe it is we." She gives a soft shrug of her shoulders.

"Don't give me hope, Trix. This list has some of my favorite things on it."

"Like?"

Her for starters. But I'm pretty sure saying that will have her running. So the list it is.

"All of it? I mean... The tattoo thing I don't know. I'm not big on them, obviously. Too indecisive to choose one. We'd have to swap out ex's brother for my brother's ex, but otherwise..."

"You're into degradation? You seem too nice for that."

"If she's into it, I fucking love it. Especially when you pair it with rough sex. But we'd have to cuddle after."

"Is cuddling on your list?"

"It's a sub-item under brother's ex only." I grin at her.

A wry little grin pops up on her face, and she looks down at the list with me.

"Cream pie? Isn't that a little...dangerous for you? A lot to gain if someone lies about birth control status. Madison would ream you up one side and down the other. She's like that scene with Dorothy in the Golden Girls, screaming about condoms if she finds out a client doesn't keep them on hand."

"I said it's one of my favorite things. Not that I do it regularly. A lot like the missionary sex."

"Where I can be your first since high school?"

"Don't tease me."

"It's not really, is it?"

"I love Lizzy, and I'm so grateful for her, but I didn't need to learn that lesson twice."

"You're making this whole *not finishing the list with you* thing hard."

"Good. Because I think you're missing out by not having me for some of these. Like the impact play? Think about how good you could have it. I could spank that cute little ass until it matches the color of your lip gloss and then you could shove my face between your legs until you forget how much it stings."

She nearly chokes on the sip of her drink she just took, and she stares at me wide-eyed.

"Cooper!"

"I have ideas for the temperature play too." I grin in response.

"I think I need them after dinner before I choke on something." Her eyes close when she realizes what she's said, and I watch as she carefully opens one eye and peeks at me to see the smirk that's spreading across my face.

"All right. After dinner we'll discuss the rest and how we make them happen."

21

B *eatrix*

I'M HEADED to the waterfall with a small picnic basket in one hand and a beach towel in the other after Cooper tells me to go ahead, and he'll catch up. I can hear the sound of female laughter in the distance as I get closer, and I grin when I hear a small screech, a splash of water, and then another barrage of high-pitched laughter echo off the stone walls. It's been interesting to see a softer side of Ramsey on this trip. One that likes to help make sandwiches and apparently tickle his friend half to death.

When I get to the fence and see the flash of them getting out of the water, I almost yell out until I realize what's happening, and I stop short. I should stop staring. Never mind staring, I should stop watching altogether, but I can't.

The rough way he handles her and the way she's clearly loving every second has me so turned on I can barely take it.

That, combined with having been in close quarters with Coop the last couple of days, sleeping next to each other and desperately trying not to touch, is enough to push me over the edge. I'd kill for a vibrator right now. Something quick to take the edge off. But this is, I'm learning, one of the downsides of camping. Outlets and power are at a premium as is privacy to recharge or use such devices.

But I'm in the middle of the woods alone with the perfect view of a show I shouldn't be watching. One that has me getting wetter by the second. I've set the basket and the towel down at my feet. I'm sliding my hand under my suit before I know what I'm doing. It won't take much, my clit's already throbbing, and I'm so turned on that the pads of my fingers slip through wetness easily as I use it to take me closer to the release I need.

I watch as Ramsey flips her over, bending to tease her pussy with his tongue and then licking his way up between her cheeks until she's moaning his name and begging for more. He slaps her ass and then uses his huge hands to spread her further before he grabs her thighs and pulls her back, teasing her with the tip of his cock.

It's the hottest thing I've ever seen, and I'm so close to coming from watching it that I let out my own soft echoing moan. One that's silenced by a large hand slamming down over my mouth and a hard male body that comes flush with my back. The other large hand wraps around my wrist and stills me in the pursuit of my orgasm. I'm ready to scream on both accounts—that I'm about to be murdered and that it's going to deprive me of one of the best self-sessions I've ever had.

"Filthy fucking girl." Cooper's voice is like gravel against my ear. "No wonder it's so easy for you to hold out. You're out here taking the edge off by yourself."

I nip the inside of his palm, and he gives a little grunt of surprise before he eases up his grip.

"Shhh," I whisper, using my eyes to draw his attention.

"Oh fucking hell," he mutters just as Ramsey slams his cock into her from behind. Then his eyes shift as he realizes what I've been doing, and they move to me, surveying me carefully like he's uncovered another layer he wasn't expecting. He wraps his hand around the ends of my hair and pulls my head back so I'm forced to look up at him. "Even dirtier than I thought. Fuck me."

My cheeks flush with his assessment, and I just give a tiny shrug in response.

"You like watching, don't you? I know it was on your list."

"He's so rough with her. It's..." I try to think of some eloquent way to put it, but I've got nothing. "I want it."

"Of course you do." His hands go to the ties on my bottoms, and he pulls on them one by one until my pink swimsuit falls to the ground between my feet. He kisses me again softly, this time at the side of my neck, before he wraps a hand around my throat and slips the other between my legs, dipping his fingers between them until he finds me soaked.

"Fuck me, Trix. You spoil me with how wet you get. The sounds I get to listen to when I touch you like this. So good," he confesses.

"I just needed something to take the edge off, you know? It's been so... tense between us since the other night." I give him my own confession in return.

He bites my shoulder and then kisses over the imprint his teeth leave there as he starts to work me over. "I know. You make me desperate too."

"I like you like this." I gasp when hits me just right, and I can feel the edge of my orgasm starting to form.

"You think you do. We should see what you say when I use every soaking wet hole you have to fill you up and fuck you right here in the dirt."

"Try me," I taunt him.

His hand tightens around my throat, and his mouth turns up at the corner in a devious smirk.

"Bend over, filthy girl. We're gonna do more than try." He slaps my ass hard, enough to leave a mark for tomorrow, and I gasp involuntarily. My stomach tightens with the anticipation, and I bend over and grab the crude wooden fence to help keep my balance on the edge of this overlook. Glancing down at our friend as he starts to fuck her fast and hard.

22

C *ooper*

HER BRAVERY IS LIKE A CHALLENGE. It makes me want to give her everything she wants and more, and when she bends like I ask, I have to remind myself to hold the reins tight. I want her a begging, come-soaked mess before I finally put my cock in her tight little cunt, and I have work to do before I get my reward.

I run my palms over her ass cheeks, caressing them softly before I slap the left one so it can match the right. She gasps again, and the sound goes straight to my cock, making it twitch, and my balls tighten just that little bit more.

"Turn around and face me." I wait and then grin when she does. "Spread. I want to see how wet you are. Want to watch you drip while we get you worked up."

She does as I ask, obedient as always. I spit on my hand and slide it between her legs, massaging her softly as her eyes close and her breathing stutters. I use my knee to nudge her legs wider, teasing the edges of her clit with the pads of my fingers before I slide them back inside her. She's so wet my fingers are coated with her, and when she starts to roll her hips for more friction, I pull them away.

"You're not in control today, Trix. We're doing this my way."

She mutters and curses my name but doesn't stop me. "I need to come so bad, Coop."

"You will. Don't worry. You're gonna come so hard, you won't be sure if your body can take another one." I'm on my knees for her a moment later.

I lean forward and take one long lick of her, savoring her taste as I start to tongue fuck her sweet little cunt. Her faltered breathing in response is one of the most perfect sounds I've ever heard. At least until I slip my fingers inside again, and she starts to moan and grind on my face. There's nothing but unintelligible muttering on her part now, and it's killing me in the best way.

I've got her in a perfect fucking rhythm a moment later, her pussy so wet she's dripping down my face, and she's clenching around my fingers. I know I'm teasing her, not giving her everything she needs, but I want to hear her beg.

"Fuck my face, sweetheart. Say my name when you grind on my tongue."

"Coop. Oh fuck... Please, Cooper." She moans in return.

My tongue slides over her, and my fingers pump in and out of her, rising to the beat of my heart, and then I give her more. The pad of my thumb softly slipping around her clit and then circling over it in a counter rhythm to my tongue, giving her the last push she needs. She comes hard a minute later, bouncing over my face like she's depraved and desperate as she grinds down for more.

"I'm gonna come. Fuck. Oh my god. It's so... So..." She's lost her words, mumbling and messy as she falls apart for me, and I can't remember ever being so hard from getting face-fucked in the middle of the day. Let alone in the woods where anyone could walk by and see it.

She's still breathing hard, lids heavy when I stand up. I grab her by the nape of the neck and pull her toward me, kissing her roughly and letting her taste herself on my lips.

"Taste how fucking dirty you are. Couldn't get enough, could you?"

"No. I loved it." Her voice is husky.

"Can't wait to see how wrecked you get when I fuck you later." I grin at her, and her throat bobs on a swallow. I've changed my mind now that I've kissed her. I want the one thing I haven't had yet. Her plush lips wrapped around my cock. "But for now—get on your knees. I'm gonna get your face as messy as the rest of you, using that sweet mouth of yours on my cock."

She lowers to her knees, and hearing the crunch of leaves and twigs under them does something for me I wasn't expecting. I pull my cock out, palming it for a minute while I watch her watch me.

"Take your top off. I want you completely naked for me out here."

She looks up at me, something flashing in her eyes before she looks over her shoulder.

"What if they...?" she trails off.

"See you being my filthy little slut? I think it's only fair they get a taste, considering you watched their whole show."

Her cheeks heat, but her fingers start to work under the top, sliding it off her shoulders and then down. A moment later, her top tumbles to the ground not far from her swimsuit bottoms, and her full breasts drop to their natural position. Her nipples are already hard, and the valley between them has me thinking of what it'd be like to fuck them and come all over her chest. Another thing I'm adding to my own mental checklist if she ever lets me.

"So obedient." I smirk. "Now take my cock."

She wraps her lips around me, and I see fucking stars. When she starts to suck and run her tongue over the length of me, I wonder if I might be having an out-of-body experience. I don't know if I've just built her up this much in my head that I can't handle having her, or if the two of us are just this well matched. Because it's like she knows everything I like without asking. Like she would do anything on earth to please me.

It doesn't take long for me. Not after the way watching her come hard worked me up. Her tongue and her hands have me on the precipice within a few minutes, and I'm too desperate to come to care about how long it took me to get here.

"I'm gonna come. Fuck, you're gonna be so pretty with your mouth full of me. I want to see it all over your lips and dripping down your chin. You hear me?"

She blinks her understanding, and I can't hold back any longer, fucking her mouth as I start to fill her up. I slide out past her lips and use my hand to work one last hot stream of come down over her chin and onto her chest. I wrap my hand around her jaw and squeeze her cheeks until my come dribbles out over her lower lip.

"Fuck. That fucking kills me. Seeing me come out of your mouth like that."

I hit my knees and kiss her. The taste of her is still on my lips, and it melds with the taste of me as she kisses me sloppily. I kneel back on my heels, and she moves closer, nearly climbing into my lap as we fall backward onto the dirt and brush, kissing each other like our lives depend on it.

I run my fingers down her neck and over her spine, and she presses into me. I wrap my arms around her until she's fully seated in my lap, and I'm holding her while she comes down from her high.

"That was so hot. I've never come like that before. It was so..." She searches for the words and I love how out of breath and sated she sounds when she speaks.

"Dirty?" I smirk as I brush the dirt off her knees.

"So fucking dirty and hot. Like being used, but in the best way. Like you had to have me."

"The best way... Especially after the way you were grinding on my face. I didn't know you had this side."

"I didn't either." She gives me a shy grin. "I mean... That's not entirely true. I knew I did, but I've never been brave enough... never had anyone that would... indulge that. You know?"

"Trixie, I will indulge any fantasy you come up with. Consider it my summer job."

She laughs and tightens her grip around my waist into a hug.

"You're so perfect, you know. It's crazy how you're so good at being so easy to be around. Be *with*."

"Likewise, gorgeous." I smile at her. We sit in silence for a few minutes just holding each other until she starts to stand and gather her swimsuit.

"Do you still want to swim, or should we go back and get cleaned up?"

Another peel of laughter echoes off the walls of the swimming hole.

"The RV's got an outdoor shower on the back. We can wash each other before they come back?" I offer.

"You even make cleanup sound sexy." She laughs.

"I mean... cleaning myself off of you is going to be sexy as fuck." I hold my hand out for her after she finishes tying her bottoms on, and she takes it.

"Cooper Rawlings, you are... something."

"Thanks, I think." I grab my hat off the ground and put it back on my head, straightening the bill in the back, and we make our way back to the campsite.

23

B eatrix

THAT NIGHT, when I step out of the RV after a post-dinner-and-shower nap, I see Ramsey setting up the picnic table with chocolates and champagne. I do my best to hold back my grin when he looks up and sees me.

"What's going on here?" I ask, eyeing the setup he's clearly created for him and the friend he has with him. "I didn't know you could be such a romantic."

"Don't get any ideas, darlin'. I don't have a romantic bone in my body. Just cold calculation on what it takes to get what I want."

"Seems like more than that to me." I raise a brow at the small bundle of wildflowers he's put in a glass on the table.

"You saw what I'm like." He smirks. "Coop said you found it inspirational."

My cheeks heat. Coop and I will be having a little chat

about oversharing. But I'm not about to let Ramsey rattle me again.

"You can't be like that and be romantically involved too? Seems like long-term having a mix of both would be a good foundation."

"I respect women enough to know that I'm not made for more. I'd only make them miserable long term. But one or two nights? I can do that pretty damn well." He winks at me.

"You flirting with my girl again, cowboy?" Coop comes up behind me and wraps a hand around my waist possessively, kissing my cheek. Hearing him call me his girl does something it shouldn't. I know he's just being flippant. Just saying that to give Ramsey a hard time. But I like it more than I should.

"Nah. Just explaining to her why we'll never get married. Too bad for me." Ramsey grins at me one last time before he goes back to the task at hand.

"He was telling me that you're being very loquacious with your reports about our day." I narrow my eyes at Cooper.

Cooper smirks in response. "Well, I had to thank him for the help."

I gently punch his arm. "You're the worst."

"That mean you don't want to hop in the truck and go do some stargazing? There's a dark sky park just down the road from here. I was all ready with blankets and snacks."

I can't help but smile. It sounds perfect. Almost too perfect. Especially after the day we've had already, and as I take Cooper's outstretched hand, I can't resist looking back at the wildflowers on the table one last time.

WHEN WE'RE LYING out under the stars, sharing a bag of candy and some pop that we've brought along with us, a text comes through from my mother, and I sigh as I read it.

"What's wrong?" Cooper asks.

"My mother thinks she's being subtle about her designs on my personal life. I thought we were out in the middle of nowhere where there'd be no service?"

"I mean, there isn't any if you turn your phone off." He smirks.

"Ha. Tempting."

"What are her designs?" he asks as he pops another sour gummy worm in his mouth.

"She and my dad want me back in Seattle like I was telling you at the fair. Doing the political thing. Very specifically, she knows I have to go back to host Xander's engagement party next week, and she was letting me know our family friends are coming and their son is in town."

"Their son?" Cooper's brow raises.

"He's my age. We went to prep school together. He was the quarterback, and I had a crush on him back then. It's all my mom remembers. Back then, he didn't care if I existed, and now I don't care if he does. The problem is... he's all grown up, football didn't work out, and his future depends on his political connections."

"And you're the obvious choice for political advantage."

"Exactly. One my parents don't hate either as his family is wealthy and has a lot of contacts they wouldn't mind having either."

"This all sounds very medieval. Marrying your daughter off for the best alliance." Cooper's brow furrows.

"Well, it is. Very medieval and very fuck what Bea wants, as long as we all get what we want. Minus my mom. She does care to some extent what I want, but she thinks I want Craig. She knows I liked him as a kid, and in her mind, not much has changed since." I sigh.

"Ah. Yeah. I get that. Mine can be the same way sometimes. She thinks she can set me up with the girl down the block, and we'll get married and be happy. Except she forgets her son is an unrepentant manwhore who never met a relationship he liked." He stares up at the stars.

"Don't talk about yourself like that. If you enjoy your life, and it sustains your happiness, then that's all that matters." I feel defensive for both of us.

"It doesn't. Not really." It's his turn to sigh. "It's just where I've always been comfortable. But then comfortable doesn't always mean happy, sometimes it just means you're content. Just content enough to not want to change anything and risk being less than content. You know?" He looks over at me and his eyes search my face.

"I can understand that. I mean… I think that's why I stuck things out in Pittsburgh for so long when I knew I wouldn't ever really be happy there. Because I was at least content. I knew what to expect every day, and the alternative was wide open space for everything to get fucked up. And well… that's exactly what happened." I can't help but laugh a little that all my worst fears have come true. I have no real job. No home to call my own, no one who loves me, and I'm essentially knocking on the door of my thirties with no plan. But at least I'm still here. There's something to be said for getting up and trying every day even when you don't feel like it.

"Yeah. I know what you mean. But for the record, I think you're doing all right, all things considered. You're figuring out your next steps, and in the meantime, you're here working with Madison, doing an amazing job for the Chaos. I'm super grateful for your little side quest here." Cooper squeezes my hand, and I glance down at the way our fingers intertwine.

"Me too." I turn my head to look over and smile at him.

He reaches over me, and he brushes my hair carefully out of my face before he leans over to kiss me softly. We're lost in each other for a moment before he pulls away and raises a brow.

"Do I need to be worried about this Craig guy stealing you away? I thought we had a pretty good setup here while we worked through our lists." He grins.

"Not on my account, but I can promise my mother is going to try to make it happen. I have no idea how Craig even feels about it."

"What if I come with you?"

"To Seattle?" I ask, surprised if he's actually suggesting that.

"Why not? Lizzy's gone at camp. We've got a break right now before training camp starts."

"I don't think you realize what you're signing up for. My family is... a lot."

"Oh, I know. Trust me, Rob bitched plenty about what it was like to deal with your brother and your father. But I'm much better at convincing people to like me than he is." Cooper winks at me, and I can't help the smile that forms in response.

"That's true, but I just feel like they'll stomp out any bit of fun between us. Ask you a bunch of questions and make things super uncomfortable."

"Easy. We just pretend we're dating already. Then you've got no time for Craig, and your parents can rest assured that you're in good hands with me."

"That easy, huh?" I raise a brow at his confidence, only slightly worried that my parents, and worse yet, my brother, will be more than he expects.

"I mean, I think it's worth a shot. The alternative is that you go and deal with Craig and your family on your own."

"Madison is coming too." It's partially a protest, but I don't know if Cooper's comfortable with people outside of Ramsey and his friend knowing our situation. Madison will be all over it if she figures us out.

"With Quentin?" he asks, and the implied statement is

there. She'll be too busy managing him to help me worry about my regularly scheduled family problems.

"Fair point."

"Good. So it's settled then." He grabs another piece of candy and leans back against the pillows to stare at the sky with me.

"What am I going to owe you for this help?"

"I'm sure we can come to an arrangement. Probably a few more items off the list."

"I suppose I can live with that." I muse, my lips turning up even as I try to suppress the smile. It seems I can't stop smiling around this man.

I lie back and stare at the sky, full of a million stars and possibilities. But there's only one I really want right now, and I worry it might be more out of reach than any of them.

24

Beatrix

STANDING outside the door to Xander's apartment, I'm starting to wonder what I was thinking when I decided to bring Cooper along. I've been thoroughly enjoying our fledgling friends-with-benefits situation, and if there is anything that can take a sledgehammer to that, it is my family. Specifically the men in my family who have an overprotective streak a mile wide. Since our cover story is that we're dating, I don't have to admit that he's my bodyguard. I look nervously at Cooper, and he smiles at me and gives me a curious look.

"I'm just wondering if I should have brought you here. If you'll survive Xander." I stare nervously ahead at the door.

"I've survived him plenty of times on the field. If I can manage that, I can manage this." Images of Xander slamming Cooper into the turf dance in my head and it doesn't help settle any of the worries currently fluttering around in my stomach.

"I don't know. There aren't any refs in there." I shake my head with a smile because my brother's temper is legendary, and if it wasn't for Xander's fiancée Harper, I definitely wouldn't bring Cooper here.

The door swings open a second later, and it's Xander, freshly showered and back from a day of practice at the field.

"Bea!" he shouts and wraps me up in a bear hug. I squeeze him tight. One of the hardest parts about being on the road the last couple of years has been being away from Xander. He's one of my best friends. Which is exactly why this next part is going to be a little rough. I see it in his eyes when they turn on Cooper.

"Rawlings." He says it like he's just stepped in something disgusting.

"Xavier," Cooper answers with a broad smile.

Xander's attention returns to me, an eyebrow quirking upwards.

"Cooper plays for the Chaos," I say, like that's supposed to explain everything as I walk in the door and Cooper follows.

"I'm well aware of who he plays for." My brother's tone is flat.

"Well, you know I've been working there with Madison," I say lightly.

"I'm aware." He's determined to make this uncomfortable, and I'm determined to ignore it.

"Perfect. Is the guest room good to put our stuff in?" Xander's guest room has pretty much been my home away from home for the last several years when I've come to town. It means I can avoid our parents and their relentless onslaught of questions about when I'll be ready to move back to Seattle. But since Harper's moved in, I don't know if it's still okay for me to sprawl out in there.

"Our stuff?" I swear I see the muscles twitching in Xander's hand already.

"Cooper's staying with me."

"You remember the guest room only has one bed, right?"

"I'm aware." I echo my brother's stoic replies.

"Are you going to make me ask, or should I just go ahead and make assumptions here?" Xander finally loses patience with playing along with the slow introductions. I realize at that moment that I can't lie to Xander, so when Cooper starts to answer, I put my hand on his arm and speak instead.

"He's here to help fend off the parents. Mom's already started in with the Craig business again, and I don't want to deal with it. Cooper volunteered to help, and I took him up on it."

"Very selfless of you." Xander gives Cooper a look that's half curiosity and half warning. "You couldn't find someone who wasn't your ex-boyfriend's brother for the task? You honestly think they're going to buy that?" Xander follows us as we walk our bags to the guest room and stops in the doorway. I see Cooper's lips turn up in amusement and he flashes me a clandestine look—one I hope Xander doesn't notice—before returning his focus to the bags.

"Be nice. And sure... why not?" I push past Xander, and he moves out of the way, following me back to the living room.

Xander looks me over before he smirks and shakes his head. "I guess we'll see."

"Can we move on now? I want to know how your trip to the Camino was. How's wedding planning going? I need all the details." I plop down on the couch and make room for Cooper, who sits next to me as Xander continues to survey both of us like we're a sideshow curiosity.

My brother sits down across from us, though, and leans back, starting with a breakdown of their flights overseas and all the gear they had to pack for their walk, and I settle in for the story.

I'M thankful Cooper and my brother even manage to get along for most of the afternoon. Minus Xander coming back from his friend Tobias's apartment upstairs in a bit of a huff just before the party—a thing I'll have to investigate later—everything is going more smoothly than I could have ever imagined for a trip home.

At least until Xander accidentally overhears me snarking to Cooper about how I'm safe from my stalker in Seattle but not my family. A comment he refuses to believe is a joke. I have to beg him to come into a side room with me to discuss it before everyone, including our parents, overhears his reaction.

"Please be calm," I beg as I close the door behind me, hoping we didn't attract attention when we left the room where everyone is celebrating. It's kind of hard not to notice when half of the couple of honor and the hostess disappear.

"How could you not tell me this?" Xander's whisper is more like a soft boom once we step into the guest room to talk.

"I didn't want it getting back to Mom and Dad."

"I'm not Mom and Dad."

"You would have worried the same. You would have sent the concerns up the chain, potentially, and then I'd be stuck dealing with them being unhinged with worry. You know Dad already wants me to come home, and I'm not ready to surrender to the family name yet."

"And I am?" He sounds exasperated with having to deal with me.

"You made the decisions you had to make. I'm not ready yet. You tell me you need me, I'll be here. You know that. But as long as I can stay away, enjoy my life as far away from the Xavier political machinations as I can, the happier I am."

"I'd be happier if you'd fucking told me you have a goddamn stalker after you. And what's Madison doing? The

Chaos? Cooper? Some fucking boyfriend, letting you fucking be exposed to a psycho."

"First of all, Cooper is not a boyfriend."

Xander flashes a look of disbelief in my direction. "This apartment isn't that big, Bea."

I glower at him.

"We have an understanding, and he's a friend. He's here with me to keep me safe."

"And what's he going to do? Charm your stalker to death? Tell him a few dad jokes and hope that wards him off? Be serious."

"I'm being serious. I feel safe with him. He's been looking out for me. He let me move in with him and his daughter so I didn't have to be alone at the hotel."

"Oh, I'm real fucking sure that's the reason he wanted you in his house. I know you've been out of the dating world for a minute, but that's one of the biggest fuckboy moves I've ever heard. Real fucking risky one, but if it pays off..."

"It's not like that."

"You sure he didn't orchestrate it to get you to move in?"

"I'm positive. Why would he keep it up when I'm already living with him?"

"To make sure you stay."

"You have a devious mind. Also, he could get any woman he wants. He doesn't have to play games to win one over."

"I just don't trust anyone. Let alone someone who claims to be a white knight when their reputation is anything but."

"Looked in a mirror lately?"

"What Harper and I have is different."

"Different in that you were lying in wait for her ex-husband to fuck up so you could swoop in and save the day?"

"Don't be a smartass."

"Then don't be an ass—suggesting someone who's been a

good friend to me has some nefarious plot. We're friends, and we have an understanding. That's as far as it goes."

"Then who do you think it is?"

"If I knew, I wouldn't be worried. I'd be calling the cops."

"You sure it's not his brother?"

"It wouldn't make sense if it was." Rob moved on easily. He was dating someone new within weeks. He replaced me so fast that I wondered if she was already waiting in the wings or if he was just that good on the open market.

"Wouldn't it make sense though?" Xander raises a brow at me.

"Rob moved on a long time ago. In record time, really."

"Until he found out you were with his brother."

"He doesn't know."

Xander lets out a low whistle. "You're playing with fire."

"How many ways are there to say ditto?"

"And my situation almost turned out badly too. I'm warning you from experience."

"Just keep this between us."

"I'm not making any promises. Frankly, I think the parents deserve to know. Should know, really. You know my feelings about Dad, but in this case, you might need extra security, and if anyone can get it for you, it's him."

"I don't want to have my father running to my rescue like I'm some overgrown daddy's girl. I especially don't want the patronizing lecture I'll get about moving home." I shake my head firmly.

"It's not about what you want right now. It's about what's going to keep you safe."

"You can't be serious!"

"I'm serious as fuck, Bea. This whole situation is fucked up. And you not telling me? You've had problems like this before. You know better. Please tell me you've told other people you work with. Madison knows? I can't believe she isn't intervening on your behalf."

"Madison has her hands full with Quentin and his career right now. Not to mention, she's got family drama of her own brewing. I can't ask her to be carrying water for me, too, right now."

"You haven't told your best friend—your business partner —that you have a potential stalker? Bea, this is insane. I can't believe Rawlings is playing along with this either. Does he have any fucking integrity or give a fuck about you at all?"

"He cares, Xander. He's doing more than he should already."

"We'll see about that." My brother charges out of the room a moment later, and I chase after him. I love him to the moon and back, but thanks to our father's frequent absences and the fact that I've been the quiet one in the family, he always thinks he has to protect me.

"Xander!" I whisper shout his name, trailing a few steps behind him. "Alexander..." I chase after him to catch up, but he ignores me, his long legs outpacing mine, and I try one last attempt. "Alexander Xavier!"

It's like I don't exist. His eyes are scanning the room for Cooper, and when they land on him, he makes a beeline there. I can't stop him before words are exchanged, and my brother nods for the door to the patio. I hurry after them into the night, thankful that a lot of the guests have already left for the evening otherwise I'm sure they'd have questions about our game of musical rooms.

"I'm going to give you all of about one minute to tell me what you're doing to keep my sister safe. Because from everything I know now, it sounds like you're just using her vulnerability as an excuse to take advantage of her."

Cooper's face flashes with a look of surprise before he regains control and shakes his head.

"Your sister is in my house so I can keep her safe. I'm as worried about her as you are."

"I highly doubt that."

"You shouldn't. I want her in my house so I know exactly where she is and so I know I'm there if she needs me. I don't want to pass that responsibility off to anyone else."

"Part of that responsibility should have been encouraging her to tell the rest of her family and friends so we could all protect her."

"I have encouraged her to tell you all. But at the end of the day, she's an adult, and I respect her ability to make decisions for herself. If she didn't want to tell you, I assume she had her reasons. Some of which are probably this over-the-top reaction you're having right now. You think this helps her? You yelling at me and threatening me when, at the end of the day, we both just want the same thing?"

"My reaction is because I already know how your family treats her. Where she is as a priority when the list gets made in the Rawlings household."

"Xander!" I want to throttle him right now, but he doesn't even bother to look in my direction.

"I'm not my brother. Beatrix and my daughter are my only priorities."

"Your brother's ex-girlfriend is your priority. Interesting. Why is that?" Xander presses, and I feel the second embarrassment shooting through my veins.

"I imagine you already know the answer to that given that your best friend's wife was yours."

"So we should start planning a second engagement party then?"

I want to die. I can't even bear to look at Cooper's face right now.

"Xander!" I shout. "Oh my god. Please stop being ridiculous. You're embarrassing all of us. Leave Cooper alone. He's been nothing but gracious to me. The second I got the first inkling of this whole stalker thing, he was begging me to be more cautious and asking how he could help. You're making an ass out of yourself, yelling at him like this."

"If he cared about you, you'd have twenty-four seven security. If this were Harper, I'd have someone on her every second of the day I couldn't be there to do it myself, and backup too. I'd have the police and investigators and anyone else I could get to have eyes on the entire thing. I can't believe you're being so casual about this."

"Nothing has happened. Just a few pictures and some footprints outside a window. The cops would have nothing to go on." I protest

"Nothing happened with Harper's ex either, until it did." Xander's eyes land heavy on me.

"What's going on out here? You have guests inside, Xander." My father's voice interrupts us, and I recoil, pinching my eyes shut.

When I open them, Xander's smile tells me he's about to bring our father into this debate. Like we're kids again, and I've finally done something wrong where he gets to tell on me, instead of the other way around.

"Bea has a stalker. For weeks now. She's done almost nothing about it, and I'm worried about her safety. I'm asking why more isn't being done." Xander's eyes shift to Cooper, and my father's follow. They both have a very unique ability to assess people and finding them wanting in rapid order. A thing my father does with remarkable efficiency as he studies Cooper.

"He has a security system. I've been careful. We don't know if it's his stalker or mine. Just that it started after they saw us together. We've been careful. I don't want an overreaction to this situation. It's embarrassing. This happens to lots of people in the spotlight. You both *know* this." I'm immediately hurrying to shield Cooper from whatever comes next, but I might as well be invisible.

My father nods once, the gray streak in his hair reflecting the moonlight.

"We're going to talk more about this later. For now, she's safe. My security is everywhere I am, and tomorrow you're coming to stay at our house. Before you return to Cincinnati..."—my father pauses to look at me—"we're going to have this resolved." He turns to Xander. "Now, please go in there and entertain your guests."

The finality in his tone is enough even to quell Xander's anxiety, and he nods, glancing one last time between Cooper and me before he heads back inside. My father silently nods for us to follow him, and we march like dutiful children to his beat.

25

C *ooper*

ONCE WE GET SETTLED in at Trix's parents' house, her father summons us into his office and has us sit down.

"I didn't want to continue the scene last night at Xander's, but I'm as concerned as he is about whatever the two of you have going on with this stalker. I've already made arrangements to have a security team help you. I have a contact in Cincinnati. He used to work for me and then he moved back east. He already does some work at the Chaos stadium so he'll be a perfect fit for you."

"We've taken plenty of precautions," Trix interjects, and I see her father's brow raise in gentle disapproval.

"Then these will just be additional fail-safes. You can never be too cautious. Among other things, they want to install cameras around the property where you're living. They'll be ready to get that finished for you as soon as you arrive home.

I've already sent them out to do an assessment, and they've noted there are a lot of blind spots on the property that make it vulnerable, so I think it's important this work happens as soon as possible."

I'm not entirely shocked that Senator Xavier is so boldly adamant about his plans, but I'm surprised at how swiftly he's put them in motion. I'm already wondering what sort of assessment they've been doing at my house. But I don't exactly disagree with his or Xander's concerns, and I want to reassure them I have her safety in mind.

"Dad, I appreciate your concern, but I think it's wildly inappropriate for you to be telling Cooper what to do with his property and—"

"It's okay." I place my hand on top of hers. I know she's trying to stand up for me, but anything that helps is something I'm willing to try. "It's extra security. Whatever it takes to keep you safe, I'm happy to do it."

Trix's mouth flatlines, and she sighs, resigning herself to the fact that the men in her life are stubborn when it comes to her well-being.

"This is beyond overprotective. You're approaching intrusive," she complains to her father.

"If you won't move back to Seattle, then I have to know you're safe where you are."

"I know you care about me, but I think this is all going to feel so silly when this turns out to be nothing. Just some overzealous fan of Cooper's, having some fun at our expense, and we'll look ridiculous for acting like it was something serious."

"I'd rather be safe than sorry." Her father says it with the kind of finality that tells me he's done discussing it, even if she does hate it. It makes it hard for me to agree with him. While I desperately want more precautions in place than Trix does, I also don't want to undermine her boundaries, and this entire conversation feels light a tightrope walk between making sure her father knows I think she's a priority and making her feel like I've got her back no matter the circumstances.

"Fine. If it makes you feel better, and Cooper doesn't object," she relents.

"Whatever keeps you safe." I brush my thumb over the backs of her knuckles.

"Good. That's settled. Now, the next bit of business is that if you're dating my daughter, I think it's important I get to know a little more about you. I've got some colleagues coming over tonight, and while Bea catches up with some old friends and her mother, I thought you could come to have a scotch and some cigars with me while I get to know you better."

If I was a ref, I'd be throwing a defenseless receiver penalty because... Fuck. I did not expect to spend the night stuck with Senator Xavier, and this sounds like absolute torture on top of it.

"I don't think Cooper has time for that." Bea tries to run interference for me.

"Well, you're only here for a couple of days, so he'll need to make time."

"Again—"

"It's fine. I'd love to chat more. I've heard so many good things, and I've been hoping to get a chance to meet you, sir."

"Then it's settled. Glad we can get all of this out of the way and enjoy the rest of the evening." Senator Xavier's face lights with the smile that tells me he's used to getting his way, so I start mentally preparing myself for the gauntlet I'm about to enter and reminding myself that Trix is one hundred percent worth it.

AFTER GOING MORE than seven rounds in the ring with Trix's father and his political colleagues with their opinions on everything from sports to the current weather, I finally see Trix crossing the room like a guardian angel come to save me.

"Thank fuck," I whisper quietly when she comes up and wraps an arm around me.

"I think you've proved you can hold your own. Ready for a little break? I can give you a tour of the house."

"Anything that gets me out of here. Do I get to see your bedroom?" I smirk.

"That can be arranged. As long as you don't judge too harshly."

"Scouts honor."

She grins and then takes my hand, leading me through a maze of hallways and staircases until she pushes open a large mahogany-colored door. I turn around in her room, and it's everything I expected and then some. The photo wall of friends, the numerous ribbons and trophies she gathered over her childhood for being an overachiever, and the aesthetic that's stuck somewhere between prep school princess and slightly rebellious fangirl.

When I see the football sitting on the shelf, I raise my brow and turn to her, picking it up out of its place and turning it over in my hand. Despite the fact it's been sitting here for years, there's not a speck of dust, and I'm going to guess that's thanks to one of the maids I saw dodge through a back hallway earlier. Her parents keep everything in here like it once was in hopes their old daughter, the one from their imagination who didn't date football players and spend all of her time on their careers, comes home and wants her old spot back again.

"Xander's not the only Xavier hoping to go pro someday?" I muse.

"Ha. I wish I could have played. I have zero coordination

with a ball. Can you imagine my dad's face if I'd said I wanted to play too? It might have killed him."

"I bet you have more coordination than you give yourself credit for."

"Maybe." She shrugs. "It's not mine though."

"Whose is it?" I'm wondering if it's my brother's or hers.

"Craig's."

"Uptight Craig from downstairs?" My grip tightens on the ball. I haven't liked the way he's been following her around all night. Although I suspect it was part of the plan, right along with the Senator holding me hostage.

She looks at something on her desk before she answers, shuffling some paper there like she's trying to distract herself.

"Yep. Like my dad was saying, he grew out of the things he thought he liked as a kid."

"Grew out of them or just wasn't good enough for college or the pros?" I hold it up, and she studies the ball for a moment like she's reliving a memory.

"He wasn't bad in high school." She nods to the ball in my hand. "That was a game-winner."

"And he gave it to you?"

She gives a sheepish smile and shrugs. "I asked for it. He was going to give it to Emily. This girl who was all but his girl-friend already. But I said if he gave it to me, I'd put in a good word for him with my dad for a summer internship. The rest is history."

"You liked him?"

Another shoulder rises and falls, and she shakes her head. "He was cute at the time. I liked him well enough."

"Enough to cockblock Emily."

"Emily deserved it. She made out with another guy she knew I liked just to prove she could have anyone I wanted."

"But Craig liked you better?"

"Craig liked my last name better than hers."

"Ah." My heart sinks a little for her. I can only imagine with a father as powerful as hers, and a brother as popular, that she was often seen as a bartering chip to get closer to power.

"It's the same now as it was then." She sighs.

"I don't think so. The way he was looking at you tonight..." I'm pretty sure she's right—Craig has all the wrong intentions when it comes to her. But I also know when I've got competition, and he's been doing everything he can to make it clear I won't get her in the end.

"Is exactly the way he looked at me junior year when he told me I'd look pretty on my knees." She gives me a tight-lipped smile.

"I hope you told him you look prettiest when he's looking up at you from between your thighs." I grin and toss her the ball.

She catches it, and her smile breaks. "No. I wasn't that fast with the comebacks."

"You do, you know."

She shakes her head and turns the ball over, end over end, in her hands. "Don't try to flatter me, Rawlings."

I close the distance between us, coming up behind her, wrapping an arm around her waist, and pressing a kiss to the side of her throat. I can feel her tense at the contact at first and then relax when she feels my lips move over her skin. Her lips part, and then she rolls the lower one between her teeth.

"Not flattery. Just truth. The way you look when you're like that, your legs spread for me while you gasp every time I run my tongue over your perfect little cunt..." I run my fingers down over her stomach. "The way your hips come up off the bed when I suck on your clit..." I slide them under her skirt and brush my knuckles over her through her panties. She takes in a breath, and her eyelashes flutter.

I slip one finger under the cotton, kissing my way down her neck, satisfied when I find her already wet for me. I slide another finger inside, feeling her shift forward, desperate for more, before I take it away again, and her brow furrows even though her eyes don't open.

"You've been teasing me all night," she says softly.

"You've been teasing *me* all night," I answer. "In that skirt. With those looks you keep giving me across the room. You're lucky I didn't bend you over the chair in the den. Let Craig walk in on you coming hard on my cock." I see her throat bob in response, and I feel my pulse quicken. "You like the thought of that? Of him watching you come?"

Her fingers tighten around the football that's still in her hands, and I smirk.

"He could see how lucky I am. How good you sound when you've got my cock buried inside you. Gasping for air. Begging for more." I tease her clit with my knuckles again, and she wets her lips in response.

"You're evil."

"More than you know." Because in her fantasy, it might be Craig walking in, but in mine, it's my brother watching her fall apart for me.

"I can't take much more. I need..." Her eyes shift up to me. I'm not about to let Craig have a single moment of her. I'm already jealous of any man who's had anything from her so far. But it gives me an idea all the same.

"You need what?" I just need her to ask for it first.

"You. Please, Coop."

I walk us slowly toward her bed until her knees hit the edge of the mattress. I reach for the football, and her grip loosens, letting me take it from her.

"Spread your legs a little for me." She does as I ask, and I slip the ball between them, turning the laces up as I press my hand to her lower back.

"Coop," she chokes out my name as her cheeks heat, and she flashes me a look.

"Roll your hips for me."

Her eyes search mine, and I raise my eyebrows slightly, glancing down at the ball between her legs. Her lashes flutter, and I lean forward, stroking my thumb over her cheek and down her jaw.

"You can do it for me, Trix. He's down there thinking you're his already. That he just has to make you see what a good little wife you'd make, standing next to him at all his political events. But he doesn't know you're up here in your old bedroom with me. Legs spread around the football you stole while you try to put yourself out of the misery I put you in. The way you let me tease you all night under the table and behind the door. Working over your little cunt until it's dripping wet."

Her eyes close, and she starts to move. Like she needs it so badly she can't help herself. I lift her skirt up so I can see more of her—watch her while her hips and her thighs work, half-bent over the edge of the bed, so desperate to be fucked.

"Look at you. So fucking beautiful. Working that clit over those laces." I have to palm myself through my pants, try to tell my cock to wait its turn. I want this. Need this so badly—to watch her so lost in how desperately she wants to be fucked that she'll do anything for it. Anything for me.

"This is so wrong." She gasps, the sound of a moan caught in her throat.

"Nah. It's perfect. You're perfect for me, Trix. So fucking sexy, I can barely take it. I love watching you like this."

"I need more." It's a breathy whisper as she grinds down on the ball again.

I step behind her, sliding my hands up under the edges of the skirt I've hiked up around her hips and grab the band of her underwear. I tug gently, and she lifts her hips from the ball just enough that I can slip them off her, moving them slowly down her legs until she steps out, one at a time. She hovers over the ball, like doing what she's been doing without that little scrap of fabric in between is too much. I grab a handful of her ass, squeezing as I lean down to whisper in her ear.

"He thinks you're a good girl. Show me you're not."

"I want you to fuck me."

"I will. I promise I will, Trix. But I want to see you take what you want. Feel the way the ribs of these laces brush over your clit. Hear how good it feels to use it."

"I shouldn't. It's..."

"Hot as fuck. I'm so fucking hard I can't stand it. Watching you like this is going to live in my head forever. Just a loop of the way your hips move and the soft little moans you make." I grab her hair at the nape of her neck and gently tug her back before I bring my lips to her ear once more. Making a confession I'm sure I'll be making a million times more. "I need it, Trix. I need you."

It's all it takes for her to move again, and I nip at her earlobe.

"That's my girl. So fucking sexy taking what she wants. What she needs." I glance down and watch as the ball starts to get slick from her wetness.

"Oh fuck... This is so... so wrong," she mutters as she rocks her hips forward again.

I can't take watching anymore. I need inside her. My own desperation demands to know that some of those moans are for me. I undo my pants and grab the condom in my pocket, tearing the foil and putting it on.

I step behind her, lining myself up as she rocks back and forth over the ball. She brushes over my cock on the next go, and the warmth of her cunt over me has me on edge. The moan she makes as she drags down me on her next move makes it too hard to hold out any further.

"You want me, Trix?"

"I need you. Please." Another soft moan escapes as she grinds down again. "Please, Coop."

I take her on the next round, sliding inside and watching as her hands grip the comforter on her childhood bed. Her moan cuts off into something more guttural, more feral, as she meets my next thrust with the cant of her hips.

"Oh fuck. That's so good. You're so fucking good, Coop," she mutters the words as her grip tightens. I fuck her harder, my balls brushing over the edge of the football, before she bats it away a moment later. I grin at how fucked up it is before I run my hand over the curve of her ass, and she murmurs another curse as I take her deeper.

I want to tell her how good she is. How sweet she is. How I can give her every fucking thing she's ever wanted. How she can be my good little wife if she wants to be. How I'd do anything for her. Get on my knees whenever she snaps her fingers. That I'm already hers.

That's how fucked up I am over her—ready to spill every damn secret I have for a chance at what I want. But it's not what she needs from me right now. Not what she wants to hear. Not how I can make her come hard like she's been begging for me to do all night.

"Fuck me, Trix. You're such a good slut for me. Taking my cock like this. Like you were made for it. While you rub this pretty little pussy all over that ball. Can barely control yourself."

There are muted gasps and moans from her, and she grinds back against me with each movement of my hips. Her fingers wrap around the comforter, tangling and wrinkling the fabric under her hands as she feverishly works her way to her own desperate release.

"That's right. Let yourself go. Like you can't get enough."

She falls apart a moment later, coming hard and taking me with her. She buries her moans in the bed, and I bite down hard on my tongue to keep from cursing my way through it loud enough for everyone in this house to hear. It's so fucking perfect I can barely stand to pull away from her.

Her breathing slows, and she climbs up onto the bed, the ball falling to the floor at my feet. I clean myself up and take care of the condom, zipping up my pants on the walk back to the bed.

I pick up the ball, grabbing an old jersey hanging over a chair in the corner of the room and wipe it down before I toss the jersey in the hamper and return the ball to her shelf.

I sit on the bed next to her and pull her body next to mine. She curls into me, leaning on my shoulder as I kiss her forehead.

"That was... wow," she whispers, and I can tell she's still feeling raw and vulnerable. The way this house and everyone in it tonight affects her is hard not to notice. I'm happy to distract her from it all for a little while.

"Sexy as fuck. That one should have been on the list. Maybe we add it so we can cross it off."

"Maybe." She laughs softly, and I take her hand, intertwining her fingers with mine.

We fit together so well in so many ways. I just hope while we work our way through this list, indulging her fantasies, that she notices it too. That she feels some fraction of the things I'm feeling. Because I think I might need more than one summer with her.

26

B eatrix

MY MOM FINDS me sitting out in the conservatory, drinking a glass of champagne after I come back downstairs, and staring out the window as the rain cascades down over the glass. She's the one who taught me about this particular escape room, one that happens to also make an excellent place to come down after good sex before you return to polite society to smile and shake hands, so she can't be too surprised to find me hiding out in here.

"It's really coming down out there tonight," she says softly as she peers out. It's noteworthy when the rain rises above a soft drizzle.

"It is. Really coming down in there as well." I give her half a smile so she knows it's because I'm worried and not because I'm trying to complain.

"You know how the men in this family are."

"I know, but he could do with a little less of the men in this family. He's been so kind to me, Mom."

"He seems like a genuinely kind person. I'm surprised, honestly, given his brother. Although, I guess Rob did survive them a bit better."

"Rob didn't register half the insults they lodged at him. He was oblivious since he was so sure everyone loved him. Cooper's actually self-aware, and he doesn't deserve it."

"You think that's a natural difference or from raising a daughter?" She muses, her eyes still lost in the distance.

"Both."

"Do his parents know you're dating?" My mother's brow furrows as she takes a sip of her own wine.

"I haven't asked." It's technically true.

"I assume his brother doesn't know."

"Of course not. I don't need to stir the hornet's nest. You know how he is. He doesn't want me, but he certainly won't like his brother having me either. Though Cooper's said he has a steady girlfriend already, so maybe he'll be too preoccupied to care."

"How does that work long term? Between the two of you? You spent a lot of time with his family, going on holiday trips and spending the summers at their family home down at that lake house of theirs. It's going to be a lot of time around your ex-boyfriend and his new girlfriend. There's a lot of history between the two of you." Her tone tells me she's worried for me.

"I haven't thought that far ahead, Mother. I just enjoy being with Cooper. We get along. He makes me laugh. I love spending time around Lizzy again." I shrug. "It works right now, and given that I don't even know where I'll be in the fall, I'm not trying to plan ahead."

"So Craig should just try again in the fall then?" She says it deadpan, but when I look at her, I can see the teasing amusement in her eyes. For all of her matchmaking and attempts to get me to come back into the fold, my mother is at least willing to admit defeat and let me have my way sometimes.

"I think Craig is in an unenviable position of following a guy like Cooper no matter when he tries."

"Ah. I can understand that. Reminds me of Ed."

"Ed?" I ask.

"Ed was a guy my friends tried to set me up with when your dad went off to law school. Your dad couldn't decide if he was ready to get married, so we went our separate ways, and along came Ed. On paper, he was great—perfect even. The kind of guy I would have had a crush on and my parents would have loved. But I'd already met Conrad Xavier." She shrugs and smiles as she stares into the distance. "And no one competed with him, even when he wasn't around." She looks back at me. "But thankfully, I hadn't dated Uncle Gerald first."

"Well, you have always been better at all this than me."

"I'm teasing you." She bumps me gently with her hip. "In the end, I just want to see you happy, Bea. Xander's finally met his match, Tobias is settling down... it seems like it should be your turn, if you want it."

"Things aren't that serious with Cooper, Mom. As you pointed out, there are reasons it probably won't work out long term. But I'm just trying to be happy for now. Live in the moment instead of trying to paint a perfect future. Every time I've tried to do that in the past few years, it's ended badly, and I'm tired of disappointment."

"Oh, honey." She wraps an arm around me and leans her head against my shoulder. "You've had a rough go of things. But I believe in you."

"Do you? You've been pretty lockstep with Dad lately about coming home." I side-eye her, and she lets out a small sigh.

"If you and Madison think you can do this thing, I'm there for you one hundred percent. Your father will come around. He always does. We just want what's best for you, and there are so many things he can give you that you'd have to fight for elsewhere. It's hard as a parent to watch you all fight so hard for ground, knowing we could help you, and you not letting us. I understand why you want to do it for yourself. I do. But I just... want to help. I want to see you happy."

"You've got to let me be happy on my own. I know it's taking me longer than either of you would like, but I'm figuring things out as I go. The things I thought I wanted... the marriage, the kids, the whole package... I don't know if I want them anymore. I'm trying to figure that out, and I don't want to run back home just because figuring it out has been a little scary sometimes."

"I can respect that. But what your dad and brother were saying about you having someone following or harassing you— you have to know that as your mom, that's different. I just want you close where we could keep you safe."

"I don't even know that they're after me. I think it's Cooper they're more concerned about. A fan of his that doesn't like that he's dating."

She pauses for a moment, taking another sip of her drink before she speaks again, and I can tell from the tone, I'm about to get a dose of reality from her.

"So to preface... I support you whatever choice you make, Beatrix. But this guy you're seeing is your ex-boyfriend's brother who you likely don't have much of a future with beyond the summer. And just to date him, you're enduring harassment from some unknown person who's made you fearful enough that you're taking your father's security recommendations seri-ously. Are you sure that's worth it?" She turns a skeptical look on me.

I take a deep breath and then swallow the rest of my champagne.

"So far, it's been the best summer of my life, despite all of that."

Her flatlined lips curl just slightly at the corner, enough that you might call it a partial smile, and she tilts her head.

"Well. Then listen to your father. If you won't come home, at least make sure you're safe where you are."

"I will, Mom."

She hugs me from the side one last time.

"All right. I'm back into the fray. Don't hide in here too long. It's not fair to leave your guy with the lions."

I grin at her, and then she disappears through the rows of plants.

27

B^{eatrix}

WHEN WE GET BACK from Seattle, Lizzy is back from summer camp, and Cooper's headed to the stadium for some of the OTAs. This leaves the two of us to our own devices most days this week, and that's meant a lot of pool and video game time when I'm finished with my half days working for Madison on Quentin's projects. I'm just winding up some emails to inquire about some local business partnerships when Lizzy meanders into the room.

"Hey. You getting hungry?" I ask as I hit send and close my laptop.

"Starving. Are there snacks?"

"There's some fruit in the fridge and some of the little baby cheeses your dad picked up from the grocery, but I was going to start making dinner. I was about to ask what you'd like—tacos, spaghetti, curry... Any of that sound good?"

"All of it, but tacos sound amazing. Do we have guacamole?"

"No, but I think we have the stuff to make it if you want to help me." We make our way to the kitchen.

"Sure. What time is Dad getting home? Do you know?"

"In about an hour, so I think we can time it perfectly." I smile at her, and we both start pulling ingredients from the pantry and fridge.

"So..." Lizzy starts. "My birthday is coming up soon, and I was thinking it would be amazing if you could make some of your signature cupcakes that you always used to make."

"I can do that. But aren't you and your dad going to the lake house for your birthday? I thought he said your grandparents had some special stuff planned for you down there."

"We are, and they do. Which is why I was hoping you'd go with us..." She gives me a mischievous grin, and when I open my mouth to protest, she cuts me off at the pass. "And before you say no, I know that Uncle Rob will be there, but it's a big house. You'll be spending all of your time with me and Dad, and we can be out on the lake and doing our own thing. So besides a dinner or two, you won't even have to see him. Plus, when he sees how gorgeous you look this summer, he'll be eating his heart out."

"Exactly how long have you been planning this ambush?" I laugh at the way she's thought out her whole argument on this.

"A while. I just really want you to come. It's sucked without you there, and this time, there's no reason you can't go. It'll just be with me and Dad instead."

"I don't know. I don't have any hard feelings where your uncle is concerned, and I'm sure it'll be fine. It's a big house, and we can both do our own thing, but it's really a family thing for you all, and I feel like I'd be intruding on that."

"I want you intruding. It's *my* birthday. I should get some say—and I want Trix hangouts and cupcakes for my birthday."

Lizzy rolls her lower lip and makes a face that lays on all the guilt.

"I'll think about it, and we'll have to see what your dad says."

"I already talked to him. He thinks it's a great idea." She grins brightly.

I start to question that premise when I hear the doorbell ring, and I frown, looking to Lizzy for answers. She shrugs like she doesn't know who it could be, and I wipe my hands and make my way to the door.

Peering out the small window, I see a man in a security uniform from the company that my father hired to install the cameras and monitor the property. True to his word, they were ready to go the moment we set foot back in Ohio, and for the last week, they've been diligently assembling everything to the specifications my father's security team outlined.

"Hello. Is there still more work?" I ask through the door before I unlock it; I'm more cautious than ever.

"Hello." The man offers me a warm smile, and his blue eyes light with the greeting. "Beatrix, I don't know if you remember me. I'm James Sharp. I worked with your father out in Seattle. He hired my team to set everything up for you, and I just wanted to come by personally and take a final look through everything to make sure it's all been done correctly."

I tilt my head and study his face for a moment before the recognition comes. He'd been part of my father's security team years ago. He'd always been funny and had been one of the good ones. He had helped me sneak away from a function or two for a breather when I couldn't take any more of my father's political contacts asking me how my classes were going or what colleges I had applied to.

"Yes!" I smile. "I remember you. It's been a while. Sorry to be so standoffish. I'm just trying to be extra careful about things right now," I explain as I unlock the door and let him in.

"Absolutely. From what your father said on the phone, it sounds like you can't be too careful. I'm just glad my team and I can help with everything."

"We appreciate it so much. You're welcome to check in on things. I assume you know where everything is."

"Yes. I've got a map here and some notes." He holds up his phone.

"I'm just making dinner at the moment, but please let me know before you go."

"That sounds perfect. Thank you, and again I'm sorry for interrupting," he apologizes again, and I shake my head to let him know he's fine before he takes off down the hall to check the cameras and security alarm.

When I return to the kitchen, Lizzy's already got a bunch of the vegetable prep going and most of the spices we need pulled out of the cabinet. I take up my spot beside her and start working on the next steps.

"So?" she asks expectantly, her question returning me to our previous conversation.

"I'll talk to your dad about it. I can't make any promises, but if nothing else, I can premake a batch of cupcakes you all can take down with you."

"Okay. But I want you there." I can hear the disappointment in her voice.

"We'll see," I say, and we return to fixing up our taco dinner until we're interrupted by James again.

"Hey," I greet him as he stands at the edge of the kitchen.

"All done. Everything is up and running and looks great."

"Thank you. I appreciate you checking everything. I know my dad and brother will be relieved."

"The man of the house too, I assume?" James's brow furrows in question.

"Yes. Him too."

"Cooper's great. We've done some work with the stadium

lately to help them harden some of their offices and tech equipment just in case. You never know in this era. But we've done a few trainings with the players so they're ready."

"Oh, I didn't know that. Well, that's good. Such a small world."

"It is. Speaking of..." He reaches into his pocket and extracts a business card. "Here's my information. My personal number is on there. If you need anything, day or night, you just call or text me. I loved working for your dad, and I just want to be sure you're taken care of while you guys work through this. Anything at all, just get in touch."

"Thank you." I wipe my hands and take the card from him, following him down the hall as we walk to the front door. "If anything comes up, I'll definitely be in touch. Between us, I think this is all a lot of overreaction for something relatively minor. But I guess it can't hurt."

"It never hurts to be extra cautious." He gives me a soft smile. "Glad we can give you all some more peace of mind. Like I said, anytime. Have a good night!"

"You too!" We say our goodbyes, and I head back to the kitchen. I'd never admit it to any of the men in my life, but I am secretly grateful they care enough about me to be this protective. I know I'm lucky to have so many people looking out for me, including Cooper.

28

ooper

THANKS TO LIZZY practically begging Trix every hour, on the hour, for the last week, Trix has agreed to go with us to the lake house for the summer family trip. I can tell she's not thrilled about having to see Rob though. I'm not excited about having to worry about how he treats her while we're there, not to mention having to pretend we're just friends for everyone else's sake is going to make it difficult. Though we've had plenty of practice with Lizzy being home from summer camp and having to retreat to our separate rooms every night she's not at her mom's.

Not having her curled up next to me at night or being able to walk up behind her and kiss my way down her neck when I get home from practice has been torture. But it's been fun watching her and Lizzy play video games and dragging them both into the pool a couple of nights a week. Fuck, even just grocery shopping with the three of us has been an adventure. So while I'm wary about the circumstances, I'm still thrilled she's coming.

A thing I grow to regret the first night we're there, and Rob and his girlfriend arrive.

Rob's eyes fall on Trix when he walks in the door. There's a flash of panic in them before it's erased by a schooled attempt to remain looking calm. Then I hear the sound of kids in the distance. I can't tell whether they're laughing or fighting by the sound, but a moment later, they're tumbling in the door behind him. I watch them navigate the kitchen, running and jumping through the hall and into the living room. I can tell Trix is trying to do the math of how they fit here, and it's quickly answered when their mom, his girl-friend, comes in.

"Bailey! Heather! Knock it off and take off your shoes!" she yells at them, and they come to a halt, one of them pouting at her before she complies with the order. Then she turns to Rob. "Babe, did you bring their bag in already? I didn't see it in the back."

"Yeah, I've got it right here." He pats the duffel hanging over his shoulder, and I watch in real time as Trix comes to the conclusion this is his new girlfriend and he's playing caretaker to her kids. She blinks and pulls her glass up to her lips, looking like she's doing her best to fix her face.

My mom and dad hear the commotion and join us in the room. They're busy greeting the kids and Rob's girlfriend, Carly. Trix looks frozen, and I wish I could put my arm around her right now and claim her as mine because I can see Rob watching her and Carly trying to make sense of who she is and why she's here. The tension in the room mounting the whole time.

Carly finally gives up wondering and reaches out a hand.

"Hi! I'm Carly. Rob's girlfriend. Are you here with Cooper?"

She flashes a grin to me before she turns it back on Trix. Before she can even answer, Rob interjects.

"Yeah. This is Beatrix. She's a family friend." Rob's eyes meet Trix's, and I can see her avoid them deftly and turn her smile back on Carly. I've dragged her into this mess and now he's going to use it to belittle her.

Fuck that. All our careful plans go out the window because I'm not having Trix dismissed.

"We're actually dating now." The words come out before I can stop them.

Trix's eyes flash to mine, and I see Lizzy look puzzled for a moment before an understanding grin spreads across her face. I get a smirk and a nose scrunch that tells me she knows what I'm doing. My parents both flash a look at us and my mom's eyebrow raises in question but drops when I flash a bright smile.

Trix, on the other hand, has more trouble recovering. Rob's eyes land hard on me, but I refuse to meet them. Ignoring him to watch her look flustered and recover with her own smile as she looks at Carly again.

"It's nice to meet you." Trix takes Carly's hand and shakes it.

"Oh, I'm so excited Cooper brought a girlfriend. We'll have so much fun!" Carly's free hand waves in the air in excitement, and the ring on her finger sparkles in the light. The kind of blinding light that my mother doesn't miss. Suddenly Trix and I aren't the most interesting thing in the room anymore.

"Something to tell us?" my mom asks Carly, and she immediately looks guilty, pulling both her hands back and looking to Rob.

"We planned to tell you at dinner." Rob looks awkward as fuck. He shifts on his feet and his brow furrows as he looks between our parents for their reaction. They won't be thrilled with that development but they also won't let it show if they can help it.

"I forgot to take it off before we got out of the car. The kids were so excited to get in, and I got distracted. I'm sorry," Carly apologizes as much to Rob as anyone else in the room. Interesting that Rob wanted her to hide it.

"Don't apologize." My mom regains her usual inner calm. "But I do need to see the ring. It looks gorgeous." She reaches her hand out and takes Carly's in hers.

Trix takes a step backward and then several more in my direction. Her face is calm, with a serene smile, and her hands are clasped like she's witnessing the most beautiful thing she's ever seen. But I can see in her eyes that it's killing her. She loved my mom, and the two of them spent a lot of time in the kitchen together during holidays and the summer. My mom used to tell Trix that she was going to get her grandmother's wedding band someday, and she couldn't wait for her to have it. So I can imagine that this feels like a gut punch, even if she doesn't want the marriage or the man anymore.

I reach out and grab her hand, squeezing it tight so she knows I'm here. At least my little verbal outburst claiming her meant I could do that much for her.

"I can't believe you didn't tell us!" My mom shoots Rob an admonishing look, and he looks sheepish.

"Should we tell them the rest?" Carly grins at him.

"Uh..." Rob's eyes land on Trix and then hit the floor in quick succession before he looks back up at Carly and smiles. "Sure. Why not?"

I can tell in my gut that whatever is coming next is going to hurt Trix, even if I don't know why.

"We're pregnant!" Carly announces brightly.

My mom squeals with delight and even my dad lets out a little yelp of surprise, patting Rob on the back as my mom pulls Carly tight into a hug. Lizzy, meanwhile, looks like she might throw up. I give her a look, telling her to fix her face. A thing she does after briefly sticking her tongue out at me.

But then I feel Trix's hand squeeze mine again, and when I look at her, she's still smiling. The picture of serenity minus the tears forming in her eyes, and now I feel a punch in my gut. She blinks a moment later, clearing the sadness from them, and turns and smiles at me.

"I just, uh... I forgot something in the car. I'm going to run and get it. Probably a good time anyway since it's a family moment." She squeezes me again and then slinks around the kitchen counter toward the door.

I do my due diligence, congratulating my brother and the mother- and-bride-to-be before I go after Trix, motioning for Lizzy to stay when she starts to follow. Lizzy thinks this is all for show, but if I'm about to find out that Trix is still hung up on Rob, we're both going to be distraught in a way that'll be hard to cover up. And I don't want Lizzy hurting for both of us.

WHEN I CATCH up to her, she's outside, past my truck and halfway down the hill to the lake, leaning on one of the old trees my brother and I used to climb when we were younger. I walk up slowly, trying to make sure that whatever questions I ask are thoughtful ones. Reminding myself that even if something's there between us now, she had a whole life with him first.

"Trix?" I say her name softly when I walk up to her, touching her shoulder gently, but she still startles.

She blinks away tears that fall down her cheeks when she turns to look at me.

"Oh. Hey, Coop." She brushes at them and forces a smile.

"You okay?"

"I'm fine. That was just... a lot. I'm sorry. This is ridiculous." She swipes one last tear off the corner of her eye and wipes her hands on her dress.

"It's okay to not be fine, Trix. I wasn't expecting that either.

It was a shock, and I didn't even date him." I try to force a smile myself for her sake.

She shifts uneasily on her feet, staring off at the lake.

"I probably shouldn't have come out here with you guys. I just didn't want to let Lizzy down, and I've gotten so used to being around you all the time. I didn't think about how weird this would be. I mean, I did... but it was a fleeting thought, and then I said what the hell, you know? But it's weird. He's definitely weirded out. Your parents are probably wondering what the hell is going on that I dated one of their sons, and now I'm after the other one. And Lizzy. Oh god!" She puts her hand over her mouth and looks at me wide-eyed.

"Lizzy knows why I did it."

"Why did you do it?"

"I'm not letting him dismiss you like you're some random person who doesn't matter to this family. Just because he didn't want you in it, doesn't mean the rest of us don't miss having you."

"You're so sweet, Coop. I don't know how I got so lucky to have someone like you in my corner." Her eyes soften, and the tears threaten to return.

"You're pretty great to have in a corner too." I wrap my arms around her shoulders and pull her into a hug.

"I can't stop crying, apparently." She smiles up at me, laughing as she fidgets, blinking away another set of tears that grow fat and roll down her cheeks, staining a trail down them.

"I'd kiss them away if I could, but I don't know if that makes sense anymore."

She frowns. "What do you mean?"

"You seem like you're pretty broken up over my brother right now. I'm not trying to make you feel bad; I'm just... trying to figure out where that leaves me."

"Oh, god, Coop... no. It's not that. Not at all." She shakes her head violently and takes my hand, squeezing it. "I don't miss

Rob. Carly seems nice. I just... him lying about it, who I was, and then finding out he lied about a lot of other things. Just felt like a gut punch."

"What else did he lie about?"

She takes a deep breath, staring out at the water for another beat before she looks back up at me.

"I can't have children. I didn't know for sure until early last year, and then they confirmed it. I was upset, but I rallied. I figured we could find a way to make it work. Maybe adopt or foster. But Rob was insistent that he didn't want to. He said he didn't want to raise another man's kids. Didn't have any interest in adoption. That it was a hard line for him. That he'd rather not have kids if that was the choice and wasn't sure if he wanted them at all.

"I wasn't ready to shut the door like that. I wanted him to at least consider adopting. Maybe take some classes and do research, but he got so pissed. I mean, you know we were always on and off. I went back to stay with Xander more times than I can count, especially when his team was doing badly. But that argument... That did us in. We'd been talking engagement rings and a future, and then he told me he couldn't marry me."

"And now he's in my parents' lake house with two future stepkids and one on the way."

"That's a pretty short timeline to change your mind on such a life-changing thing," she says softly, her shoulders falling. "So it was just me he didn't want kids with. I guess he thought I'd make a bad mother."

"Trix. No fucking way. I've seen you with Lizzy enough to know you'd be a fucking fantastic mom. Don't let this get in your head like that."

"I'm just... embarrassed." She sighs and stares out into the distance. "I can't imagine what your parents are thinking. How awkward this all is. It's obvious he doesn't want me here, and now we have to keep up a whole lie about us dating."

"It's not entirely a lie. We've been on some dates." I smile at her and tuck a piece of hair that's drifted into her face back behind her ear. "We went to the fair. Did some stargazing. There was definitely a pinic in the woods where I had a fantastic fucking meal." I'm hoping I can get her to smile at least.

"Oh my god." Her cheeks heat, and she shakes her head, laughing despite herself. "I don't think we should tell your parents about that one."

"Yeah." I cringe a little before I grin again. "Maybe we skip that one, but I'm more than happy to tell them about the others. Happy to fill Rob in on how much fun we've had this summer."

"You're evil." She says it like an accusation, but the look in her eyes when she turns them to me makes my heart somersault in my chest. "But I appreciate you more than you know. The dates. This summer. What you did in there. All of it. I hope you know that."

"I'm enjoying every second I get with you."

"Me too. You're a good one, Coop." She studies my face, and I run my fingers down her jaw before I kiss her softly.

"You're the good one. Thank you for coming here and putting up with all of this for Lizzy's sake. I know she pressured you to come, and I'm sorry it means you have to deal with all of this."

"It's okay. I wanted to be here for her, and honestly, I—" she stops midsentence and looks up at me again and then shakes her head.

"Honestly, what?" I ask.

"I've gotten used to our little... routine, I guess? I think I would have missed you. That probably sounds silly." She gives a little ground, and I feel my heart kick up in response.

"It doesn't sound silly. I would have missed you too. I'm honestly secretly glad my kid twisted your arm."

"Me too. And kind of glad you told everyone we're dating so I can still kiss you." She leans up on her tippy toes to kiss me again, and I wrap my arms around her, but her eyes suddenly flash with awareness. "Shit. What about Lizzy?"

"I'll explain it to her later. I think she's as suspicious of me and you as I am of her and Billy though, so I might be coming up on an inquisition soon anyway."

"Well, I can't say I envy you that."

I kiss her one more time and then eye the door to the house when I see a figure moving in front of it. I can guess at least some of them have peered out to see what we're doing down here.

"Think you're ready to go back in?" I ask her softly after I kiss her one more time.

"Yes. I'm ready." She holds out her hand for mine, and I take it, smiling at the fact that at least for a little while I get to pretend she's mine in all the ways that count.

29

B *eatrix*

THE NEXT MORNING, I'm in the kitchen prepping the cupcakes for Lizzy's birthday. Cooper and Rob's parents have taken off with Lizzy and the rest of the kids for the day, shopping and hitting up some of her favorite places in town before they come back here for dinner. Her grandparents are making her favorite meal, and I promised to make cupcakes for her. Cooper is still in bed, and Rob and his fiancée are having a leisurely breakfast, so I'm up whipping batter together while I preheat the oven and soften the butter for the frosting.

I'm already feeling better than yesterday, but my heart is still piecing together exactly how to feel in the wake of all these revelations. It's not that I want Rob back or that I still have dreams about getting married anymore. It's the fact that they got engaged so quickly when it had taken Rob well over a year to even discuss the topic with me. That he'd dragged his feet even after we said we wanted to get married. That no ring ever materialized, and arguments over that, among other things, led to us breaking up and then repairing things more than once.

I wasted so much time on a man who wasn't sure about me. A man who ultimately didn't want me, and I feel foolish for having done it. For having stood by hoping for something more. Something I was never going to get. Especially when I can see how easily he was able to commit to someone when he was sure. It makes me wonder whether I was part of the problem rather than it just being a difference between what we wanted in life—if the same problems will haunt me in future relationships too.

"Bea?" Rob's voice stops me mid-stir, and I'm thankful that I've managed not to actually cry while thinking about all this because the last thing I want is him thinking I'm shedding any tears over him.

"Yep?" I glance back over my shoulder to let him know I heard him.

I heard the back door that leads down to the water open and shut a few minutes ago, and I thought maybe he and Carly had gone out for the day.

"Can we talk for a minute?"

Fuck. I do not want to talk, but I don't want to look petulant either.

"Sure." I stop the mixer and wipe my hands on my apron as I turn to him.

"I'm sorry about last night. It was a little spontaneous. She was excited. I was hoping to warn you first when I saw you here."

"You don't owe me a warning. We've been over for a while."

"I know but... it's awkward with you being here. I didn't know Cooper was bringing you along."

"Yes. I'm sorry he didn't give you a warning. It's been busy for us. I didn't think about how awkward it could be when Lizzy asked me to come for her birthday. I just thought it would be fun to be at the lake house with her again."

"Oh. Lizzy." He smiles softly, and then it fades. "Yeah, she does love you. I didn't mean you made it awkward, just that it was given everything. I hope you're okay." His concern grates on my nerves because it feels more like he's probing to see if there's any jealousy on my part under the surface.

"It's fine, Rob. Truly. Happy for both of you."

"Thanks..." He stares down at the floor, and I get the feeling something else is coming. "She doesn't know about us. That we were together, and I don't really want to explain. She thinks of you as Cooper's girlfriend, and I'm fine with her believing that. I don't want any drama with her being happy right now and Lizzy's birthday, so I don't want to explain. Do you think we could keep that between us?"

I blink. Keep several years of my life to myself. I suppose it's possible, but more than a little difficult to constantly remember. Especially when I'm surrounded by people who only know me because we were together first.

"I already talked to my parents about it. We all agree it makes sense not to bring it up to keep the peace. For Lizzy." Rob adds as though he's trying to convince me.

"Okay," I agree. "I don't see why it would come up anyway."

I mean, I'm not exactly dying to reveal to his fiancée that I'm the former girlfriend and all the extra awkwardness that would create. But something about the request cuts and irritates all at the same time. Just not enough for me to want to argue.

"Are you really?" Rob asks after a beat.

"Am I what really?"

"Involved with my brother."

"I've been staying with him while I work for the Chaos for the summer. We've always been friendly."

"Cooper's *friendly* with a lot of people."

I don't miss the tone in his voice when he says it.

"I don't really think it's appropriate for us to discuss this." I'm growing increasingly uncomfortable with the direction this is going. What Cooper and I have might not be what he and Carly have, but I still feel protective over it. The last thing I want is to be discussing the details of it with him.

Rob makes a face I can't quite read, but it clears a moment later, and he looks down at the bowl in front of me.

"Cupcakes?"

"Yes." I'm happy to change the subject. I'd be even better if he'd go find Carly and leave me alone.

"You did always make the best." Without asking, he dips his finger in the batter and takes some, grinning as he tastes it. "Can't wait to have one later. Hitting the lake with Carly. See you at dinner."

I glare at his back as he leaves the room. Even if I was sad over our breakup, I wouldn't be after that. Rob has a way of doing the smallest things that irritate me to no end. Like putting his grubby hands in my batter. I dump it into the trash and go back to get the ingredients to start over, cleaning the measuring cups in the sink and pulling the eggs out again.

I mutter to myself as I do it, cursing the fact that I was ever stupid enough to date him or waste any of my life on him. That's the part that still hurts. That I can't have those years back to do something better with my life. Have some of the adventures I'm now trying to cram into one summer.

By the time I've got the cupcakes in the oven, waiting on the timer, I'm wondering why I came out here. This is Rawlings family time, and I'm not a Rawlings. As much as I want to celebrate with Lizzy and as much as I like being around Cooper, I'm an interloper. An interloper and now an accomplice to Rob not telling the truth to his fiancée. Something that makes me more uncomfortable the more I think about it too. This situation is exactly why it could never be anything else and is probably a good reason for me to clear out earlier altogether. I can probably get a flight back tonight. Give Lizzy her cupcakes and her present and then head off to go home. Get back to work.

When the timer for the cupcakes dings, I'm set on the idea. All I need to do is work out the details. I pull out the cupcakes from the oven and set them on the rack just before I hear the sound of bare feet padding along the floorboards. I look up to see a half-awake Cooper making his way into the kitchen. A lazy yawn is followed by the sweetest grin as he surveys the mess I'm making.

"I'm going to clean up." I promise.

"And I'm going to help," he answers, kissing the side of my cheek as he peers down at the cupcakes. "Morning, Trix."

"Morning." I offer a smile in return, but I'm distracted by how good he looks, by how good he makes me feel. By how attached I've gotten to having him around. It's probably another sign that I need to be careful with my heart.

"Already busy in the kitchen so early? You know you're supposed to be on vacation too, right?" He shakes his head as he opens the fridge to get some iced coffee.

"I was going to talk to you about that. I think I'm actually going to head back to Cincy."

"What?" He turns abruptly, the container of cold brew still in his hand.

"I think Madison could use my help, and after everything, I still feel a bit awkward here, you know?"

He sets the coffee on the counter, and his brow wrinkles.

"Did he say something to you? If he did..." Cooper's eyes harden with the question.

"No. I mean, yes? Sort of? He apologized for last night, but he asked me not to tell Carly that he and I used to date."

"He asked you to lie?"

"A lie of omission, yes."

"That's fucked. She's going to find out."

"Yes, but I also don't want to be a source of drama."

"You're not the drama. He is. Between not telling anyone he was engaged to the pregnancy. That's a lot to keep from everyone."

"Maybe she wanted to tell everyone in person. She didn't know his ex-girlfriend would be here."

"You're too nice for your own good sometimes, Trix."

"I just don't want to cause trouble. Especially not for your parents. I think they feel awkward about everything, too, and they were obviously uncomfortable last night. I doubt Rob is happy I'm here, and if his fiancée knew, I know she wouldn't be. It puts you and Lizzy in the middle, and it's her birthday. I think I'm going to finish the cupcakes, say happy birthday to her, and catch a flight back."

"Lizzy wants you here and so do I."

"I know, but I don't want to ruin her birthday. If someone slips and says something, and Carly finds out? Where if I'm not here there's no reason to mention me. I can give her her present and cupcakes when she gets back this afternoon and catch a ride to the airport after."

"If you don't want to be here, I won't force you to stay. I don't want you to be unhappy or feel awkward."

"It's awkward for you too."

"Why?"

"You know why." I give him a meaningful look.

"Because you like fucking me better?" he asks bluntly, and my eyes dart to the door even though I know no one is home to hear.

"I don't think he needs to hear that."

"Why not? I'll tell him. I wish he'd ask. I'd fucking love to tell him."

"He already asked about us."

"What did you say?"

"I dodged the specifics and just said you've been letting me stay with you, and he knows you and I have always been friendly."

"You don't want him to know details then?" Cooper sounds like he doesn't love the idea.

"I don't want to cause any drama when your parents just found out that they're going to be getting a grandchild and planning a wedding. It's a family vacation, and I don't belong here." I don't care if Rob knows. Honestly, I might be with Cooper on wishing he had details. I just don't want the fall out if Rob loses his temper.

"Fuck that. You're family to me and Lizzy. You belong here."

"It's fine, Coop. It's just there's a lot going on here, and I don't want anything to ruin Lizzy's birthday."

"I don't want to ruin her birthday either. You leaving... she wouldn't want that. We can all be adults about everything for a few days. Don't run off." Cooper takes an insistent tone.

"I'm not running off."

"You're allowed to be upset about the engagement and the baby, Trix."

"What?" I stop short and look up at him. "You think that's what this is about? He and I have been over for a long time."

"But they haven't been together very long. After everything he put you through. What you told me last night and then seeing them like that. No one's going to judge you for being upset. Least of all me."

"I'm not upset about Rob. I don't have regrets there. We didn't make sense. If he's happy now and ready for things he wasn't before, good for them. I'm happy for them. I just wish I could have the time back I wasted on him. The time I spent trying to make the two of us work, trying to compromise when it was never going to work out. You're smart not to date seriously. If you really think you want to now, just be careful who you invest your time in." I want to kill any ideas Cooper has about me still pining over Rob, because the only man I could even imagine wanting anything with right now is the one standing in front of me. I just worry that he might not want anything more than what we have.

"The two of you together might have been a mistake, but I don't think the time you spent with him was a waste. I wouldn't have you in my life if you hadn't been with him. And I hate what he did to you, the way he made you doubt yourself, the way he made you cry. But that I got to know you? That Lizzy got to find someone she likes so much when she's so shy most of the time? I'm so fucking grateful for that. I'm sure that makes me a selfish bastard because I only got all the good parts, and you had to suffer through the bad ones. I'm sorry for that, but it's the truth."

Tears prick at my eyes and my heart tumbles on his confession. Hope blooms in my chest, and I don't know whether to nurture it or stomp it out.

"I'm grateful for you and Lizzy too. That part wasn't a waste at all. I just know that all of this has to come to an end soon, too, and this trip feels like a window into a life I don't belong in. That I'm playing at being part of this family when I'm not."

"Whatever happens, you're always part of this family, Trix. My parents adore you. They're going to accept whoever Rob picks because he's the youngest, and he can do no wrong. But they love you. They wanted to see you two get married. They were thrilled when they heard you were coming. Fuck, I think they were hoping you might play homewrecker to his new relationship. Any awkwardness you felt last night was because they're not fans of that whole thing—not because you're here. You and Lizzy always have your thing. And as far as you and me..." Cooper's chest rises with a deep breath, and then his eyes lift to meet mine, a seriousness there I've only seen when he's worried or nervous. "This ends when you want it to end. I'm in for as long as you'll let me."

"Because flour stains and jam hands turn you on?" I laugh

as I try to wipe the jam I've just noticed on my finger on the apron I'm wearing. Awkwardly trying to distract myself because when he talks to me like this, I fall to pieces. All I can think about is how much I want him, and how someway, somehow, there has to be a version of us where it doesn't end badly.

"Yes, honestly, because it reminds me of you playing that list in my kitchen." He gives me a teasing grin.

"Oh god. Don't remind me."

"Why not?" He tilts my chin up and kisses me softly. "It's not like I can forget. Best day of my life."

30

C *ooper*

I KISS my way down her jaw, and my lips are at her throat a moment later. The way she reacts under my touch is like a drug. I'm dragged under by how much she wants me. My hand slips up the inside of her thigh, pushing her skirt up with the movement.

"Coop, we shouldn't," she whispers, but she spreads her legs wider for me and arches her back when I brush my knuckles over her through the cotton.

"I need you. Too many days I've had to go without you. We're home alone, aren't we?" I glance around the room to make sure I'm right in my assumption.

"Yes. Rob and Carly went out on the lake."

"Good." That means we have the place to ourselves, and I can have her any way she'll let me.

"But I don't know for how long," she warns as I back her up

against the vintage sideboard that sits next to the picture window.

"I'm sure he's giving her the tour, if he hasn't yet. He loves to brag about this place like it's his."

"I remember." She laughs but it makes me want to replace that memory with a better one.

"Then it's his fault if he stumbles in early." I grab her around her waist and set her up on the sideboard.

Getting to play like I'm hers instead of the summer fun we've been having sounds even better to me. I know I should be above wanting to rub it in his face that she's mine now, but I can't help the bit of rivalry that lingers. Especially when I remember the last time I heard her in this house.

"We should probably work on this whole relationship thing. Make sure they know how devoted I am to my girl. So lovesick that I can't even make it back to the room when I need her."

"Coop." There's a sharp inhale of breath as I toy with her and she says my name. "We really shouldn't."

"But you want to?"

"I always want you." That confession elicits one of my own. One I start just as soon as I confirm she's as wet as I like before I brush my thumb over her clit.

"Me too. For a long time." Her nails bite into my shoulders as I slip my fingers inside her and start to move.

"Since the blue sundress?" She looks at me like we're both in on some inside joke. Except she doesn't know the depth of it yet.

"Since the blue sundress and that night."

"That night?" Her brow furrows with the question

"When we came back, after dinner and cards and all that..." I grab her gently by the jaw and tilt her chin up, kissing her throat again while I wonder if I'm crazy for telling her the next bit.

"You and Rob must have made up. You were in his room and it was next to mine. I could hear you. Not him, just you. I was lying in bed and it was pushed up against the same wall as yours. I could hear almost every sound you made."

Her lashes flutter as I loosen my grip, and her eyes fall on me. She rolls her lower lip between her teeth.

"Oh..." I see the recognition in her eyes and the bob of her throat. "I didn't know you could hear me."

I kiss my way down the side of her jaw, and she spreads wider for me, tipping her hips as I lean in to kiss her. When I break it, there's a soft moan from her lips, and it goes straight to my cock.

"You sounded so fucking good. So fucking pretty with those little moans you were making. The way you kept softly cursing. I closed my eyes, and it was like you were making them for me. I kept wondering what it would be like if it was me. My hands... My tongue..."

"Cooper... I'm going to come like this if you don't stop," she warns, her fingers hooking into the top of my sweats, and she tugs on them like she's desperate for me.

"I don't have a condom on me. I have to go get it if you don't want—" I start to move to get it, but she halts my progress.

"I want it." She tugs me back toward her. "Besides, we don't have time to waste and I need you." She glances out the window.

It's all the permission I need, and I finish the job she's started on my sweats, tearing them off. I grab her to pull her forward on the sideboard, bringing her to the edge. I slide inside of her a moment later, and her legs wrap around my waist as she gasps a sound of approval into the crook of my neck.

She feels like fucking heaven—like I'd offer everything I have and then some just for another taste of her. I'm so fucking gone for her, and I don't even know where to start to begin processing that.

I fuck her slowly at first, trying to keep the pace that I had when it was my fingers instead of my cock. But the way she rolls her hips to counter me and the sound she's making have me more desperate than I know what to do with. I fuck her faster, and she begs for more until we're rattling the sideboard underneath us, each time I thrust is punctuated by the sound of it slamming against the wall. It's going to leave marks, but I don't care. Not as long as I can leave my mark on her and listen to her beg for more.

"Oh fuck. Your cock is so perfect, Coop..." She whimpers, and I can feel her clench down on me as she starts to come, countering me with her own rhythm. Her nails scrape their way down my back, and her lips press against my earlobe as she moans her release.

It takes me over the edge, and I'm coming hard, spilling everything I have inside her as I grip her ass to hold her still. I want her full of me.

"Fucking hell, Trixie. I love the way you take me when I fill you up like this. Can't fucking get enough of it," I whisper as I come down from the high of fucking her almost as hard as I came in the first place. I'm fucking wiped, breathing heavy with a sheen of sweat across my back and arms. The A.C. hasn't kicked on yet, and the warm, humid air rolling in off the water is just enough to make a mess of us. The same way I have.

"Didn't mean to give you a workout on vacation." She offers a joke to break the silence.

She smiles up at me as she starts to come down from her own orgasm. Her fingertips dancing little circles over my skin, starting with my shoulders and down over my chest. Her eyes fall heavy on the place where we're still connected, and I love the way she likes to watch us.

"I don't mind this kind." I pull out of her slowly, still slick as fuck from how wet she was and how much of me she took. Her eyes eat up every inch of my cock, and I could go again just thinking about the way her mouth feels. The way she knows how to use her tongue for every little thing I like.

I'm hit by a desire for more, and I slide my fingers inside her, pumping in and out as she leaks around them. I press them to her lips a moment later, and she parts for me, letting me slip them inside. Her tongue works over the pads of my fingers, her eyes shuttering, and I brush my damp fingers over her lips and down her chin as she finishes tasting us.

"That's my filthy girl. Fucking love watching you enjoy yourself like that."

She grins at me, flashing me a knowing look and then starts to move as I pull my sweats back into place.

"Wait. Just a little longer. I want to enjoy this view. You thoroughly fucked on top of this sideboard with all your fresh cupcakes around you and jam on your apron." I grin and grab one of the cupcakes as she gently swats at me and rolls her eyes.

"Those aren't even iced yet," she protests.

"Yeah, but they have jam filling, and it's delicious," I argue, biting into one, and then my grin spreads. "Speaking of."

Her eyes light when she sees me lean forward again, dipping my fingers into what's left of us on the sideboard and spreading it over the top of the cupcake before I take the last bite. I hear the little intake of breath on her part and the way she bites her lip like I've just scandalized her.

"Don't want to waste something that good." I wink at her, and she shakes her head, a laugh tumbling out. "Plus now, it's iced."

"You're depraved."

"And you like it. Enough to be sprawled out like this in my family's dining room."

"Shit." She jumps into action, standing and straightening herself out. She pulls her skirt back into position and tames her hair before she wipes her hands and catches a quick glimpse of herself in the mirror across the room. "They could be home any minute, and the kitchen's a mess."

"I've got it. Go get your shower. Just hurry, or I'll be forced to join you."

"That's not the threat you think it is." She stands on her tiptoes, kissing my cheek before she smiles at me and takes off down the hall. Something about it, the affection I see reflected in her eyes, makes my heart skip. It's not much. The slightest bit of a flutter in my chest, but it's enough to throw my world off its axis as she walks away.

It's more than just want with her. More than just our mutually beneficial relationship. It's a downright need that's flowing through my veins right now. Need to make her my girl. Need for everyone to know it. Which is a big fucking problem since she seemingly doesn't need anyone, and I never have before either.

31

B eatrix

"So how long have you and Cooper been together?" Carly asks me as we grab some drinks and snacks before we head outside to watch the fireworks the next night. Cooper's parents took Lizzy and Carly's kids into town to have front-row seats and hit some of the fair booths for treats. But the view from the deck is still pretty good, and there are two big outdoor couches and a fire pit we can all sit around. Plus, Cooper had promised additional benefits to having some alone time after the show. I smile before I remember I'm supposed to be answering a question.

I'm still hating the way I'm meant to be cozying up to Carly like another fellow Rawlings' brother girlfriend. I wish I could find a way to tell her the whole truth without causing more drama, but Rob's made sure that it would be awkward as hell.

"Not very long. Just a month or so."

"Really? That's it? You guys seem... wow. I'm just surprised."

"We knew each other before. We were friends. Seeing other people, you know how it is."

"I do. It was the same with me and Rob. I liked him from afar. His friend has been dating one of my friends for forever. But he always had a girlfriend. She never came out with us, so I never met her, but when they broke up, I figured it was my chance to shoot my shot, you know?"

"Yes. I get that." Is this what hell is like? Forced to talk to your ex's new girlfriend about their meet-cute like you're besties in a bar bathroom? I mean, I don't dislike her, nominally speaking, she seems like the kind of person I would get along well with. It's just very awkward forming a friendship in this particular scenario.

"Need any help?" Cooper comes inside just as I'm trying to gather up everything onto trays, slightly worried about whether I can do it without dropping anything.

"I think we have it," Carly answers, overly ambitious in her own endeavors. "I was just telling Bea here how cute the two of you are. I can't believe you've only been dating for a month."

"Well, I mean... When you know someone's your person, you know, right?" Cooper gives her his most charming smile as he comes up behind me, tugging my ponytail gently and kissing me softly on the mouth.

"That's what I was just saying to her about me and Rob!" Carly laughs, but I'm too caught up gazing into Cooper's eyes when he lets my hair go to answer. His eyes search mine for a moment until we hear someone clear their throat.

Rob's standing on the other side of the kitchen, his eyes burning into Cooper and me until Carly turns around and greets him happily, and his scowl fades to a furrowed brow.

"Fuck," I whisper as I return to gathering up the ingredients.

Cooper wraps an arm around my waist and leans over me until his lips brush the shell of my ear.

"Oh, I will fuck you later. We can make it loud enough for him to listen to if you want." He says it low enough so only I can hear before he grabs a marshmallow and pops it into his mouth, smacking my ass as he walks away and winking at his brother before he grabs some of the drinks and heads for the door.

I can see Carly giggling and whispering something to Rob out of the corner of my eye, so I quickly finish my prep and hurry after Cooper. I'm glad Rob's happy, and Carly seems like an absolute sweetheart, but this trip has met my awkwardness quota for the entire year.

BEFORE THE FIREWORKS EVEN START, we've demolished a round of s'mores and had some sweet wine and sangria. The wind coming off the lake is a little cold tonight, and Cooper's brought out a blanket for us. He pulls me into his lap and tosses the blanket over both of us before he settles back on the pile of outdoor pillows he's created at the back side of the couch.

There's been a subtle, almost imperceptible vibe between the two of them ever since Rob walked into the kitchen. It's like they're pacing around each other waiting for the other to make a wrong step. Cooper, for his part, seems more than amused by the development of getting to play my doting boyfriend in front of Carly than anything else.

When I look over at Carly, she's lying in Rob's lap, already softly breathing like she's asleep. I imagine being a mom to two rambunctious girls is a lot. I'd probably be sneaking naps in whenever I could, and I smile a little at her for having the chance to have a night off. The more we talked tonight, the more I think I like her. She just has unfortunate taste in men, not that I can judge. My eyes shift to the mistake in question. Rob's half-asleep, too, his eyes struggling to stay open in a way that makes me think he'll be out cold soon.

There's a distant boom though that draws my attention to the sky. Brilliant red illuminates it, followed in quick succession by white and blue. A moment later, there's a barrage of starry fireworks, one right after another, making the dark, navy-blue sky look like a brilliant backdrop.

"You're so pretty, Trixie. I love watching all those colors light up your eyes," Cooper whispers, wrapping an arm tight around me, and I lean back against his chest, looking up at him and smiling. The man gives me butterflies, and I can't help how much, in moments like this, I wish we could be something real. Something more than a secret summer fling while I hide out.

I run my hand down his thigh and watch the next round of fireworks light up the lake. His hand runs over the small sliver of skin that's been exposed between my shirt and the top of my shorts, and his thumb slips back and forth. It's an absent gesture, or so I think, until I feel his fingers creep under my shorts.

"I know I promised later, but I think I might be too impatient. Think you can be quiet enough to let the fireworks drown you out?" He grins.

"We shouldn't."

"Then tell me to stop," he says softly, his fingers creeping lower, dangerously close to the lace band of my panties. "Say, 'Please, don't make me come,' and I'll do whatever you want, Trix."

"Touch me," I dare him instead of telling him to stop because, apparently today, I don't care about rules.

He slips under the fabric of my panties, and his fingers brush over me, drawing circles over my skin until the pads of them get slick. He starts to massage my clit, and I bite down hard on my lower lip to keep from making any sort of noise.

The fireworks are just loud enough, and the two of them are a good ten-plus feet away from us on the other side of the fire pit, but it still feels dangerously close.

His fingers work me over in a slow rhythm. He takes his time working me up, and his breath against my neck and his heartbeat follow the same pattern. It doesn't take much for him to get me to the edge, the desperate way I feel for him and the proximity to my ex enough that I'm already ready for him to push me over it.

"Oh fuck. You're so sweet like this. You getting close for me?" he asks quietly.

"Yes," I whisper back. "Please." It's take everything I have not to writhe in his lap and draw more attention to us.

His fingers splay over my clit, the pads of them working the sides and then pulling in and circling to a tight heavy rhythm that has me gasping when the next firework explodes. I turn my head, burying half my face against Coop's T-shirt as I start to come hard.

"Let him hear you. I want him to know how well you come for me." Cooper's voice is husky and rough.

There's another loud boom, and I open my eyes to watch the firework explode at the same time I do. But instead of the brilliant flash of red in the sky, it's Rob's sharp blue eyes that are on me. My heart skips a beat and I gasp when Coop pinches my clit and gives me one last wave of pleasure in the process. I'm lost in it, too overwhelmed by how good it feels to care about the opinions of the audience.

"The sounds you make wreck me," Coop whispers before he slips his fingers into his mouth, and I nearly burst into flames. I can feel Rob watching us, the way he's working out what we've just done and the fact that Cooper knows my body well enough to get me off this easily.

"Fuck, you taste so sweet, Trix. You think you're ready for bed yet? Or you want to make me give you another round first?

Let me edge you a little this time." Cooper's voice is quiet but he kisses the side of my neck, and I feel the answering shiver down my spine.

"I'm ready for bed." Hoping we can sneak away for a quick round before his family returns from town.

When I stand, Cooper jumps up, grabbing me and tossing me over his shoulder as I giggle. The noise wakes Carly up, and she stirs, opening her eyes and giving us a sleepy smile. My eyes flash to Rob again of their own volition, and he looks furious, but Cooper playfully slaps my ass and carries me away before I can have another thought about him.

32

C ooper

WHEN I GO OUT to the kitchen to get us some water, Rob's there in the dark. The small nightlight Mom keeps plugged in under the cabinets is the only thing lighting the room. He looks up when he sees me, almost like he's been waiting for me to show up. He downs the last of his drink and pushes it across the table.

"That was some great acting with Bea tonight." His eyes lift, and there's a challenge in them.

"Acting?" I want to bait him, tell him he might not be able to recognize the real thing when he sees it on account of how many times she had to fake it for him. But I hold my tongue. Trix didn't want drama, and for her I'll try not to cause any.

"I assume she told you I wanted to keep the past in the past." He ignores my question.

"She mentioned it." I'm weary of where this is headed.

"So you thought you'd what? Take advantage of that? Press your luck?"

"Is it luck or advantage, do you think?" I taunt him. I know I shouldn't, but I can't help myself. That he's out here waiting to fight tonight is too much.

"I think you'd better keep your hands off her."

"I don't think you get to decide that."

"I think I do. Whatever the fuck that was out there, you don't do it again."

"It's a little late for that. My hands have been all over every square inch of her, reminding her of how perfect she is, even if there were people in her past too stupid to know it."

Rob stands and kicks his chair back. It slides across the floor, almost silently, and his nostrils flare.

"Stay the fuck away from her."

"Why? Having regrets now that you remember how much better she is than anything else you've ever even had a shot at having? Realizing you pissed it all away for nothing?"

"She's mine. Always was. Always will be. Just because we're not together anymore doesn't mean that changes. *You* can't change that no matter how hard you try, brother."

I can't help the laugh that rumbles out of me, and he hates it, pressing in closer to me from across the room.

"I can't change the fact she picked the wrong brother first. You're right there. But I can definitely do my best to help her pick which one she wants last. *Brother.*"

He moves to tackle me a moment later, and I dodge it. I always was faster than him, and I smirk at the fact that time hasn't changed it.

"I'm not fucking fighting you in this house. Lizzy's sleeping."

"Then let's take it outside." He shoves my chest, and I stumble backward.

"Fuck that. Act your fucking age for once in your life, Rob!"

His big beefy arm is around my neck a moment later, and despite a hard punch to his ribs and another to his kidney, he manages to drag me to the doorway before I can shove him off again. He slides the glass, and we end up pushing and shoving our way out through it. I'm just thankful there's no one to see us acting like children.

"I am acting my age. Why don't you fucking act like a brother instead of going after my ex?"

"I didn't go after her. She came to my city. Showed up at my stadium. Needed my help."

"And she just fell on your dick in the process?"

"No. She just realized I could give her all the things she'd been missing with you."

His face twists, and I think I've somehow managed to actually wound him. It seems to be confirmed when he charges toward me and slams us both into the dirt. We tumble for a moment, limbs tangled as we each try to best each other before we shove away again.

"It's fucked you would ever try. Fucked that you'd bring her here and rub it in my face." He pulls himself up to his feet again.

"Lizzy fucking wanted her here. I wanted her here. Fuck... our parents want her here. Had nothing to fucking do with you, and if you want blunt fucking honesty, it's you and your replacement girl who don't fucking belong." I try to brush the dirt off my knees as I glare at him.

"She's not a replacement girl."

"Which is why you ran to knock her up and put a ring on her finger."

"It was an accident that we're making the best of. You should be familiar with that. Yours is what... fourteen now?"

My fist collides with his mouth a second later, and he stumbles backward and trips to the ground. He wipes the blood where his lip is bleeding.

"You ever talk about Lizzy like that again, I'll make the damage permanent."

We stay like that for long minutes. Him staring at me silently, and then at last, he shakes his head and stands.

"You're right. That was fucked. But you're a piece of fucking shit for this. And for what? Just because you needed to get your dick wet, and she was there? She'll never pick you in the end. You might be able to give her the kid she wants, but you'll never be able to give her the life she wants. She wants the real thing. The ring. The marriage. The big house filled with family at the holidays. Someone her family respects. The only thing anyone knows you for off the field is how many women you've fucked. You're a rebound she'll just be embarrassed of someday."

My heart pounds in my ears. I want to hit him again. But not for what he said wrong this time. For what he said that hits too close to home. For what he might be right about, and I don't want to face.

"What is going on out here?" Trix whispers harshly, her voice just loud enough that the wind doesn't carry off the words.

I turn around, and she's closing the sliding door behind her, wrapping a cardigan tightly around her shoulders to help keep out the wind coming off the lake. Her silk sleep set shimmers in the dim light, and her eyes bounce between the two of us. Then she notices the blood smear across Rob's face, and her eyes widen.

"Oh my god!" She moves toward him out of instinct, and I don't miss the way he relaxes when she touches him. "Seriously. What is going on?"

She looks to me for answers, and I shake my head, pissed that she's touching him and annoyed he's created a scenario where he looks like the victim.

"Ask him what he said about Lizzy," I spit out, giving him a derisive look.

"Lizzy?" Her accusation turns to him, and she steps back.

"I shouldn't have said it. But he's out here bragging about fucking you."

Her lips flatline, and her eyes hit the ground like she's ashamed, and he smirks at me so subtly you'd almost miss it— if you weren't his sibling, you definitely would. But I recognize it. The one I got a million times growing up when he made me look like the fool in front of our parents.

"I'm going inside. Going to make sure we didn't wake anyone else up." I turn on my heel and head inside, my heart ricocheting around in my chest. If I've come this far with her to lose her now because I walked straight into his fucking trap, I don't know how I'll live with myself.

33

B eatrix

I WATCH Cooper storm back into the house, clearly pissed. Even once he's gone, the energy of his presence is still electric, still surrounding Rob and me as we stand out here in the late summer humidity. A frog croaks noisily in the distance, and heat lightning dashes across the sky before he says anything.

"He'll only hurt you. He'll play whoever he has to to get what he wants out of you, and then when you need him, he'll be nowhere to be found."

"Sounds familiar." I fold my arms over my chest.

Rob's jaw goes slack, and his eyes turn down, a deep sigh coming out of him.

"I fucked up a lot. I know that. I know you hate me for a lot of things, and I'm sure this week didn't help. But I do still care about you, Bea. I still want to see you happy."

"I don't hate you. I learned a lot about myself and what I

want in the future. I'm a little confused about your current situation given what you told me about kids that aren't yours, but it's also none of my business."

His shoulders sag, and he tries to roll them back again like he's aware he's wilting under this pressure.

"I started seeing her shortly after we broke up. She said and did all the right things."

It stings a little. The idea that she was capable of filling desires of his that I never could. But then I feel the same way, so I can't exactly blame him.

"So does Cooper."

"Which is why I'm trying to warn you." There's a sincerity in his eyes. Enough that I don't doubt that he thinks he's being the white knight right now, but I don't need or want it.

"I don't need any warnings. I know who Cooper is. He's not some guy I met at a bar."

"Who are *you* right now? Because that? Out here with him? That's not you. The Bea I knew—"

"The Bea you knew isn't the Bea standing here now. She's gone. No one stays the same forever, you of all people should know that."

"That's who you are now? Letting some guy finger fuck you in public?"

I hold my breath and bite my tongue for full seconds before I respond. I know it's jealousy making him lash out. I don't have the patience for it, but I also don't want to stoop to his level.

"We were in a private backyard under covers. But yes. This is who I am now. Someone who enjoys things in the moment and doesn't apologize for getting what she wants."

"My brother," he says bitterly.

"Yes. I want your brother. I enjoy every second I'm with him, and he makes me happy."

"So what, you wanted him when we were together too?"

"I wanted you until you wanted me to be less. Then I found someone who wanted me exactly the way I am." I shrug.

Rob makes a scoffing sound and shakes his head.

"He only wants more until he realizes where that ends. What you really want, and who he is? It doesn't work. He's not that guy, Bea. He's the guy who leaves you in the morning and fucks the next girl that night. He sure as fuck won't be able to deal with your family."

"He's already met my family, and he did just fine."

Rob's smile sharpens. "I'm sure your dad loved him."

"My dad likes him well enough. Cooper did an apology tour that wasn't his to make thanks to sharing your last name."

I see Rob's jaw tick, and he shakes his head, staring off into the distance.

"I know you're mad, Bea."

"I'm not mad. I'm tired. Standing outside in the middle of the night because you two are fighting like children."

"I just want him to stay away from you."

"It's not your decision to make. Go back inside to your fiancée, Rob." I turn to go inside, and his arm darts out, grabbing mine.

"Bea, please. I fucked up. I hurt you. I know all of this with Carly is hurting you, and I hate it. I can't fix those things, but I can stop you from getting hurt again if you'll just listen to me. I know you see a family with him. A future with him. But if he couldn't do it for Lizzy's mom, there's no way he can do it for anyone else. He loved her and couldn't make it work. There's a reason he's never had a real relationship since, and I don't want you to get hurt again. You deserve a good guy. One who treats you right. One who can make up for all the shit I fucked up. I don't want to see you alone, Bea. I just don't want to see you with him."

"I can take care of myself. Focus on you and your own future, Rob. Make sure you're making the right decisions for yourself because asking the rest of us to lie for you to your fiancée seems like a problem that should have all of your attention right now. She seems like a very sweet person, and I'd hate to watch her end up hurt too."

"Fine. Fuck him if you have to then. But don't fall in love with him."

I want to laugh at the audacity of him giving me permission and telling me what not to do—particularly when it's a thing I couldn't help if I wanted to.

"It's too late."

I open the sliding door and slip back inside, pulling it shut behind me but not locking it as I watch Rob turn on his heel and walk toward the boat dock. The house is dark and quiet, and I'm hoping that means everyone else missed the show. I only discovered it when I went to find Cooper after he didn't return with drinks.

I head to our room now and knock softly before I open the door a crack. I can't see much in the dim light, but I can tell he's sprawled out over the bed. His feet crossed at the end closest to me.

"Coop?" I whisper.

"Yeah." It's a low, flat response. My stomach takes a soft roll on the anxiety I feel swirl there.

I step inside and close the door behind me, walking toward the bed.

"Are you okay?"

"I'm fine."

"Are you really?"

"As good as I can be."

I sit down on the edge of the bed, and it sinks a little under my weight. I reach over and touch his shoulder and look at him through the darkness. The moonlight is just enough to hit the highlights of his brow and cheeks. The man is beautiful even when he's grumpy.

"I hope that wasn't about me."

"He wants you back. He's doing the math to figure out how he can make that happen," Cooper grouches.

"He doesn't want me back."

"He does. Surprised he didn't get on his knees and beg the second I went back in the house."

"I think he loves Carly in his own way. Maybe he has some regrets about me. But he doesn't want me back, Cooper."

"Do you want him back?"

"Absolutely not."

"You sure? Because you stayed out there with him."

"He was bleeding, and you obviously hit him. I was just trying to figure out what was going on."

"Yeah, well he fucking deserved it. For talking shit about my daughter. He's lucky his jaw's still attached."

"He's an asshole for saying anything about Lizzy. I can't believe he would do that. He loves her, and it's such a low blow."

Cooper groans and runs a hand over his face.

"I... might have done a little bragging. Maybe a little taunting too."

"I figured he wasn't completely lying about that. I mean... what we did outside. It was asking for trouble."

"But it was hot as fuck." I can see him grin even in the dim light, and it's infectious. I shake my head despite myself.

"It's probably given him a complex." I glance toward our door, half worried he'll come back in and lecture one of us some more.

"That and then some based on what he said to me." Cooper's amused tone returns, and he relaxes for a moment before he grows serious again. "What did he say *to you*?"

"Nothing I didn't already know."

My heart hurts staring at Cooper because I know this might end soon. It'll end badly if we keep dragging it out like this, and

I desperately want us—maybe even need us—to stay friends after it's all over. I care about him and Lizzy too much to imagine anything else. As long as I still have them in my life, I can be happy with with memories of this summer. Or at least it's what I keep telling myself.

"I care about you a lot, Trix. I would never *ever* hurt you. You know that, right?"

"I know. You've been nothing but good to me. You've gone above and beyond, and I'm so grateful for you. That I've had you this summer to confide in and help me deal with all the craziness. I don't know what I would have done without you."

"No fucking way would I let you do that alone." He wraps his hand around my wrist and pulls me down next to him. I put my arms around him and rest my head against his chest.

"I don't know what he said to you that rattled you that much, but he just wanted to hurt you. Even he doesn't mean it. You know that, right?"

"Oh, I'm pretty sure he meant some of it. But he's still my brother at the end of the day."

"Don't ever let him tell you you're anything but good, Rawlings."

Cooper kisses the top of my head.

"I know. I have you to convince me of that."

34

B *eatrix*

THE REST of the summer flies by and before we know it, Lizzy's back in school and football season has started. We've been so busy with Cooper at practice and games, me helping Madison deal with all the Undergrove and Westfield drama, and Lizzy adapting to life as a high school student that I've barely had time to think about anything else.

The stalker's been quiet too. I don't know if the extra security measures have been noticed and are serving as a deterrent, or if maybe they've finally just decided to leave us alone but I'm thankful. It had been like this before when my dad would run for office. There'd be a sudden flurry of interest; notes in the mail, threats online, and strange cars driving down our block. Then as soon as it started, it would stop. It was like they had gotten bored of us. I hope whoever this was had grown uninterested in Cooper and me finally. I'm hopeful that maybe I'm back to something approximating a normal life, even if that new normal might mean reevaluating if I need to be living with Cooper.

Today though, my focus has been Madison Westfield and Quentin Undergrove, because despite the fact it's midseason and the middle of the week, the two of them have finally made their way back to an altar. Or more specifically, they've made their way back to a courthouse, and the rest of us are spending the day celebrating. I'm so happy the two of them have finally admitted to the world that they can't live without each other.

It's been a long day though of dresses, hair, makeup, vows, photos, and last but not least, a friends and family dinner at West Field. By the end of it, we get a ride home from the post-wedding celebrations because I did my fair share of toasts, and Cooper hasn't been light on the drinks either. It's unusual for him since the season's started, and I haven't seen him drink since the summer. He's quiet on the car ride home, and when we get in the door, he takes his shoes off and leans against the store frame studying me like he's looking for answers. He stares at me for a full minute before I raise my brow.

"What is it?"

"I have to show you something. I don't want you to be mad. I didn't want to show you earlier with the wedding today. I wanted you to be able to enjoy it with Madison and Quen. Just know that I had good intentions. I'm just real fuckin' worried you're going to be mad now." His voice is soft and my heart drops into my stomach with dread.

I don't know what he could possibly do that would make me mad. Not this otherwise perfect man.

"Show me. You're making me nervous."

He blows out a breath and then takes my hand, bringing me to his office. There's a large manila envelope addressed to him sitting on it. It's already been opened. He pulls out the contents

—at least a dozen photographs—and scatters them over the desk.

I stare at them because it takes full minutes to process what I'm looking at. It's Rob and me. We're standing outside the lake house. Me in my PJs and him bleeding, barely lit by the lamps at the back of the house and the moonlight. The shots are zoomed in though, some of them action shots with light trails obscuring half our faces.

Another of him grabbing my arm and pulling me close. One where I look like I'm lost in whatever he's saying. One of me telling him something. Another of Rob looking distraught, and the next one where he's alone, and he's crying. If I didn't know the contents of the conversation, I'd think—

"You're still in love with him," Cooper blurts out the accusation, and I hear the strain in his voice.

"I am *not* in love with him."

"It looks like it."

"Well, I don't know what to tell you. But I'm not." I look at the photos, and then I feel sick. "Who took these? How did you get them?"

"They were sent to me. I assume whoever's been stalking you followed us to the lake house. I've already hired someone —"

"How long have you had them?" My chest feels tight.

"Just since this morning. I don't know why they waited until now, but I only got them this morning." He holds up his hands like he's defending himself, and I must look as crazy as I feel. "I promise. I got an investigator on it immediately. Should have done it a long time ago, but I didn't want you to get upset. But we have to now. You see that?"

"Yes... Oh my god... The lake house? How'd they even find us there?"

"I don't know. That's what they're going to find out. I talked to the security team too. I want someone here personally. I want someone watching the house at all hours. With you and Lizzy in the house, we can't be too safe." His voice is raw, and I can see the worry in his eyes despite how angry he is about the photos.

"I agree."

"You need to come clean with Madison too. She's leaning on you and her family for help. You need to lean on her. They're together, and they're happy now. She can handle it." Cooper gives me a meaningful look, and I know he's right.

"She's going to be pissed."

"She's going to be more than pissed."

"Don't sugarcoat it or anything." I give him a grumpy look.

"I'm not in the mood to sugarcoat things." He looks back at the pictures again, and I can tell he's been on a low simmer about this all day.

"Who was the envelope addressed to?"

"Me."

"So they did it on purpose. They wanted you pissed. They wanted you thinking this was something when it's not." I point to one of the pictures where Rob's touching me.

"I mean, he's got his hands on you. The two of you look like you're locked in a pretty emotional conversation. Be honest with me, Trix. I just need to know so I can fucking process it." I can tell Cooper's holding back; his voice is calm, but his eyes say that he's hurt.

"I told you that night. We were going back and forth about the fight you two had. I was telling him he was being immature."

"This looks like a woman who still has feelings." He holds up one of the photos, and I hear the subtle crack in his voice. "So what is it? Still carrying a torch for him but I'm a better fuck, so it's best of both worlds?"

"You can't be serious." My jaw drops, and I turn to look at

him. This isn't the Cooper I know, and I can't believe the photographs have rattled him this much.

"Oh, I'm dead fucking serious. You never look at me like this." He tosses the photo down on the table.

"I've never looked at you like that because you've never acted like a petulant child. It's been a long day. You've had a lot to drink tonight, and I think it's warping your perception." He steps toward me while I take a step back, until my ass hits the desk and his knuckles brush alongside my cheek.

"I had to celebrate my QB getting married. I only drank every time I was told to toast to their happiness. There was a lot of it to go around. Meanwhile, I had to watch you all night knowing these pictures exist." He grabs me by the hips and pulls me up on top of the desk, some of the photos falling to the ground in the process. "The only consolation was knowing that I got to come home, take this dress off, and fuck you on top of them."

His eyes go heavy, and a dark smile replaces the concerned look he's had since we came in here. His hands go to his belt, and he undoes it, whipping it out of the loops with one hand and slamming it onto the desk next to me. His fingers tighten around it, and I can see the muscle twitch in his hand and the way his jaw moves in anticipation. I can feel my pulse in my throat and my mind, heart, and clit are all in disagreement with how we feel about this development—but they're all throbbing to the same beat at least.

"Should have just taken you to the bathroom and fucked you over the sink."

"Cooper," I say his name softly, like I'm trying to calm a startled horse and it's the wrong thing to do.

"No. You're not getting out of this by whispering in my ear about how sweet I am. Saying my name all soft like you do. I *know* I'm good. I *know* I fuck you better than anyone ever has. Definitely better than anyone who shares my last name. I just want you to remember that while you beg for me. While I have this tight little cunt quivering around my cock, and I get your ass that perfect shade of red that we both love so much." His hand wraps around my throat, and he kisses me roughly, making his way up my jaw before he pauses just beneath my ear. "Then you can say my name as much as you want when you tell me which brother you belong to."

He steps between my legs, and I scoot forward and spread wider, desperate to feel him.

"Fuck..." I whisper when I reach out and palm him through his pants.

He grins against my lips and then nips my lower one.

"Undo my pants," he demands.

I do as he asks; my hands are shaking in my rush to touch him. This side of Cooper makes me want to do anything he asks, and I'm already his to order around most hours of the day, if we're honest. I wrap one hand around him and stroke him gently under the fabric, restricted by the tightness of it but still able to tease him. A guttural sound rumbles out of him before he bats my hand away.

"Don't fucking start. Take your panties off and then turn around and bend over the desk."

I think I may have issues because angry Cooper is hot as fuck. I do as he asks, and then I go for the belt, my fingers hovering over the buffed black leather for a moment before I take it and hold it out for him. He wraps his hand around it, looping it over once and tightens his grip.

"You want this?" he asks, seeking permission even though he's already promised it.

"Yes."

I hear a muttered curse, and he steps back. I can feel his eyes on me, surveying me in this position—vulnerable and spread out for him.

"Who fucks you best?" he asks as he drags the belt down my

lower back, over my ass cheek, and then down between my thighs, teasing me with the edge of it.

"You."

"Louder." He cracks it over my skin, and I feel the harsh lash of it zip through my nerve endings and straight to my clit.

"Fuck! You do." I say it loud enough it echoes off the walls, and I'm thankful that we're alone in the house tonight.

"That's better." He leans over me his lips ghosting down my neck, kissing and biting in intervals. His fingers splay over my back and drift down my spine. "So fucking good for me when you listen. So perfect when you take everything I give you. Think you can take one more before I fuck you?"

"Yes. Please," I beg because I want it. I love when he's like this, desperate to give me all the things we both need.

The leather comes down hard on my flesh one last time, and then he drops it, grabbing my hips instead and lining his cock up with me before he slams inside. I gasp at the counter sensations, pleasure and pain mixing, and I have to grab the desk to keep my balance.

"Fuck," he curses. "You're always so fucking wet. Dripping for me like my good little slut."

"Always." The words are half mumbled because he's got a perfect rhythm already, and he's hitting everywhere I need. "Feels so good."

He palms my ass, and his fingertips brush over the spot where he's left me red, and then he grabs my hand, threading his fingers with mine and pressing them both down on top of the pile of pictures.

"I hope your sweet little chat was worth it, and you got to tell each other you love each other one last time."

"I told him it was too late when he asked about you." It's my turn to blurt out things I shouldn't be saying.

He stops, goes stark still with his dick still inside me and me bent over the desk. Regret sets in instantly. I've ruined this—

ruined us—by admitting the one thing Rob warned me he couldn't handle hearing.

I promised myself I wouldn't make this awkward between us when the season started, and we hadn't resolved things properly. I know how important their mental state is when they play after growing up with my brother and then working with so many other guys. I know he's already worried about Lizzy in high school and a million other things. I told myself I could be happy just stretching out our friends with benefits a little bit longer. It hadn't stopped being fun, even if I started loving him somewhere in the process.

"Too late for what?" he asks after what feels like an eternity.

There's no use in lying now.

"He told me not to fall for you," I say it so softly I'm worried he's going to ask me to repeat it again, and I don't think my heart can take it.

Instead he grabs my shoulders, standing me up as he pulls out of me, and turning me to face him in the process. His eyes search mine, and I wait for the inevitable.

"Is it true or did you say it to hurt him?"

"It's true." I give him a wary glance.

"Why didn't you tell me?"

"I figured as long as we stay friends and this is just sex, then..." I shrug. The silence drags on for a moment after. His eyes studying me while we wait in it.

"Broke my fucking heart today when you didn't even want to catch the flowers." His fingers thread through my hair.

"I didn't want to make it awkward for you. Have you thinking that I wanted more than what you can give. For the record, I'm fine with what we have. I don't need more right now, and I know you're in season. You've got bigger things to worry about."

"Jesus Christ. The biggest thing I worry about is you. You

and Lizzy. I just want the two of you to be safe and happy, know that I'm here for you whenever you need me."

"I know," I say softly.

He lets go of my hair, his fingers skate down my jaw, and his thumb slides over my lower lip.

"Actually that's a lie. I want more than that. I want every last piece of you, Trixie."

"I need someone who can be mine too," I confess. I want to be Cooper's more than anything, but I desperately need to know that it goes both ways. I'm so far gone on him that I know he could break me—in ways no one ever could have before.

"I've been yours since that day we were on the boat. I just didn't think you could ever be mine."

"I'm yours." I smile at him, my chest tight with how full my heart feels.

35

C *ooper*

HER FINGERS CREEP up my tie, and her lashes flutter. My heart's still pounding in my chest from the combination of hate fucking her over the pictures of my brother and feeling like I was freefalling the second she blurted out that she's mine. Hearing her admit it was like being pushed out of a fucking airplane with no parachute. I've wanted it so badly, but I've spent so long assuming it would never happen that I didn't come prepared for it.

Her palms slide down over my chest, and she kisses her way up my neck, nipping at the spot just beneath my ear where the skin is tender. In return, my hands run up over her hips.

"Tell me what you need from me," she whispers. I hear her pulling the zipper of her dress down. A moment later, it hits the ground, and she's naked except for the bustier she had on underneath and the heels she hasn't taken off yet. I can worry about telling her how much I love her when I'm done because right now I want to fuck her like I don't. I just need a fucking minute to regroup first.

"Get back up on the desk and spread your legs for me. I want to watch you play with that pretty pussy until I fuck you again." I sit back in my chair and grab my cock, running my hand down the length of it.

She sits up on the desk and spreads wide so I can watch her when her fingers slip between her thighs. She's already wet enough that I can hear her when her fingers start to massage her clit. It's one of the sweetest sounds in the world, and my eyes fall hard on the sight of it.

"So fucking wet already. You need me that badly?"

"Yes. I've needed you all day. I wish you would've fucked me at the bar."

"Next time I will. You just have to ask."

Her eyes roam over me, landing on where my hand moves.

"I can't do this much longer, or I'll come." She half says, half murmurs the words, and a soft moan follows.

"That feel good? You touching yourself for me?"

"Yes. But I want more of you."

I grab her thighs and scoot the chair forward, leaning down and taking one long lick of her before I press my lips around her clit and suck. She kicks my chair in surprise and then wraps her foot around the leg of the desk. I feel her fingers twist in my hair.

"Oh f-uck... I'm going to come. You have to stop or—fuck..." Her voice fades to moans, and her nails sink into my scalp as she relents. She rocks against my face, and I tighten my grip on her thighs as she rides through her release, eventually sinking back against the desk and releasing me. I lean back in my chair and watch her come down from her high, her breathing slowly returning to normal and her focus back on me.

"You look gorgeous like this." I nod to her mostly naked

form and grin at the heels she's still wearing. She props one up on my knee.

"You think so?"

"I know so."

"You look good too. But you'd look better with these heels dug into your thighs while you fuck me." She smirks.

"You have a smart fucking mouth." I can't control the laugh that bubbles out of me.

"I'd be talking less if your hand was around my throat."

She's outright baiting me, and I fucking love it. I have no idea how I got this damn lucky. But I'm not wasting time wondering when I could be enjoying it.

I'm on my feet a moment later, grabbing her and dragging her to the edge of the desk. True to her promise, her legs wrap around mine, and I tease her with the tip of my cock for a moment before I fuck her in earnest. The gasp she lets out as her nails rake down the back of my neck is enough to bring me close, and I have to pace myself to keep from just coming right here and now. But it's like she knows and wants to bring me to my knees tonight, and her muscles tighten like a vice grip around me.

"Fucking hell. Your cunt is so fucking greedy for me."

"I know. I need you. Finish what you started and fill me up."

"Oh, I will. Until you feel me leaking down your thighs when I turn you around and spank your ass for being such a fucking brat."

I run my hand up her stomach and over the bustier, coasting softly across her rib cage, and then wrapping my fingers around her neck while she spreads wider for me.

I've never had a woman this responsive, this easy to please, because we love all the same things. It's like we were made for each other, and I can't get enough of it. I start to fuck her hard, and she whimpers but hangs on, begging for me to go even harder. The desk rattles underneath us, and I'm half-afraid it'll collapse from this kind of abuse.

Her hips rock, and I can tell she's searching for more. I slip my hand between us and use my thumb on her clit. She moans her approval, and her eyes flutter closed, her fingers gliding up my forearm.

"Such a good little slut. Always letting me know how desperate you are for more of me."

"Oh god. I'm going to come again."

"Good. Use that tight little cunt on my cock and take me with you."

She does exactly as I ask, and I fuck her harder as we both come, almost in sync, and I fill her with every last drop. I barely let her catch her breath before I move again.

"Turn around and spread. I want to watch me leak out of you while I finish what we started with the belt."

She stands slowly and places her palms on the desk before she bends. My come is already slipping down, making a mess of her thighs, and I grin as I grab the belt and gently tap her with it.

"You can do better than that," she taunts me, and I crack her hard, one last time for good measure. She cries out, and I rub my palm over the red mark before I bend down and kiss it.

"Better?" I tease her back.

"Much." She turns to look at me, a softness in her eyes I don't remember seeing before. "Completely sated."

"Good." I kiss her, pulling her into my arms to hold her. We sit like that for several long minutes. Me muttering how beautiful and perfect she is while she nuzzles against the crook of my neck. I'm so lost in her, lost in the control she has over me, that I don't know that I'll ever recover from it.

I break the silence. "I'm going to start the shower for us. But first I need to tell you something."

Her brow furrows, and she studies my face like she might

be able to find the warning of what's to come there. Her lip worries between her teeth, and I tilt her chin up so she's looking at me.

"I love you."

It comes so easily that I can hardly believe I'm capable of it. Words I've never been good at that now feel as uncomplicated as telling her she's pretty and smart. It's just the truth. And with her, the truth is easy.

"I love you too. For a while now, I think." The sweet smile she has makes my heart pound in my chest. I don't know how I got this lucky.

"I don't know how this works. It's new for me. But I want it to work. Okay?" I'm nervous about this part. Worried about navigating the complexities of her being a vet at relationships and me being a gangly, confused neophyte still trying to find his footing.

"We can go slow, and we can figure it out," she reassures me.

"I can do slow," I agree. I place one last kiss on the tip of her nose. "I'll go start the shower."

"That sounds good," she answers, but when she bends to pick up her dress, she reaches for one of the photos that's fallen to the floor instead.

She picks it up, and I see a note scrawled on the back that I hadn't noticed before. To be fair, I'd been too upset at the contents to look much past the images themselves. A thing I feel silly for in retrospect.

She deserves better than a Rawlings. Either of you.

"Oh shit," she whispers as her hand goes to her mouth.

We were distracted, and the bubble bursts abruptly—the reality hits all over again. Our confessions that we love each other don't change the fact that we've still got someone following us, photographing us, stalking us—stalking her.

A cold shiver of dread runs down my spine as I look at it. They want her, my girl, and it makes me sick. I can see the worry on her face, and I pull her close to me, wrapping my arms around her.

"They won't get anywhere near you," I say it firmly enough that we have to believe it.

"What about you?" She looks up at me. "Seems they don't care for you much either."

"You let me worry about that. The investigators from this morning are on it. I'll give these to them when I meet with them tomorrow. You'll get Madison on board. We'll talk to the security team. By the time we're done, they won't be able to get anywhere near us."

"Let's hope." She shakes her head at the note and surveys the rest of the photos. I can tell she's getting stressed out all over again. I know I am, but it won't help us tonight. Tonight, I just want to focus on the fact she's here, and she's safe with me.

I kiss the top of her head. "All right. There's nothing else we can do about this tonight. For now, I just want to get you cleaned up and tucked in bed."

I pick her up into my arms, and she drops the photo back to the desk, wrapping her arms around my neck as I carry her to the shower.

36

B*eatrix*

WHEN I SIT down with my bestie, she's glowing despite all the ongoing trouble with her father and the stress it's been causing —she finally has her man. Seeing them together makes my heart so full. Knowing that despite all the years and their family baggage, they've been able to make it work. It has me thinking it might be possible for Cooper and me too. If we can figure things out, and if I can get to the bottom of this stalker situation. Which starts with the investigators Cooper hired and by telling the best fixer I know.

"Marriage looks good on you." I smile at her as I watch her sending a text that must be to Quentin.

"Thank you. It feels good. Just ten years in the making." She laughs softly, and I grin.

"Better late than never. I also feel like I should be able to get a 'told you so' in here."

She rolls her eyes and shakes her head. "Fine. I guess that's fair."

We laugh for a few minutes, and she tells me more about how things are with her family and her post-married-life bliss before I break my own news to her.

"So. I have something I need to tell you. I'm hoping you're not going to be mad at me. I kept it from you because you've had so much going on in your own life, and I didn't want to add to your stress."

"Okay..." Her face clouds with concern, and she looks me over carefully.

"I think I have a stalker. Or Cooper and I do? It's hard to know for sure. It didn't start until I was around him, so I've been thinking it might be a fan of his that thinks I'm his girl-friend. But now I don't know."

"What do you mean you think you have a stalker?" I can see my best friend going into business mode.

"It started a few months ago with pictures on social media of Cooper and me at the fair. Someone clearly following and watching us. Then it stopped for a bit until there were foot-prints outside his house a few nights after I swear I saw someone staring at me through my bedroom window. We installed cameras and got security—someone my father worked with and had on his team before he moved. He actually works with the stadium as well. I felt better after that, but we just got another round of photos. These ones were a lot more disturbing. They were sent to Cooper."

"Disturbing how? How were they delivered? Any chance of prints on them?" Madison is hyper focused on the details as always. It's almost like she's taking mental notes and connecting dots for me already.

"Well... this is where I admit the next thing. I suppose you've already kind of guessed. Cooper and I have been sleeping together. Not in a relationship. Or, well, we are now, but we weren't before. I went with him to his family's lake house a few weeks back before the season started, and naturally, Rob lost his shit when he figured out what was happening. They had an argument, and I went out and tried to help break it up. The person who's been watching us took photos of me and Rob. Ones that made it look like we were having some sort of lovers' quarrel even though we weren't. The stalker sent them to Cooper, and they got here on your wedding day. He didn't tell me until that night because he didn't want to ruin anything but..."

"Holy shit, Bea. I wish you'd told me sooner. This is crazy. They sent them to Cooper, so they've been watching you enough to suspect you're in a relationship of some sort then?"

"Yes. I mean... we've tried to be discreet, but I guess if you were following me regularly and saw us enough, maybe you'd know?"

"I haven't been around you that much, and I had my suspicions. So that doesn't necessarily surprise me but that they would try to drive a wedge between you with those pictures... I see why you think it could be a crazy fan of his. Has he had that issue before?"

"He said he's never had any fans who have harassed him at all. A few people here and there who message him too much or he sees regularly, but nothing that would make him think they'd be capable of this."

"An ex of any kind or maybe a hookup he had that went wrong?"

"He says no to the hookups, and he's never really dated seriously since I've known him. But maybe you should talk to him and see if he'd be more candid with you. I'm sure there are details he'd rather not share with me." I try to put my PR hat on even though it's my boyfriend we're talking about because, at the end of the day, getting to the bottom of this is more important than him being worried about hurting me. "This last time though. There was a message scrawled on the back about me deserving better than a Rawlings brother."

"So maybe not a fan then?" Her confusion deepens and I'm glad I'm not alone.

"Maybe not. Cooper's never thought it was a fan. He's always thought it was me."

"Does he know you're talking to me?"

"Yes, he's been telling me to talk to you the whole time. He basically insisted on it, and I finally agreed. I just hope I'm not adding more stress to you, Mads. I know it's a lot to deal with with everything you have going on."

"Bea. Please be serious. You've been helping with the stuff with Quentin and with my dad, and you've been amazing. If I'd known all this was going on—" She gives me a remorseful look. "I feel awful you didn't think you could come to me."

"No! I wanted you to be able to lean on me. I'm here for you. Helping you makes me feel better and helps me get my mind off things. We're a team."

"If we're a team, you should have told me." She gives me the eye.

"I know, I know. I should have. I'm sorry I didn't. Like I said, it was the best of intentions."

"All right, well, like we tell clients... no use in crying over the past. We just have to move forward from here. I'll talk to Cooper. Meanwhile, give me everything you've got in writing. The timeline, copies of the photos, any suspicions, or gut feelings you have. Have you talked to the cops yet?"

"No. I briefly asked around about that, and they told me the cops were unlikely to do anything. With no name and no leads, they'd just file it away and move on. I didn't want to bother. But Cooper has hired a private investigator in addition to the security team. He wants as many people as we can get looking into it."

"What about your family, do they know? I feel like your dad

would have opinions."

"He does, and he did. He eased up a little after we hired the guy who used to work for him, but he's still adamant about me moving home. I told him you and I just started planning to start our own PR firm. I'm not about to abandon you just because of this."

"Well, first of all, I wouldn't consider it you abandoning me if you had to do something for your safety, Bea. Your dad definitely has more protection and security than the average person does in their orbit, and unlike some fathers, he actually cares about you and Xander, even if he's got a shitty way of showing it sometimes."

"I know he cares, but he's still insistent that he knows best when Xander and I are fully grown adults."

"I get it." Mads nods and smiles at me. "But let's hope we can just get to the bottom of this between the security folks, the investigator, and me... I think we can figure out what's going on and, hopefully, get the authorities to handle it from there."

"Thank you. Truly. I'm so glad to have you in my life." I reach over and squeeze her hand. It feels like a huge weight lifted off my shoulders just telling her.

"Likewise. I don't know what I'd do without you. Especially in the last couple of months. You sticking with me while this was all falling apart. But I'm so excited about our PR firm and our plans. I think we're going to break so much ground."

"Toast?" I raise my water glass, and she laughs.

"Oh my god. You and your toasts lately." She gives me a look but it crumbles into a smile and she raises her glass in response.

"There's been a lot to celebrate!" I say defensively as I clink her glass. We down some water and then finish our orders, going back to discussing our PR and client agenda, and talking about all the holiday plans she has now that she's moved in with Quentin.

37

Cooper

QUENTIN, Ramsey, and I are headed into a bar to grab a bite to eat after a particularly brutal practice and a round of ice baths.

"I'm getting too old for this shit," Ramsey grumbles as he sits down. "Shoulda been like Davis and skipped practice."

"That's just going to make socials go crazy with rumors he's quitting the team. But you're not too old." I flatten my lips and shake my head at my old friend.

"You're both younger than me, so I don't want to fuckin' hear it. Davis better get his ass to practice tomorrow. I don't give a fuck what his agent thinks he can press for by holding out. We're either a team or we're not." Quentin raises a brow at his menu. He's quickly become the leader around here and the mounting wins in our favor despite some rather heinous trials for him personally mean he's gained a lot of respect.

I'm flipping through the menu and too busy thinking about Trix to even get involved in that argument right now.

"Something off with you?" Quentin asks.

"Madison didn't share?" I was hoping to let Trix give the newlyweds as much of the news as she felt comfortable. She'd given me permission though, to discuss it with whoever I felt comfortable telling now that her best friend finally knew.

"She mentioned something's going on with Bea that she's worried about. A stalker or something? I didn't get to talk to her much because we were running in opposite directions this morning."

"Yeah. We've had a stalker the last few months. It's been intermittent. Gets quiet for a while. Then something happens. Then quiet for a while. It's been escalating though."

"Escalating how?" Ramsey raises a brow because I haven't filled him in on the latest development either.

"The day of the wedding I had pictures delivered in an envelope. They were from my parents' lake house. Images of Trix and my brother outside."

"Oh fuck." Ramsey gives me a sympathetic look and Quentin follows suit.

"No. No." I shake my head. "I mean, yes, they were intended to look that way, but it wasn't what it looked like. Trix explained everything."

"And you believe her?" There's a hint of suspicion in Ramsey's tone.

"She wouldn't lie. But the pictures were rough. Whoever sent them—that was their intention. To make me think she would lie. That she still had feelings for him. Which means whoever it is has been watching us enough to know something's been going on and wanted to try to stop it."

"So someone who's got a thing for one of you then?" Quentin's brow furrows.

"I guess? Trix thinks it's a fan of mine. I think they would have made themselves known by now if it was a fan. I think it's someone who wants her."

"Your brother?" Quentin asks.

"Rob? He's engaged and has a baby on the way."

"I'd still be fucking pissed if my brother went after my girl. Fuck, if he looked at her wrong, I'd set his shit on fire for thinking it." Ramsey tosses his menu down on the pile at the center of the table.

"*My girl*. And you've never had a girl."

"All the more reason if I did. Your brother's a prick. I don't think you can rule him out," Ramsey says.

"Nah. I knew Rob pretty well when I played with him in Pittsburgh." Quentin shakes his head. "Pissed, sure. Grumble about it, definitely. But spending his time stalking her? No way. Plus, the pictures had him in them, right?"

"Yeah."

"So what'd he do, take pictures of himself?" Quentin looks to Ramsey.

"Hired someone. Put some cameras in the woods. Can't imagine that it's that hard to set something up if you're dedicated to the task." Ramsey shrugs.

"He wouldn't have had the opportunity to hire someone. He didn't even know she was coming with me. No way he set up cameras in the woods. He had a lot on his plate with the pregnant fiancée and the two kids in tow." I shake my head.

"Honestly, it's more fucked up if it wasn't him, given that it means some stranger neither of you know about is dedicated enough to follow you out to the middle of nowhere."

"I know." I down a long drink of my beer before I set it on the table again. "I don't want Trix to know, but I'm starting to lose my shit that we can't figure this out. I'm just desperate to get to the bottom of it before someone gets hurt. I hate being away from her for a single second. I only feel comfortable being here because I know she's with Madison, and Madison's read in on everything."

"They're at East's place tonight. Bea's safe. Don't worry." Quentin gives me a sympathetic look.

"I can't let anything happen to her. Not after everything. I've never felt this way about anyone, and Lizzy just fucking loves her." I can feel my heart rate kick up in my chest just thinking about something happening to her.

"Madison's great at this stuff. She has lots of connections. You guys have gotten investigators involved, right?" Quentin asks.

"Yeah. But it doesn't feel like enough. Sometimes, I wonder if her father is right about her being back with him, where he has a whole security team to watch her. But I can't stand the idea of her being across the country. I don't feel like anyone is gonna watch her the way I will, you know?"

"I get it. I'd feel the same about Madison." Quentin nods.

"You're doing everything you can. And like I said, you need an extra set of hands at the house, I'm there whenever you need me." Ramsey gives me a nod. Ramsey doesn't talk much about his life before football or his family, but I know enough to know that it wasn't the same sort of middle-class suburban life I'd had growing up.

"I hope it doesn't come to that."

A moment later, the waitress is back to take our orders, and while Quentin gives her his, I drift off to thoughts of Trix again. Hoping that I'm doing right by her. Because I can't lose her, not now that I finally have her, and we have a shot at something real.

38

C ooper

"Fucking Christ," Ramsey curses loudly as he finishes tying his cleat, and I look over at him. He's got his phone in his hand and is shaking his head.

The look he gives me is all I need to see. It hits me like a ton of bricks straight in my gut. I have no idea what's happened, but his look is enough to tell me it's fucked.

"What?" I manage to ask, dread filling my veins.

"I don't fucking want to show you man." He takes a deep breath, pressing the phone to his jersey.

"What is it?" There's impatience in my voice that even I can hear.

"A DM I just got. It's got pictures in it, and it's you."

"Me?" I'm confused.

"You and Bea... in a compromising position." Ramsey winces as he tells me.

I hear a choking sound on the other side of the locker room, and then a rush of laughter behind me. I glance up, and everyone in the locker room seems to be looking at their phone screens or me.

Seems like a lot of people in this room got similar DMs, or I'm having one of those waking nightmares that Bea gets. Instead of naked in a classroom, it's naked on the phones of all your teammates right before a game.

"Let me see."

Ramsey hands me his phone reluctantly, and I see the anonymous name on social media and a string of photos that have been sent to him through it. It's me and Bea in my office from the other night. I feel sick, so much so that I think I might actually vomit. I grab my stomach, tossing Ramsey his phone, and move through the hall to the bathrooms.

I wretch the second I get through the door, my stomach twisting but my throat and mouth come up nearly dry. Just the taste of bile and the room spinning keep me feeling like I've been hit by a truck. My mind is racing with how anyone could have gotten those pictures. There must be cameras in the house we don't know about. There must be someone accessing the house that we don't know about.

Panic floods my veins because Trix didn't travel with us. She stayed back with Lizzy so they could work on a school project she has due tomorrow. She'd promised to watch the game on TV, and it means both my girls are sitting ducks in my own home. I race back down the hallway, bumping into Ramsey on the way.

"Whoa. Where you headed?"

"My bag. I need my phone. I have to warn her."

Ramsey jogs down the hall with me.

"She didn't know about the pictures? You didn't take them?" Ramsey frowns.

"Fuck no. They're not ours. There's a camera in the house."

"Holy fuck." I've never seen Ramsey look shocked before.

Nothing seems to faze him, and yet now, he's standing stark still as I slam my finger down on Trix's number. It rings. Once, twice, and then finally I hear her voice.

"Coop?" She's confused at why I'm calling, knowing I'm about to start a game.

"Get out of the house."

"What?" Her voice is tight with confusion and shock.

"Get you and Lizzy out of the house. There are cameras inside, and someone has access. I don't know who or how many. But there are photos of us in the office."

"What are you talking about?" The panic seeps into her voice.

"There are photos of us from the other night in the office. They—the stalker, whoever it is—they sent them to my whole team through social media DMs. Ramsey got one. I saw it. It's bad. You and Lizzy... you're not safe, and you need to get out."

"Okay. Okay...." I can hear her thoughts racing through the phone, the stuttered nature of her breathing. "Okay, I'll get her packed, and I'll get her to her mom's. Do you think that's okay? To take her there?"

"Yes. Take her there. I'll text her, and let her know something's going on and you're coming."

"Okay."

"RAWLINGS! RAMSEY! Let's fucking go guys. We got a game to play!" Coach Undergrove yells. I look up and most of the team has already disappeared from the locker room.

"Just a fucking minute!"

"Excuse me?" Coach's tone shifts.

"He's got a good reason, Coach. We can explain. He just needs a minute." Ramsey steps between us.

Quentin stops in his path up to the stadium and turns and looks at me. "Everything okay?"

"No. Nothing's okay." I shake my head.

Both Undergroves close in on me.

"Trix, I gotta go. The game. But just... You're getting out of there? You'll text me when you're safe?"

"I will. I promise. I'll get Lizzy to her mom's."

"And you?"

"And me. I'll go to Mads's house."

"Okay. Let me know when you're safe. I love you. Tell Lizzy I love her too."

"I love you. We'll be okay. Don't worry about us. Just focus on the game."

I don't have time to argue with her that that's impossible, so I just repeat myself and hang up the phone. Questioning looks surround me, and I scrub a hand over my face.

"We have a stalker. We've had security involved for a while. Investigators. Even Madison," I nod to Quentin. "But we can't get to the bottom of it. Or haven't yet, at least. I just found out they have cameras in the house. Trix and Lizzy are there alone, and I had to tell her. Give her a chance to get out and get somewhere safe."

"Does Madison know?" Quentin's furrowed brow grows deeper by the second. "She can come stay with us. They both can."

"That's what she said she's gonna do. She's taking Lizzy to her mom's house."

"Coach?" One of the assistant coaches yells to Coach Undergrove, questioning why we're not getting our asses upstairs where we belong. They'll be barreling out of the tunnel to start the game any second, and I can't even think straight right now.

"Just a minute!" Coach Undergrove yells, and then he turns to me. "Did you call the cops?"

"I'm sure she will." My mind races with questions about the best course of action. If I should have told her to call them first.

"You should make sure she calls them," Quentin agrees. I look at Ramsey, and he shrugs.

"I hate the fucking cops, but if they're alone it might be her only choice." Ramsey shrugs.

"I'll send a text to Madison." Quentin nods.

"Quickly. Then get upstairs!" Coach Undergrove gives us all a stern once-over and then looks at me. "Can you play? We need you out there, but I need you to not be rattled out on that field, especially considering who we're playing today."

"I can play." No way am I letting this fucker get the best of me, whoever they are.

"Half the team has the photos on their phones. Probably should tell them to delete that shit or face consequences." Ramsey speaks matter-of-factly to Quentin, and he nods.

"I'll handle it," Coach Undergrove says. "You just focus on getting this shit handled so your heads are on straight when we get out there. Got it?"

"Got it." I nod.

It doesn't last long though because when we're on the field, my brother is lined up across from me, and he doesn't waste time letting me know he got the same photos my teammates did. He follows me back toward the line of scrimmage after the next play.

"I told you this would fucking happen. I told you you'd ruin her and should stay away. But you wouldn't fucking listen, would you?"

"I've got it handled."

"Yeah, well now we've all seen how you've got it handled."

"Shut the fuck up!"

I turn around and shove him in the chest without thinking.

I'm ready to rip his helmet off. We can finish what he started at the lake house.

Refs and other players come flying over to us from across the field. Garner and Ramsey pull me backward while he continues to shout something unintelligible. The referees warn us this is our first offense, and we won't get another warning.

I get the signal to come off the line, and Coach subs for me. I slam my helmet on the back of the bench and sit down. The guy next to me looks at me like I've lost my shit. One of the offensive coordinators comes over and crouches in front of me.

"Tune him out. You've got to leave your personal problems off the field, or we won't get through this game. You're here now. The only thing you can fix now is what happens on that field, so focus on that. Worry about the rest after the game, got it?"

I nod like I understand him because it's impossible to explain that I can't possibly worry about the rest later. Not when my girls are in trouble, and not when I'm failing them by being here instead of there when they need me most. Having a family member who wants to rub that shit in on top of it just pours salt in an already fresh wound.

39

B eatrix

"Lizzy. I need to take you over to your mom's. Something's come up, and I've gotta run to Madison's house."

"I can stay here on my own for a while. Dad and I have already talked about it now that I'm in high school."

"No. We need to get you to your mom's. Your dad is letting her know that's where we're headed."

She drops the stylus to her tablet and looks up at me, her brows drawing together.

"Why are you being so weird? You look... panicked or something. What happened? Is someone hurt? Is dad hurt?"

"No. He's fine. He's completely fine, and he's getting ready to play. If we get you to your mom's soon, you can probably still catch some of the first half while you work. I'm fine too; I just have some... work emergency stuff that's come up that I want to take care of." I didn't mean to scare her. I thought I'd kept my tone in check, but apparently, I'm transparent in my worries.

Lizzy eyes me warily, but she starts to pack up her homework and put it back in her school bag along with her computer and tablet.

"Do you have stuff to stay overnight?" I ask quietly as I start to gather my own things from around the room.

"Overnight?" There's a hint of incredulity to her tone.

"I might have to stay at Mads's house to finish working on things, and if you've got all your stuff and that happens, no one will have to run back. You know your dad will be in late when he gets home after the game."

"I guess. I just have to get some things out of my room."

"Okay. Just be quick, all right? And thank you. I appreciate you doing this for me. I'm really sorry. I was looking forward to working on this with you."

"It's okay." Her eyes search my face, and I can tell she knows there's more going on, but she's being kind enough not to press the issue with me. Which I'm more grateful for than I can say because I'd love to get out of this house without bringing any attention to why we're doing it. Knowing that the stalker could be watching us even as we pack up has me rattled.

My heart races in my chest at what all this means as I pack my own bag. By the time we get in the car, it's hitting hard that there are pictures of Cooper and me circulating out there somewhere. That people we don't know have them and could release them to anyone. My heart skips a beat. That Lizzy could accidentally stumble on them or worse that someone at her school could have them and taunt her about it. Kids are fucking cruel in high school, and I don't wish her any of that heartbreak, let alone the kind that we've inadvertently fueled. I know Cooper must be panicking about all of it.

I can only imagine what my own father will think when he

finds out because it's not a matter of if but a matter of when. When the tabloids or the opposition get wind of it, they'll use it to smear him. Paint a picture of what an immoral, reckless heathen I am and how our family doesn't deserve where his career has taken us.

There's going to be so much fallout.

My phone rings with a call from Madison, and I answer it despite not wanting to in front of Lizzy. Because if I don't answer, she'll go into a full-blown panic.

"Hey, Mads. You're on speakerphone. I'm driving Lizzy to her mom's house, and then I'll head your way so we can get started on the work thing." I try to prepare her and pray that she doesn't slip up and say the wrong thing.

"Oh good. Just wanted to make sure. The client already called, and I'm just worried about timing is all. I'm glad to hear you're on your way."

Despite her catching and landing that perfectly, Lizzy's eyes are still on me, giving me a once-over that tells me she still doesn't really buy our little ruse. We're pulling into her mom's driveway, though, and I'm hopeful that that's going to give me the break I need.

"No problem. Hey! I'll call you back. I'm in the driveway to drop her off."

"Sounds good. Talk to you in a few." Madison disconnects the call, and I look to Lizzy.

"Text me if you need anything, okay? I'll still be around." I see Lizzy's mom in the doorway and I leave it up to her if she wants to chat about this in front of Lizzy.

"But you'll be busy." Lizzy's eyes are on me and mine soften as I look back at her. I feel like I'm disappointing her. I want to explain everything so she knows I'm not just ditching her tonight, but I want her parents to have the say in how much she knows.

"Yes, but I'm never too busy for you, and you know I want to help with this. So if you need anything, text me." I make a face, letting her know I mean business, and she nods.

"All right. I hope whatever's going on with your client gets resolved."

"Thank you. Have a good one at your mom's."

Lizzy hops out of the car and waves before she goes up the driveway. I watch her pause and talk to her mom at the doorway. She ushers her inside, and then her mom walks down the steps and heads toward the car. My stomach tumbles, and my nerves start because I've only had brief interactions with Lizzy's mom so far, and this seems like a terrible time for us to have our first real conversation.

"Hi," she says flatly as she approaches the car, a small smile appearing and fading almost immediately.

"Hi. I'm so sorry to bring Lizzy by so abruptly. I hope Cooper had a chance to explain."

"He told me the basics. I'm honestly really frightened for Lizzy, and I just wanted to make sure to say that I hope the two of you will communicate with me more freely in the future. Cooper and I have had a really good run of co-parenting, and I hate to see that breaking down now. I understand you might have privacy concerns, but nothing should be trumping Lizzy's safety."

"Oh, I'm not sure what he told you, but we didn't know any of these details until today. The second he told me what was happening, I got Lizzy out of there."

"You had no idea you were having these problems before? Someone just installed cameras in the house out of nowhere?"

"Well, no, we had cameras installed as a security measure after some strange things happened. We thought that and the extra security around the house would help if he had an overexuberant fan. Cooper told me he'd explained that to you."

"Cooper told me you were having issues that required extra security. That there had been social media messages, which I understand can happen with people of your celebrity, but I didn't realize you two believed there was a physical threat at the house. I would have insisted Lizzy stay with me until you resolved it."

I open my mouth to speak and then close it again. I'm not sure what to say, and the last thing I want to do is get between Cooper and her on how they handle Lizzy and her safety.

"I'm sorry for anything I've done to make you feel that way. I will talk to Cooper when he's home, and hopefully, this will all be over soon."

"Tell Cooper to call me when he gets home. I need to make plans if she needs to stay with me for the foreseeable future. I also need reassurance that my daughter isn't on any of these cameras in a way that's going to endanger her or her future. I need that to be higher on his priority list than it seems to be at the moment."

"I'll tell him."

"Thanks for bringing Lizzy home."

I nod at her, and she turns and walks back up the driveway. I let out a long sigh and let my head hit the back of the seat as I try to let my nerves return to normal. I'm not cut out for this; being in the middle of parental arrangements and feeling like I'm the asshole when I've been trying to do everything right. If I'm the reason Lizzy was put in danger, I'll never be able to live with myself.

BY THE TIME I get to Madison's house, I'm in tears. She pulls me inside and wraps her arms around me, giving me a tight hug before she leads me into the living room and has me sit down. The game's playing on the TV in the background, but it's muted. I have to stare out the window because I can't bear to see Cooper right now.

"What do you want to drink? Wine? Iced tea? Something stronger?"

"Just some tea, maybe."

Madison disappears into her kitchen for a few moments and reappears with two glasses of tea before she sits down across from me. The look on her face is thoughtful, but I can tell she's worried.

"Do you want to talk or just sit for a bit?"

"I just came from dropping Lizzy off. Her mom is furious. I think she blames me, and I don't know that she's wrong."

"Oh, Bea, you can't blame yourself for this."

"I mean, whatever's happening... it's because of me. It wasn't happening to Cooper before. It's obvious whoever is doing this doesn't want me with him. They've done everything they can to make that happen, and now they're going to hurt everyone else around us. Can you imagine being Lizzy right now? Her mom is going to have to explain to her. I'm sure it's going to be the talk of school tomorrow."

"That's assuming it gets out of the locker room."

I give her a look that tells her we both know that it's impossible it won't. Some of the guys might have a conscience, but inevitably, one of them will slip up and share it with a friend or a nosy tabloid willing to pay a price.

"Even if the pictures don't, everyone will still be talking about it. Some of the other students are bound to hear, and the rumor will spread."

"The rumor that two adults who are dating were having sex in their home unaware they were being violated by having someone film them and disseminate the photos?"

"What if they filmed Lizzy too? Someone's going to have to sweep the house to see where all the cameras are. I can't believe the security team didn't check for that. I guess... I guess they couldn't have suspected at the time. We didn't suspect, but still."

"Do you want me to send someone over? I have some connections I've been working on in town for when we launch the PR firm. If Cooper's investigator isn't able to do it, I've got someone."

"I don't know. We didn't discuss everything the person he has on it is doing yet. We didn't get that far with how busy this week has been. If you have someone, yes... I say let's get them over there sooner rather than later. I want to make sure there's nothing that could hurt Lizzy. I'm sure Cooper would feel better knowing that as well."

"All right. I'll make some phone calls. You sit tight, okay?"

I nod and take a sip of my tea, watching as she moves to her office and picks up her phone. She paces the room as she talks, and I'm grateful I have a friend like her to run to. Out of the corner of my eye, I see a commotion on the screen, players involved in a scuffle, and my heart skips when I see the two Rawlings brothers are at the center of it.

I don't have to have the sound on to see how loudly one of the refs is blowing the whistle or hear the yelling that's taking place as they try to pull them apart. Yellow flags are flying through the air, and now even the coaches are on the field trying to break up the mess.

Tears form in my eyes because all of this is because of me. If I'd just stayed away from Cooper, if I had leaned on literally anyone else for help, they wouldn't be getting penalized in a game right now. Lizzy wouldn't be at her mom's, and her parents wouldn't be stressing over what sort of life-altering photos or information is lurking out there in the hands of someone who wants to do us all harm.

My phone buzzes in my purse and jolts me back to the present. I pick it up and see that it's my mom.

"Hello?"

"Bea? Honey, are you okay?" My mom immediately launches into sensitive mode, and for a woman who's well practiced at maintaining a calm and poise demeanor, it chills me to hear it.

"Yes." My heart bottoms out. She knows. Somehow, she already knows. "How do you know already?"

"They sent the images to your father as well. To his phone somehow. His team is already on it."

"Oh my god." I start to cry. It was humiliating enough to know a whole football team I worked for had seen me half-dressed, but knowing they sent them to my father too? "I could die. Did they send them to Xander?"

"I don't know, honey. You know he won't care about that. Your dad doesn't either. Someone violated your privacy. He's furious on your behalf. Whoever is at the bottom of this, we're going to make sure they pay for all of it. Don't you worry."

"Mom... It's impossible not to worry right now." My voice is shaky from how hard I'm trying not to sob into the phone. "Cooper. Dad. Lizzy. Everyone is going to suffer from this, and I can't do anything to stop it. I kept thinking it was nothing, and I didn't do something fast enough. I should have told Madison. I should have done more. I should have gone home when you asked me to."

"Honey... None of that matters right now, okay? You did the best you could with what you knew at the time. You're a strong woman, and you have a lot of people who love you and will help you get through this. None of this is your fault. Absolutely none of it, do you hear me?"

"I wish that were true. But I've ruined so much just being here." I can't help the flow of guilt and self-flagellation that follows, and I just start bawling while she sits with me on the phone. She's mostly quiet, telling me in intervals it's not my fault. There's a flash on the screen that distracts me.

My eyes lift to see it's already halftime. The banner at the bottom of the TV declares, "Rawlings Brothers ejected from the game."

"Oh my god." My heart drops in my chest.

"What is it?"

"Cooper and Rob were both ejected from the game. I told you. All of this for what? Because I was stupid and selfish."

"Bea?" Madison enters the room again and looks at me with worry. Her eyes dart to the screen and back to me, and she hurries over and hugs me. "Who are you talking to?"

"My mom." I barely get the words out because my throat is so scratchy, thick with mucus, and my eyes are swollen as I rub at them again.

"Okay. Let me talk to her for a minute, and you just sit here with me." Madison pulls me onto the couch next to her and takes the phone from me. I curl my legs up under myself and lean my head on her shoulder. I'm busy worrying about Cooper's likely looming suspension and fines. How the team, and more importantly Coach Undergrove, must be feeling given that Westfield and Rawlings have gone back-to-back weekends with more drama than most teams have in an entire year—on a team he's desperately trying to reform into a playoff team.

Worse yet for Quentin, who is doing so well despite everything. Another rack of guilt runs through me. Cooper is a good guy. He doesn't get into trouble. No fights and certainly no ejections.

Madison and my mom would never blame me. I have a solid record of always being the good one which gives me passes for situations like this. But objectively, this is my fault. I could have done more. I should have done more. I would've scoffed at a client trying to play this all off like I did.

I barely hear anything Madison says after she gets off the

phone with my mom. At some point, she helps me up to the guest room. I curl up, and she puts a blanket over me, promising me that she's going to fix everything, and I have nothing to worry about. But it feels like everything is coming apart at the seams, and I have no faith that even our dynamic duo can fix it this time.

40

C *ooper*

WHEN I GET HOME, the house is empty, and I drop my bags before I collapse in the entryway. I pull out my phone and sit on one of the steps. There's a message from the security team letting me know they've disabled all the security cameras, and they've done a sweep of Lizzy's room and bathroom, and it's come up clean. It gives me relief to see it in black and white, even though Trix and Madison already told me, and I passed the message on to Lizzy's mom.

I send another message to her, thanking her again for keeping Lizzy until we decide on what the next steps should be and reiterating the information about the cameras that I passed on to her earlier. She responds shortly after expressing her own relief, and I close the chat for now.

I groan as I stand. My whole body still hurts from the fight Rob and I had, one I'm sure is going to continue when we're on speaking terms again. The stress isn't helping and I collapse at the counter in the kitchen with a bottle of water. The heaviness of everything finally hits me so hard I feel like I might crumble under it, especially in this dark, empty house.

I stare down at my phone, scrolling through the messages I've sent Bea that have gone unanswered. I glance at the dozen or so messages of support I've gotten from teammates and friends and open the one from Madison again, where she assures me Bea's safe with her.

Madison told me she was upset, not wanting to talk to anyone, and not leaving bed. She asked Madison to keep her phone so she didn't have to know about anything else happening for a while. I can only imagine that she's been inundated with messages. I was torn about whether I should go straight to Madison's or not when I got home, but I told myself to give her a little space first. I don't want to be another voice overwhelming her, even if I'm also desperate to comfort her.

I make my way to the kitchen and grab a bottle of water from the fridge. The light illuminates the room and catches on a white envelope sitting on the kitchen counter on top of a pile of mail. "Beatrix" is written across the envelope, and my heart bottoms into my stomach. I walk toward it slowly, turning it over to see it's partially unsealed—the corner is torn up at the side. I can see there's a letter inside, handwritten, and my heart feels like it's going to pound out of my chest. Thank fuck I told them to get out of the house.

I finish opening it, not thinking about the potential consequences until I've already gotten it torn open. Then, I slide the small piece of paper out and unfold it the rest of the way so I can read it. In for a penny, in for a pound.

BEATRIX –
I HOPE YOU KNOW I'M ONLY TRYING TO HELP YOU. I

KNOW YOU'VE BEEN STRUGGLING LATELY. I CAN SEE IT WHEN I WATCH YOU. I KNOW YOU NEED HELP, AND I'M HERE FOR YOU. I CAN BE THERE FOR YOU IN EVERY SINGLE WAY YOU NEED IF YOU JUST LET ME.

YOU'RE MAKING A MISTAKE. ONE BROTHER AFTER THE OTHER. HE'LL FUCK UP JUST LIKE THE LAST ONE. I DON'T KNOW WHY YOU CAN'T SEE IT.

YOU BEING HERE IN MY CITY IS A SIGN. IT'S MEANT TO BE. WE'RE MEANT TO BE. I DON'T WANT ANYONE TO GET HURT, LEAST OF ALL YOU.

LEAVE HIM. BE WITH ME. I CAN FIX EVERYTHING FOR YOU.

I'LL FIND YOU WHEREVER YOU ARE. THIS WOULD ALL BE SO MUCH EASIER FOR US IF YOU JUST LET ME IN.

I FEEL sick all over again. But I take pictures of the letter and set it back down. If there's any chance there are fingerprints on it besides mine, I want the cops to have the evidence. This whole house could be full of it. But I need to talk to Bea first.

Before I know what I'm doing, I'm hurrying to grab my keys and race for my car. I can't stay away from her tonight. I want to be with my girl. I want to hold her and tell her everything is going to be okay. Then, I want to get to the bottom of this. I want us to figure out who this is and have him behind bars before he ever even thinks about touching her.

———

WHEN I GET THERE, it's late, but the lights are still on, and I ring the doorbell. Quentin appears at the door a few moments later, looking worse for wear from being on the road but still dressed like he isn't ready for bed. Madison appears behind him and gives me a sympathetic look.

"I need to see her."

Quentin nods for me to come in, and Madison shows me upstairs. She knocks softly on the door and opens it. I hear the soft exchange of voices, and then Madison motions for me to go in. The room's dark, and I can barely see any details other than her form curled up on the bed.

"Trixie? You okay?"

"Coop." She holds her arms out, and I join her on the bed, wrapping my arms around her and holding her tight.

She starts to cry again, something I can tell she's been doing most of the day from how hoarse her voice is and how swollen her eyes and cheeks are, and my vision starts to adjust to the dim light. I just keep holding her. Telling her I love her and that everything's going to be okay. She squeezes me back, and finally, after a few minutes, we sit up. She leans back against the pillows and headboard and shakes her head, staring down at her hands as she plays with her nails.

"It's awful. I don't know how we fix it."

"What if we could figure out who it is?" I pull the images of the letter up on my phone.

She sees her name at the top, and she frowns.

"What's this?"

"It was on the countertop when I got home. It was unsealed, so I opened it and took photos."

"From who?" she asks as she reaches for it.

"The stalker," I answer, even though we both already know.

"They were in the house again. Holy fuck." The tears form again at the corner of her eyes, glistening in what little light there is in this room. I reach out and wipe one away as it starts to fall.

"That's why you're right about you and Lizzy needing to be

away to be safe. But I think there might be clues in this that could help us." I nod to the phone.

She looks down and rubs her breastbone as she reads it, her lip worrying between her teeth and her brow furrowing. I reach out and take her hand, and she squeezes mine.

"This is so unhinged." She shakes her head, lifting her eyes as she finishes, and her hand and the phone drop to her lap.

"But it confirms it's you they're after. That they knew about Rob. It sounds like they knew you before. Any guesses?" I frown as I look back down at the letter.

"No. I really don't know. I had some boyfriends in college and high school, obviously, but none that would write something like this. Most of them are married too. Of the rest... I don't know of any who live here."

"What about something unrequited? Maybe someone similar to the situation with Craig?"

"I can't think of anyone. But... we should take this to the cops. Maybe it'll help them. Whoever took the photos and wrote this obviously had access to the house, and they were in it multiple times. Maybe there are fingerprints."

"That's what I was thinking. But I wanted to come here first and show you, prepare you before I started all that. Madison told me it's been a rough day for you, and I wanted to come see you first. Are you okay?"

"I feel guilty for putting Lizzy at risk. Your career. Your reputation. Your family and parents..."

"Lizzy is okay. Nothing happened to her. She's safe with her mom. We'll figure things out, and it'll all be fine. As for the rest of that... I don't give a fuck about any of it."

"I don't think it'll all be fine. Lizzy's mom was furious. She was polite, but I could tell. I felt like a complete fuckup who should never have been put in charge of a child in the first place."

My heart twists for her. After all her worries with Rob and

kids, I know this must be hurting her. None of it's her fault, but I also can't blame Evelyn for being upset. I would be too if the tables were turned. I just wish she'd taken out her frustration on me instead of Trix.

"She was upset. I was upset. You were upset. We were all just worried about Lizzy. Lizzy's mom has never had a bad word to say about you, Trix. She was just scared and worried. I'm sure we can all talk and work through it."

"Lizzy can't move home as long as I stay with you. Whoever this stalker is, they don't want us together, and clearly, they're willing to do anything to keep us apart. They could go after her next. You know that's what her mom is thinking. It's what I'm thinking. I'm sure you've thought it too."

I can't argue. I am worried about it. That whoever this psycho is knows that Lizzy is a soft spot for Trix and will press it for leverage over her. I'm not sure how this is going to work, but somehow, I hoped we could figure it out.

"That's what I thought," she says softly.

"I am worried about Lizzy. I need to talk to her mom and work things through about how she wants to handle this. But we've always figured things out before, and we'll figure things out again. As far as my career and my reputation, I don't give a fuck. That's the least of my worries. We were attacked— violated in our own home. If people can't understand that, fuck them."

She squeezes my hand again. "You're a good man, Coop. I'm glad you think you, Lizzy, and her mom can work through everything. But I can't be in a relationship with you, Cooper. I can't do that to you and Lizzy. I love you both too much. I can't be the reason problems start happening with your co-parent-ing. I can't live with Lizzy resenting me because I moved in, so she had to move out. None of that is okay."

"We'll catch the stalker, and then it'll be over. This letter has clues." I'm desperate for her to see it my way, for there to be some way out of this for us.

"Not many."

"It tells us he's here in the city. From here. That he's someone you knew."

"That doesn't narrow it down much. He could be one of thousands of people. If we open it up to anyone I could have crossed paths with.. who knows how many? I was with my father at a lot of political events. Politicians and their families have issues with these kinds of parasocial relationships. People think they know us when they don't."

"Once the police are involved—"

"It'll help. But it'll get more complicated. Bureaucracy and red tape. My dad's had to report enough things over the years that I know how this goes."

"You're resigned to this then," I say, almost bitter.

"Not resigned. I just want us to be realistic about what this means for us. I was hopeful before that it was just some fan of yours that didn't like our relationship. That they'd find someone else to crush on soon enough and move on. But this is obviously not that, and now, who knows how deep it runs or how long it'll take to unravel."

"Just don't give up on us yet. At least give me that."

"Coop, I told you. I'm in love with you. I'm not giving up that easily, but I'm scared. This letter scares me even more. What if they go after you next?"

"I'll be fine."

"You can't know that."

I know she's right. Half of this battle is going to be keeping her mind at ease. Making sure she knows Lizzy and I are safe. I know what that means for us, but I'm still struggling to accept it. Tears burn at the back of my throat.

"We can wait and see," I try to bargain.

"We can't. They're escalating. Taking photos in your home,

Coop. Following us to your family's home. Who knows what they'll do next. We can't wait."

"I'm not okay with this. I'm not doing this. There has to be a way," I say the words even as I'm accepting that she's right. She usually is.

"I've been lying here for hours trying to think of a way. Any possible way it can work. But..."

I can see the desperate way she looks at me, and I know in my heart if this woman thought there was a way to fix it, she'd do it in a heartbeat. She'd fight for me—for us. So if she's not, I can't fight her. I can't make her hurt even more for trying to do what she thinks is best. I take her hand in mine, lacing our fingers together. I close my eyes and try to just appreciate the fact that I have her at this moment. For this fleeting bit of time we have left, she's mine.

41

B eatrix

LIFE AT MADISON'S is busy, and I'm thankful for it as I don't have as much time to think about Cooper and Lizzy, or the status of my unknown stalker who seems to have gone quiet since the release of the photos—at least temporarily. But that hasn't changed the fact that my mom has insisted on coming out and checking in on me. She's settled into her hotel, and we're waiting for her to arrive at Madison's for dinner.

"You guys just got this house, and now you already have me and mom descending on it. I'm sorry!" I apologize as we plate the takeout meals we ordered to keep things easy.

Quentin's out with a bunch of the guys after practice, continuing to get to know them, so it's just us girls tonight. I'm thankful at least that he doesn't have to listen to me getting babied by my mom and best friend. Although I'm sure Cooper is one of the people he's out with, and it hurts my heart that he gets to see him and I don't.

"It's no worry at all, Bea. I'm glad she's coming. You need support right now." Madison's eyes are full of sympathy.

"I'm fine. I know I had a little breakdown there for a minute, but I've rallied. You did your fixer thing and got rid of the pictures and put the hammer down on anyone trying to sell them. I'm still not sure I ever want to see the inside of a Chaos locker room again, but beyond that, it's like it never happened."

Madison gives me a look that tells me she knows me better than I think she does.

"I know you're strong Bea, and I have no doubt this is gonna be in your rearview soon, but until we find out who is doing this, it's not fine. So I still wouldn't mind having your mom and her security connections as backup support right now."

"I guess that's fair. I just feel like we've settled the whole me going out to Seattle conversation, and I'm worried it's going to reignite. With us trying to stay focused on the new PR compa-ny..." Now that I knew Cooper and Lizzy were safer without me around, I'd redoubled my focus on work. I'm not about to let the stalker take that from me too.

"I'll make it clear to your mom that I've got my own security people I'm working with and explain how we've beefed up security here. We needed to do it anyway with Quentin doing well, the extra publicity thanks to my family's shenanigans, and people starting to care about his comings and goings. It just makes sense all around. Plus the cops are involved now. That report's filed and hopefully there's progress soon."

"All right. As long as we've got a plan to keep her happy."

As we make our way through dinner, Madison and I explain the situation to my mother. She nods her way through our discussion until she abruptly stops us.

"Wait... what name did you say your dad gave you for security in Cincinnati?"

"James Sharp." I repeat his name, and my mom goes stark still, the color in her face draining.

"Does that mean something to you?" Madison asks.

My mother looks between the two of us and sets her drink down.

"You remember that he used to work for your father? Around the house?" my mom asks.

"Yes. I liked him. He used to talk to me. We'd joke around. Honestly, I kind of had a bit of a crush on him. He was older and kind of hot with all the bodyguard-ish vibes he had going on."

"Yes, well..." She presses her lips together like she's just tasted something unfortunate. "He had a crush on you."

"What?" I pull back, my brow furrowing as I try to process that information. He'd been well into his twenties, and I was still sixteen or seventeen at the time.

"I overheard him talking to you one day. Complimenting you on your dress and telling you how smart you were. You'd just broken up with your boyfriend at the time when you found out he was going to a different college than you. I was worried that if he kept flattering and fawning over you that you wouldn't see through it. Nothing he said was inappropriate. Nothing I could point to to get him fired, but I just had mom senses, you know? That something was off with the way he looked at you. I didn't want to tell your father though because it was in the middle of an election cycle, and nothing had actually happened. So I talked to the head of security, and I had him reassigned away from you and the house. I don't even remember the reason I gave. I heard he quit a few months later anyway."

"Oh. Wow. I never thought he thought anything of me. I just thought he was being nice to me like some of the other security team had been in the past."

"You always were kind of oblivious as a girl." My mom pats my knee and smiles. "But I just... Like I said. There was something about him and the way he was. I didn't like it. That he's the one who's here makes me really nervous. I'd tell your investigators to look into it, if not the cops."

I think about it for a moment. The conversation we had when he came by the house to check up on things, the final sweep he completed of the house when Lizzy and I were there, and when he gave me his personal number and told me to call him anytime. After he set up cameras inside the house. He was able to watch us on all of them, knew our comings and goings, was able to access Cooper's house whenever he wanted. Worse yet, he had access to the stadium too. He had access to everything the stalker would have needed because we trusted him. I'd naively assumed he was one of the good ones.

"Oh my god..." I mumble, feeling sick suddenly.

"What?" Madison looks at me.

"He's the one who installed the cameras. I mean, him and his security team. Plus, he's one of the heads of the same company that runs security at the stadium. He would have had access to all of the places the stalker had."

"Oh, Bea," my mom says, patting my knee again and giving me a reassuring look. "It's my fault. I should have asked your dad."

"I'm texting the investigator his name now." Madison pulls her phone out.

"It's not your fault, Mom. You couldn't have known. What are the odds? Besides, it started before Dad ever got involved.

Half the reason we used him after Dad suggested him was because his company is contracted with the Chaos's stadium."

"Still. I wish I had said something. I should have told your dad when it originally happened." My mom starts to tear up, and it makes my heart hurt.

"Mom. Don't be hard on yourself. You were trying to protect me and Dad at a stressful time. You thought you'd managed the problem. You had no way of knowing. I'm just thankful you're here now. That it came up. It means we have a lead." I pat the back of her hand to reassure her and then lean in for a hug when she starts to cry harder.

"We're going to get to the bottom of this. Don't worry." Madison gives me a sympathetic look as we exchange glances.

The rest of the night is spent making sure the cops, investigators, and the current security team are on the right trail. My gut tells me it's him, everything he said and did reframed in the light of the new information has me sure of it.

IT DOESN'T TAKE LONG for him to find me. It's only a couple of days before a note addressed to me shows up in Madison's mailbox. She brings it in with the rest of the mail and hands it to me, a nervous look on her face.

It's typed rather than handwritten this time, and I assume it's an attempt to try to cover his tracks. That he doesn't want us to have any more evidence; it's him when the walls are finally starting to close in.

Beatrix —

I need to meet with you. I need a chance to explain. You're confused about what I'm trying to do. He's confused you. I'm not trying to hurt you. I'm trying to help you. I was there for you all those years. Watching out for your family. I'm still trying to look out for you now.

We were friends, remember? I think if you talked to me, if you let me have a chance to explain, to get to know me—you'd see that I'm right. You'd see that I love you and want the best for you.

I know it's Cooper convincing you to do this. Making you have them try to ruin my life. Please just meet with me and let me explain.

I SET the letter down as a chill runs down my spine. A number is typed at the bottom of the paper, and Madison shakes her head as we reach the end of it. I'm pulling out my phone to see if it matches the number James gave me at the house.

"We have to get this to the police. They might be able to trace the number. Him saying he worked for your dad, that's more evidence that leads to him." Madison reaches for her phone.

"Agreed, but this isn't the number James gave me." I hold up the contacts list where I entered his number next to the entry "Security James" when I met him in the house during his last camera check. "So I can almost guarantee that's a burner phone."

"It's worth a shot. It's still evidence that will help them put the puzzle together." Madison plays the devil's advocate.

"That's true. I wish they'd hurry. It's freaking me out that he's already found me here."

"Not to make it worse, but he's been following you for a while. He'd have seen you at the stadium and here; he'd probably seen you with me plenty of times. If he works in security, then it's not unusual that he'd be able to track down someone's address." Madison's nose scrunches as she stares at the letter.

"That's the thing about all of this. He works in security. It makes me feel sick that he thinks he's protecting me. I'm worried, too, about the way he talks about Coop in this. I worry he'll start going after him." I press my hand to my stomach because it's tumbling on the anxiety. I wish I could protect Coop in a more meaningful way instead of feeling so helpless.

"Cooper can take care of himself, and he's getting new security set up at the house for him and Lizzy. I gave him information for another company. The one Quentin and I have been using is great, and they're well vetted. It's awful the stadium was employing him, but then I guess they get through the background checks sometimes."

I feel some relief at that, knowing that Coop and Lizzy are going to be safer than they were before. It's killing me not to be with them, but I still want to do right by them.

"I just want the cops to have enough to arrest him." I sigh.

"I know." Madison reaches over and hugs me before she dials the number to the local station. "We're going to get this to them right now. Every step is a step closer to this being over."

42

Cooper

LIZZY and I are in the midst of serving the pizza we picked up on the way home from her friend's house when she drops a bomb on me.

"I miss Trix. Friday nights aren't the same without her here. Her character's just sitting there in the game waiting." Lizzy sighs.

"We can play if you want." I knew she was upset, but she'd been quiet, and I hadn't wanted to press her to share more if she didn't want to.

"I love you, but it's not the same. She likes doing all the side quests you hate. Sometimes we just spend hours in the little towns collecting things." A small smile erupts despite the sadness there.

"I can spend some time sightseeing in the towns if you want." I offer, studying her carefully.

"And then make sundaes with me while we talk about hair masks and our favorite skin care regimens?"

"Sure, why not?" I grin despite myself.

She gives me a look that tells me I'm not impressing her.

"I know you miss Trix, but you know why she's not here." I hedge.

"I know. She wants us safe. I understand, but I still miss her."

"I'm sure she misses you too."

"Do you miss her?" She lifts a piece of pepperoni onto her plate and looks up at me.

"Of course I miss her," I answer, trying not to let how much I miss her seep into my tone when I say the words.

"Were you ever going to ask her to be your girlfriend?"

I nearly drop the piece of pizza as I put it on my plate and manage to catch it before it tumbles to the floor. I grab a napkin and wipe my hands and the counter before I look up at Lizzy. The look on her face says everything—that I'm completely and utterly transparent and always have been.

"I did ask her."

"She said no?" Her tone is incredulous.

"She said yes, but then everything happened right after. We didn't get a chance to tell you. It was kind of over before it really started," I say softly, thinking back to the feel of her fingers wrapped tightly around mine, and wondering if I'm really going to have to go the rest of my life never feeling that again.

"Over? For good?" she asks, and I can hear the sadness in her tone.

"I don't know." I can't explain to Lizzy all the nuanced details of this, how complicated this all was to begin with before there was a stalker, and an angry mom, and photos of the two of us sent to an entire football team.

"I know you don't like relationships, but I thought Trix was different for you. You seemed so different around her. So happy."

"Trix is different. But sometimes that's not enough. You'll understand better when you're older. Sometimes different isn't enough."

"You didn't love her then?" Lizzy looks at me thoughtfully, and I can tell she's genuinely trying to figure out why things didn't work, but answering her questions feels like I'm breaking my own heart all over again.

"I do love her."

"Oh." She says the word softly, and then she stands and wraps her arms around me, pulling me tight in a bear hug. I wrap my arms around her and kiss the top of her head. I can feel the tears burning down my throat, and I'm desperate to choke them back. "You're allowed to be sad, Dad. I'm not going to stop thinking you're a badass just because you cry in front me. I wish you would, honestly. It'd make me feel better. I've cried a few times over her being gone."

"What?" I pull back and look down at Lizzy. "I didn't realize. I mean, I knew you were disappointed she left, but you could have told me you were that upset."

"I wasn't sure what happened between you. Whose side I was supposed to be on. I'm always on your side. But if you broke Trix's heart..."

"Oh god, Liz. You can always tell me how you're feeling. You don't have to protect my feelings."

"Did you break up with her?"

"No. I didn't break up with her. The circumstances were just a lot for her to take. Right now, all her focus has to be on us all staying safe and them getting to the bottom of the investigation. When that's over, we can see where things are."

"You're not seeing anyone else in the meantime, are you? I think she's had a crush on you for a while, and I've been scared for her." If only she knew how long I've wanted her, she wouldn't be scared—at least not for Trix.

"No. I'm not seeing anyone else." I shake my head. "I can't imagine anyone else but her."

"Good. Because I want her back as soon as this is all fixed. I know you two have stuff to work out and all, but if I get any vote, I want her back."

Lizzy looks visibly relieved and I guess as much as I knew she liked Trix, I didn't realize how invested she was until now.

"I want her back too. But I'll keep that in mind. Might have to use it as leverage since I think you might have some extra points with her."

"Just tell me when you need me to turn up the pressure. I love you both, and I think you guys are so much better when you're together. Especially you. But she was so much happier pretending to be your girlfriend than she ever was with Uncle Rob."

"Well. Let's not say that in front of him." I chuckle at her boldness.

"I know. But I'm saying that to you. In case you were wondering. Objective bystander opinion and all."

"Oh yes, very objective." I smirk at her.

She sighs and looks me over like I'm a project she's evaluating. One she finds satisfactory despite some deficiencies.

"I love you, Dad. I hope everything works out for you both."

"I love you too. And I hope so."

I hug Lizzy one more time for good measure. The older she gets, the less moments like these I'll have, so I'll take one whenever I can get one. And right now, I can use the hug. I'm so grateful I have such a sweet kid, and knowing she's rooting for us, makes me feel like I did a few things right lately. Maybe there's still a chance of this working out for all of us.

43

B eatrix

It's the fourth game of the season, and they're playing back at home in Cincinnati. Madison's attending the game, and she's brought me with her. She claims it's because she wants to keep an eye on me, but I think she's also hoping it'll distract me from everything else going on right now.

After we discovered that James was the likely suspect, we turned all the evidence we had in to the police, and they've been investigating it. But since all they have to go on for threats are photos and a few vague threats, it's been an uphill battle. Especially since the individual we're accusing had permission to access all the places he might have used. They've told us to prepare to wait, which is the last thing I wanted to hear. In the meantime, I'm stuck in limbo, worried that James is going to find out we've named him as a suspect, and constantly worried he'll still go after Coop.

The game is largely uneventful. The first smooth win of the season without any ejections or antics. When it's over, I follow Madison down to where the families usually wait for the players so I'm not walking through the city streets to the car alone. I linger on the periphery since I'm still not excited about being remembered as the woman from the pictures with Cooper.

Cooper was suspended after the game against the Pittsburgh Rivermen where he and Rob were ejected, so I don't plan to run into him down here. Which is why when I see him in his sideline gear, his hat on backwards as he leans against the wall talking to Ramsey and some of the other guys in the hallway, a smile on his face from the win, my heart stops in my chest.

I want to run to him. Hug him. Tell him how much I miss him and how scared I am right now. But then I realize the whole reason he didn't play today was because of me, and my heart breaks all over again that I've put him and Lizzy in this situation. I need a minute away from all this if I'm not going to have a public breakdown.

"Hey, I'm just going to run to the restroom," I say softly to Madison, motioning over my shoulder before I turn.

"Okay. Do you want me to come?" Her brows knit together with concern. I must be doing a poor job of hiding my emotions.

"No. I'm good." I flash a bright smile at her because I want to go and have my freak-out alone. As sweet as my best friend has been lately, I don't need her seeing every breakdown I have.

"Okay. See you back here in a couple?"

"Yep. Back in just a second."

I risk one more glance at Cooper, and it's a mistake because, before I leave the room, his eyes catch mine. I watch his smile fade as he sees me, his eyes falling over me and then meeting mine for a moment again before I hurry off. It's too much, and I can already feel my tears clawing at the back of my throat, so I pick up my pace down the hall.

I'm in such a hurry, I'm not even paying attention to who else is around me or even where I'm headed. So when I slam into a hard body and their arms wrap around me, I jolt back in surprise.

"I'm so sorry. I wasn't watching. I'm sorry," I apologize as I start to step back.

"Yeah. You never watch. Never pay attention. That's the problem with you, Beatrix."

My head snaps up, and I realize it's James. I start to move backward, glancing behind me and hoping I can run fast enough, but his grip on me tightens.

"No. You're not going to fucking run off, you little bitch. I try to help you, and you repay me by ruining my life."

"He—" I start to scream for help, but his hand slams over my mouth, and he drags me around a corner and shoves me up against a concrete wall. His hand tightens over my jaw and it feels like he might snap it if I thrash too much.

"Scream again and when I'm done with you, I'll gut your boyfriend and his daughter too. Is that what you fucking want?"

I shake my head no, the fear that I'm going to die like this welling in my gut. His eyes glint with a hatred I haven't seen before as he studies me. I don't want to know what he's thinking. What he's about to do.

"You're leaving with me today. We can do it the easy way, or the hard way." He points to his hip and I see the flash of a gun holstered there. I push back, terrified he'll use it as he wraps his hand around it. I don't think. I just act. Probably for the worse, but I've always heard that you never let someone take you to a second location. I'd had enough education from my dad's team to know that much. I shove hard again and I bat at his arm. The gun clatters to the ground, and he's forced to release me to reach for it.

It gives me just enough space that I take the opportunity to lunge away from him, making it almost back to the main hallway where someone might be able to hear me scream. But his hands are on me again, dragging me back while I try to fight him, and he pins me up against the wall.

"Just for that I'm going to take a trophy. Make you bleed low and slow. Let you think about what you've done while the lights fade out on you." He grits his teeth and shoves me harder against the concrete wall, pressing the oxygen out of my lungs.

He pulls the gun and raises it to my temple, his eyes flickering with an even darker intent. Nothing but hatred pooling in them. So much for the love and understanding he was begging for in his letters. I think about fighting again, but I worry he'll slip and pull the trigger even if he's not trying.

So much flashes through my mind. I'm stupid for not having realized it was him sooner. I wish I'd been able to call my family—especially Xander—one last time to tell him I love him, and that he did the best he could to protect me. He was smarter than me, and I should have listened. Wishing I could tell Cooper that even if it was just for a summer, he was the love of my life, and that being a friend to Lizzy meant the world to me. Tell Madison that I know she'll take our PR firm to all the places we hoped it could go.

"Trix!" I hear Cooper yell my name and the sound of footsteps pounding on concrete. I think I must be imagining it until I see Cooper's fear-stricken face running toward me.

"Stop!" James yells.

Cooper doesn't stop fast enough for James's liking, and he fires the gun into the air over our heads. My ears ring with the sound, and I yelp in response. Cooper throws his hands up in the air, yelling at James to calm down and telling him we can work this all out.

"Stay the fuck away. She's mine now. The two of you thought you could ruin my fucking life and get away with it? Go back to your happily ever after? Fuck that!" James yells and points the gun back at Cooper, waving it at him and then turning it on me.

The tears come then, fast and hard. I want to be strong. I want to stay calm. I keep asking myself what Madison would do in this situation, but I can't stop the way they pour down my face, hot and staining. I can feel the flush of my skin underneath them. Cooper sees it, and I can see him fighting with what to do. Whether to run for help or try to take on James himself. I'm terrified James will kill us both, and I give a subtle shake of my head.

Another set of footsteps is barreling down on us from behind a moment later. James fires off another round of shots into the air, threatening whoever is headed for us before he turns around, pressing the barrel of his gun to the side of my head. I feel the hot singe of it on my hair and skin, and I scream, terrified I'm next. He's too distracted by the person behind us to notice or care, and I hear Cooper's voice again, yelling at him to let me go. His grip on me tightens, and I cry out again as he presses the barrel to me once more.

Cooper lunges forward, and James whips back in his direction. I barely have time to register what's happening as he lifts the gun and fires it at Cooper. My heart bottoms out of my stomach as I watch him fall. It's all happening so fast, but the reel in my mind is in slow motion at the same time. My mind's barely able to keep up, and then I hear a loud shout from behind us, and James and I both go tumbling forward to the ground with force.

He collapses on top of me and the gun clatters across the concrete as he tries to catch himself. The concrete skins my knees and palms as I struggle to get away. Everything is a blur of bodies as we both scramble on the ground. Both of us are fighting to get up and gain control before I hear another loud grunt and look behind me to see Ramsey standing over James and me. He grabs James a moment later, wrapping his hands around his neck and pulling him back from me. It gives me just enough room to crawl out from underneath his weight, grabbing the gun and rolling over.

I've fired one once or twice. My dad's security team gave me the opportunity at a range before but it's been years, and I pray I still remember how to aim and shoot.

Before I can do anything though, Ramsey's hands are wrapped around either side of James's head, and he wrenches it to the side. There's a cracking sound, like a branch breaking, and James falls limp at his feet.

My heart skips in my chest and I hear the insistent thud of it against my eardrums. It drowns out every other sound. My breath catches in my throat and then I remember Cooper. I scramble to my feet, hurrying to his side.

He's sprawled out across the ground, bleeding heavily, and I rush to kneel next to him. I pull his head into my lap and survey the damage before my fingers search over his bloody shirt for the entry wound. I don't know much about first aid. I've never learned, but I know I have to stop the bleeding. It's too much blood. Far too much blood for such a short time.

I look to Ramsey. Hoping that he has answers. That he might know what to do to save Cooper. But his eyes go dark when he sees Cooper laying limp on the ground. Fury is painted over his face as he turns back to James.

I'm screaming for help at the top of my lungs, pressing my hands into the wound on Cooper's shoulder. There's so much blood, and it's everywhere. Soaking through his shirt, seeping over my fingers, and spilling onto the concrete floor beneath us. It starts to pool at my knees, staining them and the stone. I scream louder like somehow that'll make this all end. That I can wake up from this nightmare if I can just yell for help loud enough. But just like it's failed me every time before in my sleep, it fails me now.

I look to Ramsey one last time for help, but Ramsey's not with me anymore. He's not willing to let it go. If he can't fix it, he's determined to destroy what caused it.

"You fucking piece of shit!" He yanks James's body forward underneath him, the flutter of James's lashes the only sign he's still alive, and then he starts to pummel him. One fist after another. Left then right. Bruising and beating James's face until it splits and bleeds. I want to yell for him to stop. Tell him that he has to come help me with Cooper. But I can't move. I can't speak. Trapped in sleep paralysis in broad daylight.

But I *have* to move. I have to save Cooper. It's just me and him here, and I won't lose him. I can't lose him. I see movement in my peripheral vision and I yell for someone to call an ambulance. The person, whoever they are, because I don't bother to look up, yells back that they have. Another person shouts that they're going to get stadium security.

Cooper's eyes are closed, and I beg for him to stay with me. I can't lose him. Not now, not like this. I can't let Lizzy lose her dad, and I refuse to be the reason for it. I should have left the city when I had the chance. I should have gone home like my father told me to, and none of this would have happened. My own selfish desire to still be close to him is going to kill him, and it would all be my fault.

"You stupid, stupid man. You should have let him shoot me." I can feel the tears streaming down my face, dripping onto my dress and the tops of my hands as I press my fingers into the wound, trying to keep the blood in his body. Praying there's going to be enough to keep his heart beating until the ambulance gets here.

"Bea! Oh my god, Bea!" It's a voice I recognize. Madison. Madison is here, and she'll know what to do. She can fix anything. She can fix this.

"Maddy!" I cry out for her, and she wraps her arms around my shoulders, surveying the situation.

"Oh, Bea. Oh god. Don't worry, okay? There's an ambulance on the way. It's going to be okay." She turns her attention to shouting at people around us. "Go downstairs, take two lefts and the physician's office is down there. See if he or any of the trainers are there. Ask for any supplies they have. Tell them what's happened. You! Go get security. I don't care if someone else went. You run the opposite direction and find someone. Run like his life depends on it."

I can hear the distant sound of sirens, and I pray that they're on their way here, but the sound is drowned out by male shouting. Quentin.

I look up, and it's Quentin trying to pull Ramsey from James's limp and bloodied body. Using all his force to attempt to stop an out-of-control Ramsey from crushing the man's skull in.

Another team member is shoving Ramsey at his shoulders while Quentin pulls back, and eventually, they're able to pull him off James. The three of them tumble to the ground in a heap while Ramsey screams that he'll kill James's whole family. Quentin tries to say something to him. Something I can't hear. But whatever it is, it's not enough, and Quentin and the other guy are forced to physically pin Ramsey to the ground while they try to talk him down.

"I got you, Bea. I got you." Madison hugs me tightly. "Help is coming, and you're doing such a good job. Help is coming."

"He can't die. Lizzy needs him. I need him," I sob as I stare down at Cooper, my vision blurring from the tears and the hopelessness.

"He's not going to die. We're not going to let that happen," Madison promises me, even though we both know she can't keep it.

44

C ooper

WHEN I WAKE UP, it's a blur. There's pain in my shoulder like I've never experienced before in my life. The room's dimly lit by flourescent overheads, and I can hear the sound of a monitor beeping quietly in the distance. It's enough to know I'm in the hospital, lying in a bed, and the pain is probably the reason why.

I groan and close my eyes when I try to move. Trying to remember how I got here. If I got hurt on the field or—and then it hits me. The stalker. Trix. Ramsey. The flash of the muzzle, and the searing pain in my shoulder. I feel panic swell in my chest, and I want to jump up. Want to run to find someone who can tell me what happened, and see if she's okay. If Ramsey is okay.

I blink when I feel the weight of something against my side, stopping me from sitting up, and I turn my head to look down.

Trix is there, curled up on the edge of the bed, wedged between me and the rail. Her eyes are closed, and the soft sound of her breathing tells me she's asleep.

Asleep means she isn't dead. My head falls back against the pillow, and I can feel the tears well in the corner of my eyes. I run my hand down her back, thanking every damn star in the universe that somehow we're both still here.

"Dad?" I hear Lizzy's voice, and I turn my head, realizing she's sitting in the chair to my left.

"Lizzy?"

"Oh. You're awake." She stands up abruptly and comes to the side of the bed, worry fading to a smile as she studies my face. "Do you need anything? I can get a nurse."

"I think... I think I'm okay right now. But yes maybe a nurse so I can talk to them." I need someone to explain what's going on.

Trix stirs, and her head raises, blinking before her eyes widen, and a smile forms on her lips.

"You're awake." She grins.

"I'm going to get a nurse," Lizzy announces, moving toward the door. She pauses there and looks back at us, her eyes darting to Trix and then me before she smiles and takes off down the hall.

"Are you okay? Do you need painkillers? The nurse said when you woke up she could give you more if you need them. You just have to tell her."

"I'm fine. Are you okay?" I see the bandage on the side of her face, and I reach for her chin, turning her head so I can get a better look.

"I'm fine. It's nothing." She gives me a soft half smile. "But you... you took the brunt of it."

"That why my shoulder feels like it's on fire?"

"Yes. Do you remember being shot?"

I nod silently.

"The ambulance got there just in time. The training staff saved your life. I was so scared." She swallows back her tears, and I run my knuckles along her chin.

"I'm still here. Can't get rid of me that easily."

"I was terrified. I love you so much, Coop. I don't know what I would have done." She buries her face into my good shoulder, giving me half a hug that's careful to avoid the bad one.

"I love you too, Trix. I'm so glad you're okay. Did he hurt you though? Your face?"

"Just a singe from the gun barrel. It'll heal."

"And Ramsey?"

"Ramsey is—"

"You're awake!" The nurse greets loudly, and our attention is turned to her. "How are we feeling?"

I'm distracted from my conversation with Trix as the nurse puts me through my paces and calls in the doctor a few minutes later. They talk me through my injury, discuss the surgery they performed, and walk me through my recovery process as well as tell me what medications I'll be taking in the meantime. They warn me that they'll have to see how my wound and rehab progress goes, and they'll adjust their recommendations based on that, but I'm very lucky to be alive and need to just focus on getting well enough to leave the hospital.

"So obviously, I'm out for the season." I say the words out loud, but I'm hoping the doctor is going to tell me that I might make the last couple of games if I heal faster than usual. Somehow, I always want to believe I've got the superhuman ability to do what other people can't.

The doctor's mouth flatlines, and he shifts on his feet, clearing his throat before he looks at me. His brow furrows just as he opens his mouth to talk, and it's almost like I can feel a shift in the temperature in the room. I glance at Trix, who has taken a seat on the far side of the room while the doctors work, and her eyes are on the floor, her face etched with sadness, and then I know. I know before he even says the words.

"I think we have to see how your recovery goes. But I want to be honest with you that the rehab needed is extensive—months at least, possibly a year or more, depending on your progress. It's going to take time for you to get back to anything close to normal."

"A year?" The word croaks out. It doesn't even sound like my voice.

"Yes. It's possible. I hope it won't come to that, but the nerve damage you have is significant."

"When you say close to normal... what are we talking?" The panic is welling in my gut, and I feel sick from it.

"Right now, you just need to focus on getting rest and healing. We can address all your concerns as time goes on, and you make progress. But the best way for you to help your future self is to focus on your recovery now." The doctor gives me half a smile and tucks my chart back in its holder, nodding at everyone in the room before he takes off again. His words are nonsense. A slew of weasel words meant to comfort me when the underlying lack of positive affirmation on my recovery tells me I'm in fucking trouble.

"I'm glad you're awake. Just let me know if there's something I can do." Lizzy smiles and pats my leg once everyone is gone.

What I need her to do, as much as I love her, is not be in this room right now. Because the panic in my gut is threatening to make me sick.

"Could you actually go get us some snacks down in the cafeteria? Some drinks and whatever sounds good that they have? I just realized I haven't eaten, and I think your dad might want something other than hospital food." Trix saves the fucking day like she can read my mind.

"Of course. Anything in particular you want?" Lizzy grins at me.

"Nah, up to you, kid. Whatever sounds good. You know what I like." I grin back at her, swallowing down the bile and panic for a few more moments shouldn't be too hard.

"I can do that." She turns and practically bounces out of the place, happy to be able to do something after what I'm sure was hours of her just sitting around waiting and watching.

When her footsteps have disappeared down the hall, I let the tears come. My chest feels like it's on fire, and a sob escapes before I can stop it. The bile climbs its way up my throat again, and my stomach churns like a vat of boiling acid. My heart feels like it's going to pound out of my chest, and I'm not sure I won't have a heart attack on top of everything else.

It takes me a moment to say the words I'm dreading.

"I'm never going to play again, am I?" I ask the ceiling.

Fingers wrap around my hand in response, and her palm covers the back of my knuckles, brushing over them gently. The warmth of her hands radiates up my arm, and she squeezes.

"We're going to do everything we can to try to make it happen. If anyone can, it's you."

"And if I can't?"

"Then you're still Cooper fucking Rawlings. You're going to figure out whatever it is you're doing next, and you're going to crush it the same way you do everything else."

I risk a glance at her, and when my eyes meet hers, my heart breaks its insidious rhythm and starts to slow. Because the way she looks at me, she believes it—every single word she's saying. She believes in me. I squeeze her hand in return, and she tightens her own hold on me.

"It's going to be okay, Coop. I know you must be thinking a million things right now. I know you're in a lot of pain. But Lizzy and I are going to be here for you every step of the way. Helping you figure this all out. Helping you get better. Not just us either. Ramsey. Quentin. Madison. The whole damn team would be in this room if I let them, but I insisted they go home as loudly as Lizzy insisted to the nurses that I be allowed to stay in here. She is fierce as hell by the way. I don't think you have anything to worry about with her and holding her own in high school, or anywhere else for that matter." Trix laughs, and it's infectious, making a soft roll of it escape me before I know what's happening. She grins when she hears it despite the tears in my eyes.

"I'm glad she fought for you to stay. I need you."

"I need you. You saved my life. You're a hero, you know. You and Ramsey. The news channels can't stop talking about you. They all want an interview as soon as you're feeling up to it. Madison's been fielding all the press for us."

"Ramsey, is he okay?"

"He's... going to be okay. He... uh..."

"Just tell me. I know I look like I'm about to break, but I'm good. You're here, and I'm good." I take a breath and try to fix my face, calm my outward appearance to match the way my anxiety is starting to slowly recede.

"In the process of trying to stop James, he... James is dead."

"He killed him?" My heart slams against my chest again, forgetting all the worries I have.

She presses her lips together and gives a half nod as her eyes drift downward.

"Holy fuck. Is he... the police? What's happening?" I stumble over my words.

"He's out on bail this morning. He has a lawyer. The team has already issued a statement saying the two of you were heroes who saved lives. Madison and I are going to do everything we can. You know her, she's already got a plan."

"Fuck me." I let my head fall back against the pillows, staring at the ceiling for the second time in less than an hour, wondering how the fuck we got here.

"It'll be okay. It was self-defense. He was saving my life. Your life. Like I said, the news can't stop talking about what heroes you both are. He has the best lawyer money can buy, and they've already said your jerseys sold out overnight after the news broke."

"Jerseys won't save him in court."

"I know but—"

"Nah, Trix. You don't understand. He's... got a colorful family. A background that'll come up when they go to prosecute him. They'll obliterate him in court and outside of it." I don't know how to tell her his family runs a criminal enterprise that goes so deep it's caused him one tragedy after another in his life.

"Then our job is to make the PR campaign so strong they don't have a choice but to decline prosecution." She shakes her head. "Trust me when I say Madison and I are going to do everything we can. I'll be on every single channel and news outlet I can find saying how you both saved my life. Plus, my father has wide-reaching connections, and he's incredibly grateful for everything the two of you did for me. I promise you don't need to worry. You had my back all summer. I've got you and Ramsey right now."

"I love you." I don't have any other words. Just those.

"I love you," she echoes and leans over to kiss me.

45

B eatrix

Two Months Later

"I hope we've done enough." I stare at the TV screen in Madison's and my office. It's muted with the captions on as a group of talking heads discuss Ramsey's fate on the nightly news.

Thanks to investments from Cooper, Quentin, Ramsey, and a few other team players, Madison and I have not only been able to start our own PR firm separate from the Chaos, but we've also been able to get our own office space downtown and hire our own administrative assistant to help us run the place. The three of us have been glued to the television as they've geared up to start Ramsey's trial.

"Well, they've declined to prosecute on the manslaughter charge. That's huge right there. The mandatory minimums for that meant he'd never play again." Madison sighs as she stares at the TV.

"Not to mention what it would mean for the rest of his life." I lean back against my desk.

The prosecution had declined the manslaughter charge, claiming that it was justified in the wake of the attempted kidnapping and murder. I'd given a witness testimony along with other players and family members who'd seen the aftermath to support Ramsey's character and chances at staying out of prison.

However, the brutal beating Ramsey had given James, even once he broke his neck, had been filmed by one of the staff on-site, and having reviewed it, the prosecution did proceed with assault charges.

I've been sick with worry ever since. So has Cooper. We were all nervously waiting to see if our friend's good deed would go unpunished or if he'd have to suffer more than the suspension from the league that he's serving now.

"I think they have to let him off, don't they?" Penny, our administrative assistant, is much less jaded than Madison and I are.

"We can hope," I say, shrugging. I glance down at the time on the screen. "Shit! I've got to go. I have to pick up Lizzy from her after-school coding thing."

"Cooper still not up to driving?" Madison asks.

Cooper is home from the hospital and is slowly rehabbing his shoulder. The prognosis for his future is grim, but he's been absolutely dedicated to his rehab, and his attitude through everything has been amazing.

"He's starting to, but I'd rather he didn't. Plus, her school is on the way home for me."

"All right. See you tomorrow. Don't forget to look at that stuff I sent you about the new program they're starting over at *This Week in Football*. I think it's an option for Cooper. They'd be excited to bring him on, and their timeline seems like it might work with his rehab schedule," Madison reminds me as I gather my purse.

"I'll let him know."

ONCE WE'RE HOME, Lizzy's off to talk to her friends in her room about her latest idea she was working on today while Cooper helps me make dinner in the kitchen. As I toss the onions and peppers in the frying pan, he comes up behind me, kisses my cheek, and then makes his way down my jaw.

"You and Madison plot to take over the world today?" He grins as he snags one of the leftover peppers on the counter and pops it into his mouth.

"I wish. Mostly, we just filled out paperwork, answered emails, and watched the coverage for Ramsey's pretrial stuff."

"I talked to him today. Told him to keep his head up, and we'd do whatever it takes. I reminded him we got the best lawyer money could buy, and the best PR team too." He smiles at me.

"I'm just so worried for him. I wish I could promise him it would all be fine, but that video was... ugly. They play that for a jury, and it's going to be hard to explain away."

"That's what we're for," Cooper reassures me.

"At least we'll get to speak on his behalf." We've agreed to be character witnesses for him, and it gives me some comfort that I can try to fight for him.

"You're doing a lot more than that, Trix. You've got to stop blaming yourself. You know what the therapist said." Cooper gives me a knowing look, and I nod in response. We've both been in therapy since the shooting, and I've been working hard on letting things go, but the anxiety of Ramsey's trial has ratcheted all my old fears and insecurities back up again.

Cooper must see it on my face because he wraps an arm around my waist and pulls me away from the stove. He kisses me softly and then holds my eyes with his.

"Ramsey doesn't blame you. I don't blame you. No one blames you for what happened. James did this," he says firmly, and his hand rubs a small circle on my lower back. "You and I are doing everything we can to help. Which is all we can do."

"I know." I close my eyes, and he kisses my forehead.

"So let's talk about something else then." He moves to the fridge to pull some more of the ingredients out.

"Madison brought up the *This Week In Football* opportunity again. She wants me to talk to you about it because we need to give them a response."

"Tell her I'll call them tomorrow."

"Really?" I drop the spoon I've been using to stir the pan and turn back to look at him. I'd expected a no. Because a yes meant he was accepting that he might not play again.

"I might as well. Even if I could somehow miraculously play next season, I'm getting close to my last anyway. I need to figure out what's next after this. That was the goal when we started this, right? You were going to help me with my image, and I was going to plan for the future."

"Yes, that was the plan." I study him because he seems like he's in a good mood, and discussions about his future have understandably had a mixed reception in the last couple of months.

"Well, this is my future." I can't quite read his tone, and I worry he's keeping up a good show for me.

"And you're okay with it? Be honest."

"I've got a gorgeous and insanely clever live-in girlfriend who runs her own business and finds me jobs where people still want to hear me talk football even if I can't play it. A kid who's doing amazing in school and is probably going to conquer the gaming world. And my image went from playboy to hero overnight thanks to you—not to mention a badass scar that gives me one hell of a story to tell for the rest of my life. So yeah, Trix, I think I'm pretty happy with it." He flashes a bright grin.

"Good. Because I love it." I smile in return. "A lot."

"Me too. Now we just gotta plan our next checklist. Unless you've already got one going on that phone of yours," he teases and pulls me close, wrapping his arm around me before he kisses me one last time, and I melt into him.

EPILOGUE

Beatrix

THE NEXT SUMMER

We've just finished having a delicious picnic lunch Coop's mom made for us, and I'm ready to crash on one of the loungers and fall asleep listening to the sound of the waves on the lake when Coop grabs my hand.

"Ah. Ah. You're coming with me." He smiles.

"With you? Where are we going?" I cover my eyes from the sun to look up at him.

"Out on the boat for a bit."

"Oh, okay. I might fall asleep while we're out there though." I lace my fingers with his as he leads me down to the dock.

"We won't be gone long. Plus, I think you'll be able to stay awake."

"What does that mean?"

"You'll see."

"If this is like the other day when you tried to race that guy, I don't think I can handle seasickness post lunch," I warn him as we climb into the boat.

"No. It's nothing like that. Just trust me." He looks back at me and smiles as I slide into the seat, and he finishes prepping the boat.

I smile as I watch him bend and work, so grateful for how well he's healed since the shooting. It's a miracle he's even still here. The sheer luck of timing on the part of the ambulance and his will to live are what's kept him here. He always tells me it was me that kept him alive, that somehow he knew I was there the whole time, and he had to fight to stay for Lizzy and me. I just feel lucky that I have him at all, and I've turned just as sappy as Madison when I think about him.

He pulls away from the dock and takes us out onto the lake a little way before he kills the engine, and turns back to me.

"Everything okay?" I ask, surprised that we aren't going farther out or taking a tour around the lake like he usually likes to.

"I'm about to find out." He smirks, and he's holding a hand out for me again. I take it, and he pulls me to my feet.

"What are we doing?" I laugh nervously because I can't figure out what he's up to.

"Remember I told you when we got together that it was us out on the boat that day, the sundress, and you just spending the day with me fishing that made me realize I wanted you?"

"Yes. I remember." My brow furrows as I look up at him, still a little confused.

"I'd always thought you were gorgeous, but that day, I just realized how alike we were in so many ways, how much you made me laugh, and how smart you were. I told myself I needed to start finding things about you I didn't like because you weren't mine to have. But when I tried, honest to God, Trix, I couldn't think of anything." His eyes meet mine, and I feel like I might melt under the weight of his gaze. No matter how long we're together, that part never changes. "I still can't think of anything. I love every single thing about you, and this last year, when you've been so patient with me, even on the hard days during recovery, even when I was still trying to figure out this whole relationship thing, you stood by me."

My heart twists with all the sweet things he's saying, and I press my free hand to my chest.

"Well, you did take a bullet for me. Kind of hard not to be patient with a guy who will do that for you."

"I'd take more of them. I'd do anything for you, Trix. I hope you know that. I hope I've shown you that over the last year. You might not have been mine to have, but you were mine to earn—mine to gain if I could do this right and show you how much you really deserve and how willing I am to be that guy every single day for you."

"Coop, you know I love you. You're the best thing that's ever happened to me."

"Well, that's good to hear because I need to know something."

My heart skips a beat in my chest. "What's that?"

He spins me around, having me look back to the shore. Standing there holding a giant sign is Lizzy and the rest of his family, including Rob, Carly, and their kids.

Will You Marry Me? is painted in huge letters, and I'm shaking. I can't believe this is real. I turn back to look at him, and there are tears in his eyes too. He's holding out a small black box with a gorgeous ring. I start bawling like a baby the second I see it.

"I can't imagine anyone else but you forever," he says softly.

"Yes. Of course, yes." I take the ring and slip it on before I wrap my arms around him; he crushes me in a hug and then leans down to kiss me. I can hear the hollers and chants from the shore as they realize I've said yes, and Coop holds up a thumbs-up and waves back at them.

"I love you so much, Coop. I don't deserve you."

"You deserve the world, Trix. I'm going to do everything I can to make sure you get it."

Cooper

A little while later, after she said yes, and my mother, Lizzy, and Trix have already planned our entire wedding over the course of a couple hours, I head downstairs to grab a beer out of the fridge. Rob is sitting there staring out at the water, and I pat him on the back as I walk by.

"How's fatherhood treating you? Getting any sleep at all?" I ask.

"A little bit here and there. Enough anyway. Trying to take some of the pressure off of her so she can get some and we don't both feel like we're on the edge of sanity. This shit is no joke. I didn't give you enough credit for being able to do that and play ball and take classes. In retrospect, I don't fucking know how you did any of it."

"I had to do it for Lizzy. It was hard, but it was worth it." I shrug.

"She's thrilled today, huh? She about died when Bea said yes. So much screaming." Rob laughs. "I don't know how you top that birthday present next year."

"Next year, she might get a car if she keeps her grades up. She's already been window shopping with Trix." I smile thinking about it because I think Trix is almost as excited for her as Lizzy is.

"I'm happy for you both, you know. I wasn't always. I know I was a dick about it at first. I said some fucked up shit. I still say it was kind of a dick move on your part. But seeing the two of you together—how happy she is—I get it."

It's the most he's ever said about the matter since last summer. We've mostly just avoided the subject, sticking to safer topics like football and the weather when we talk.

"I'm glad you're in a better place on it." I choose my words carefully. "I love her. I can't imagine life without her."

"I figured that, what with the career-ending injury for her and all. That doesn't bother you ever? No regrets?"

"I'd do it all over again if I had to."

"Well, like I said. I'm happy for you." Rob tips his beer in my direction, and I tap the neck of my bottle against his in a toast. I don't know that Rob will ever completely forgive me for it, but I'll take peace with him if I can get it. In the end, he's my brother, and I want Trix to know she has a home with our family.

"What are you guys drinking?" She grins at the two of us. "And can I get one? Your mother and Carly have been showing me all the different table-setting options they think would be perfect for us, and I need a breather."

"Just some local beer. I can get you one. You want to watch a movie?" I ask as I go to the fridge.

"Sounds good to me. You and Carly want to join? Did Sienna go down okay?" Trix looks to Rob. She's been trying to make peace with him and smooth everything over. Carly's firmly in her corner, even after finding out the truth about their history, but Rob's only recently come around.

"Yeah, she's good. I've got the monitor. We can watch. Or we can play some cards." He taps the baby monitor.

"Let's not do anything competitive today, maybe?" Trix winces a little at the thought.

"Fine. Just don't make us watch another one of those romcoms," Rob grumbles.

"Carly likes them!" Trix argues.

"And so do I. The part where he gets the girl to finally admit she wants him? Fucking love it." I wrap my arm around Trix's waist as I hand her the beer, and she leans into me, smiling up. Her ring flashes when she takes the beer, and I grin at it.

"You would." My brother side-eyes me, but there's the slightest hint of a smile as we make our way back upstairs to find Carly.

Trix squeezes my hand though and pauses me on the step, waiting to make sure Rob's out of earshot.

"Everything good?" she asks.

"Yeah. He said he was happy for us." I shrug. "I don't know if I completely believe it, but it's progress."

"Good. I'm glad you're getting along again, at least. Talking more," she says softly.

"So is my mom driving you mad yet?"

"No. Overwhelming me a little with options. My mom would have picked a few and had me choose my favorite. Those two are going to be an interesting mix when they get together." She smiles.

"I think they're going to make an amazing team planning everything so that you just have to show up and say you'll be mine for the rest of your life."

"Let's hope so. With all the new clients, I don't know when I'll have time to plan it properly. We have to talk about a date."

"My only input is the sooner, the better. I can't wait to call you my wife. Gonna say it like fifty times a day just so I can hear it and know it's true." I kiss her softly, and her eyes open slowly, studying my face as I pull away.

"How did I get so lucky?"

"Easy, you suffered through the wrong brother for a few years until you picked the right one."

. . .

WANT MORE of Cooper and Beatrix in the future? maggierawdon.com/mine-to-gain-bonus/

ALSO BY MAGGIE RAWDON

ACKNOWLEDGMENTS

To you, the reader, thank you so much for taking a chance on this book and on me! Your support means the world.

To Kat and Vanessa, thank you for your constant help, support, and patience. I'm so grateful for you. There's no way I'd ever get a book out without you!

To Autumn, for all of your tireless work to help promote and support my work. So thankful for you!

To Thorunn, thank you for always keeping me sane through the hard writing days.

To Shannon, thank you for all of your humor and your support getting me through my first signings this year!

To Emma, Jenn, Ashley, Jaime, Mackenzie & Maggie, thank you for your feedback, humor, and support.

To my Creator Team, thank you so much for all the support you give my characters, my books, and me. I wouldn't be able to do this without you, and I'm so incredibly grateful!

ABOUT THE AUTHOR

Maggie Rawdon is a sports romance author living in the Midwest. She writes athletes with the kind of filthy mouths who will make you blush and swoon and the smart independent women who make them fall first. She has a weakness for writing frenemies whose fighting feels more like flirting and found families.

She loves real sports as much as the fictional kind and spends football season writing in front of the TV with her pups at her side. When she's not on editorial deadline you can find her bingeing epic historical dramas or fantasy series in between weekend hikes.

Join her newsletter here for sneak peeks and bonus content:
https://geni.us/MRBNews
Join her readers' group on FB here:
https://www.facebook.com/groups/rawdonsromantics

facebook.com/maggierawdon
instagram.com/maggierawdonbooks
tiktok.com/maggierawdon

Printed in Great Britain
by Amazon

43596074R00192